The Sweetest Passion

NORMA WEST-GREEN

outskirts
press

CHAPTER ONE

The scene was grotesque and brutal with rage that had a kind of vibration permeating the room and its occupants who seemed as lifeless as the blood-bathed corps that was once a man.

Someone really hated this poor bastard, thought Detective John Garrison who was more than annoyed at having to be there since he was planning his vacation to visit his children in Seattle.

If he had not allowed his ex-wife talk him into a later flight to accommodate her, he would be in the air and someone else would be cleaning up this gruesome madness.

His frustration paled against the fury that occurred in this room earlier.

He watched and listened to the forensic team go about their work, annoying the medical examiner's attendants standing around waiting to remove the body for the last two hours.

Garrison stood over the faceless, handless body and could feel the frenzy that caused this carnage.

The detective was infamous for his pensive demeanor that signaled do not disturb. When he approached a crime scene, he was never approached, but rather observed for his direction and point of view. His focus was always complete and severe, as if centered in meditation. He's been known to observe a scene more than an hour before saying a word; listening to smooth jazz through the earphone.

The killer either knew the victim or knew something about him that was provocative enough to generate enough rage to destroy everything that would aid in identification, he determined staring at the skin and bones that was once a face and head.

The victim's face had been beaten beyond the capability of fists. Every bone in his face and head were crushed into small pieces. Skin and muscle was torn apart to the point of leaving a hole where his face should have been.

John saw his partner, Andy Becker walking out of the bedroom, talking to one of the forensic team.

The music played on in his head as he walked through the apartment, talking to no one—paying attention to everything.

The medical examiner inspected the body while wearing his miniature glasses too close to the tip of his nose with a look of bemusement that was constant. His consistent frown and squinting kept his glasses in place as he worked without speaking.

A search of the apartment did not reveal a weapon of any kind. His face would have to be beaten with some kind of a blunt object. There were no knives, axe or saw to remove the hands. There was no blood. Where *was* the blood, John thought?

There was no wallet, money, or keys in the victim's pockets. He was naked. There was no sign of the clothes he had worn—only a sheet of paper lying on his chest with the words: FEEL THE PASSION. THERE WILL BE NO MORE.

The apartment was small with one bedroom, a bathroom, kitchen, eating area and living room. It was fully furnished with comfortable, cheap, but stylish commercial pieces.

The bathroom looked unused. How did the killer wash himself, thought Garrison? The towels were clean and hanging straight and white. The soap in the dish was unused. The tile surrounding the tub as well as the shower door was dry and spotless.

There were no clothes or luggage in the closet and all of the dresser and nightstand drawers were empty.

The kitchen was spotless—untouched. There were no dishes, glassware, pot, pans, cutlery or food anywhere. This could have been used as a model apartment had it not been for the body on the neatly made bed.

The apartment was on the first floor under the stairs leading to the second and third floors. The plants hanging over the window were well cared for and freshly watered. There was a small bar-b-que pit that looked new. There were two lawn chairs with a small table between them next to the pit on the patio. The front door faced a parking lot. Beyond the parking lot was a wood fence. The parking space in front of the apartment was marked with the number 101 indicating the space allocated for the tenant in apartment 101 that contained the deathbed of the victim.

There was a covered walkway from the parking lot. The killer could have entered the apartment without being seen, since it was located at the end of the building and the windows next door were behind a patio fence.

"This is a secondary crime scene—he wasn't killed here. Chad Bailey said, still examining the faceless body. "There are no fingerprints anywhere in this apartment. Every surface has been dusted; my house should be this clean," he said while frowning; looking at no one, "even the light bulbs are clean."

There was no blood or bodily fluid of any kind revealed using Luminol and an alternate light source.

"Shit," Chad exhaled, "what the hell happened here?" He had to have been killed somewhere else and brought here. Nothing happened in this place," he said to no one.

John thought about the killer and his victim—about the precision of this murder, and the sterile crime scene. It didn't look like a crime scene—more like a mausoleum. Nothing indicated a break in; nothing disturbed, except of course the body on the bed.

"He's been dead at least thirty hours", the medical examiner finally spoke as he stood and removed his gloves. "It's Friday afternoon and I'm not going to get into this today. I'm taking the weekend off just because I want to; so don't call me for anything;

I don't care who dies."

He walked through the doorway and to his car with his glasses still perched.

No one said a word because they also had weekend plans that did not include official work. Not even this bizarre case prompted anyone to consider overtime. John was sure it had nothing to do with the weekend; no one knew where to start solving this murder.

The faceless, headless body had been released and removed to the van and driven away.

Outside, Chad Bailey turned to John Garrison and repeated, "he didn't die in there". "Have a good weekend."

John watched the last official vehicle disappear and walked toward the apartment manager's office, followed by Andy Becker.

"Why did he move the body to that apartment?"

"He didn't. The killing and mutilation took place right there."

CHAPTER TWO

I should get there no later than three o'clock, he thought as he drove north on highway 45. Traffic was light in spite of the highway construction that has been going on as long as he could remember.

He drove along feeling relaxed and free and grateful for the time alone on the road. The spring weather was mesmerizing. He drove with his window down and felt the luxuriant wind kneading his face and filling the Range Rover.

He went over the contents of the back seat in his head again and again until he was certain that he had everything, and nothing was left behind.

He had wrapped the vacuum cleaner in two plastic garbage bags. The baseball bat, handsaw and scalpel were wrapped in paper and plastic then taped. The kitchenware was neatly packed in a box. The tarps were wrapped around the clothes and shoes. The hands were in separate plastic bags. The apartment was left move-in ready.

It was after two o'clock and he felt the pangs of nothing to eat all day. He reached in the paper bag on the seat beside him and pulled out a sandwich he made before he left home. He finished the sandwich and the apple and put the apple core in the plastic sandwich bag and returned it to the paper bag on the passenger seat. He opened a bottle of water and washed his lunch down feeling satisfied.

He turned down the road that led to the deer lease. The dirt road was smooth from the vehicles driving back and forth for decades.

He pulled around to the back of the lodge and parked.

He put on a pair of rubber gloves, emptied the back seat, and went about destroying the contents of the bags.

The hands had to be sawed in half-length wise to fit into the chipper. After disposing of both hands, he put the saw handle and the baseball bat in the chipper.

He emptied the woodchipper and poured a small amount of lighter fluid on the chips and lit the pile.

The fire started fast.

He burned the tarps and clothes with the shoes. He unwrapped the vacuum cleaner and removed the bag, placing it on the fire. He stood over the fire until it burned out completely and nothing was left except the ashes. He removed the vacuum brush and pulled the small amount of hair and carpet from the bristles and threw it in the fire. He then put the brush back in place in the vacuum and returned it to the floor in the rear of his vehicle.

He scooped the ashes into a shovel and spread them in the nearby brush, then took the hose attached to the faucet on the side of the lodge and washed the shovel.

He took the shovel into the thick brush and turned over the ground to dirty the shovel and returned it to the tool shack behind the lodge.

He drove to the front of the property and looked around remembering the trips he made with his father to prepare for hunting season without him. "Men only," his father said each year, and by the time he was a man, he was never invited or encouraged.

The pain from those trips and contempt for his father had long since absorbed into who he had become.

He drove down the road toward the highway feeling no regret that this was his last visit and headed south to Houston.

He saw a church ahead where there were no cars parked in the driveway. He tried all three doors that were locked, then put the box of kitchenware at the door on the side of the church and drove away.

When he stopped for gas, he threw the bags containing the apple core as well as the lighter fluid and rubber gloves in the trash beside the pumps, just as the attendant picked it up to empty it into the dumpster.

As he drove out of the gas station, he saw the garbage truck he had seen earlier, enter for pickup.

He arrived home at seven fifteen and parked in the garage. He put a new bag in the vacuum cleaner and returned it to the utility room.

He knew he had to hurry if he wanted to keep his eight thirty reservation for dinner. He took a shower, dressed, fed the fish and left to pick up his dinner date.

CHAPTER THREE

John saw Janice Harding standing outside of the apartment when he arrived and knew she was the manager by the way she was dressed and coifed. She was twenty something, thin, with blond hair falling on her shoulders. She was tastefully, if not slightly seductively dressed in a white tee with a hint of cleavage tucked into tailored navy linen slacks, with a faux alligator belt and shoes.

Her smile was wide and professionally maintained surrounded by bright glossed coral lipstick.

She seemed to be in denial about what she saw on that bed. There was no sign of distress. No fear. No horror.

John identified himself and Andy and accepted her invitation to sit in front of her desk overlooking the pool that was obviously the meeting place for actively hormonal residents with bodies homed in gyms from 4pm to 7pm every evening during week.

He declined her offer of coffee or a soft drink and noticed the absence of anything personal in the office. It was a marketplace for the building. There were hard candies wrapped in paper exhibiting the apartment complex logo. Brochures for renter's insurance and the cable company dressed tables along with brochures of the complex that included each floor plan.

"What was the name of the tenant in apartment 101?" John asked her.

"There was no tenant in 101."

"I don't understand."

"That apartment is one of eleven apartments we lease to Executive Suites Corporation. They use the apartments for executive housing on a short-term basis. Their tenants usually stay three to five days. ESC provides maid service every other day during their stay, as well as all of the furniture, television, radio, towels, dishes silver ware and pots and pans. We have no contact with their tenants. We have no reason. Our lease is with ESC, and per their contract with us, they must notify us when they check in a guest, and when they leave, so that we can inspect for damage."

"When was the last time that apartment was inspected?" John asked.

She stood and walked to a filing cabinet and pulled a folder.

"Two weeks ago, on the 7th. ESC cleaned after their last tenant vacated and called me for an inspection."

"If your lessee is responsible for the apartment, why do you inspect after their tenants vacate?"

"We have to be sure the carpet and walls are not soiled, plumbing and appliances are in working order—it's part of their contract with us. If the carpet needs cleaning, or the walls need painting within one year; we charge them labor and materials. There is no charge for any other repairs." She closed the folder and returned it to the cabinet.

"Did you inspect apartment 101 after the last guest check out?"

"Yes, I did, along with the maintenance supervisor, Matt Porter."

"Was anything missing from the apartment, or was anything left behind?"

"No, the apartment was in good condition—nothing was missing or left behind. The apartment was clean without any damage."

"Who found the body?" John asked, watching for a reaction.

"Our maintenance man, Matt Porter saw him first; then I saw him when I heard Matt calling for me from the bedroom."

"Why were you in the apartment?"

"I usually check the vacant apartments once a week for light cleaning needs."

"What did you do when you saw him on the bed, Ms. Harding?"

"I screamed and ran to the office to call the police. It was so sickening; so disgusting. He was lying there naked, with his face smashed in and his hands gone, and I couldn't breath. It was so horrible. I can't stop seeing it. There was nothing left of his face."

She had no idea that her tears were dripping on her desk. Her hazel eyes were filled and closing, and nose had turned dark pink as she transformed into a panic-stricken woman.

John knew she needed to express her fears and distress. He let her cry without saying a word and watched her become aware of her condition as well as her appearance. She was embarrassed, but grateful for the moment.

"I'm so sorry," she said, pulling a tissue from the box on her desk and patting her face, "I just can't stop seeing him and I don't know how to handle this."

She excused herself and went into the bathroom, adjacent to the office and closed the door. He could hear her lightly blow her nose while she cried. She turned on water and continued to cry. Andy stood and walked to the patio door overlooking the pool, thinking that would give her more privacy.

She returned to her desk looking controlled but pale. She was calmed and seemed to have brought herself into the present saying, "I don't usually break down; I just lost it, but I'm better now, thank you for your patience."

"Ms. Harding, you are a victim of this crime and you might want to talk to someone about what you are feeling", he said handing her a card with the name of a counselor for crime victims.

"Thank you, Mr. Garrison, but I'll handle this."

Her embarrassment was distracting, and he thought that continuing his questioning of her would benefit them both.

"How can I reach Matt Porter?"

"He's off today, and I don't think he is on property right now, however, he will be here Monday morning."

"I would like to meet with him Monday morning at 10:30 if he is available." John declared with a smile that sent the message that there were no options.

"He'll be here, and so will I."

"How do you know there was not a tenant within the last two weeks?"

"The company has to notify us when they lease."

"Who has keys to the eleven apartments leased by ESC?"

"We have a master key in our office, and so does the maintenance, supervisor and the lessee."

"Does ESC have a master key?"

"No, they have individual keys for each of the apartments as well as card keys for the front gate."

"Where do their guests get their keys?"

"They have to go to the ESC office to sign in and make payment."

"We'll need the address and phone number for ESC, and a contact."

John took the business card from the manager's hand thanking her for her cooperation while noticing her attempts at seduction.

"We need Chad's report to confirm the time and cause of death. The time will give us an idea of how long the killer was in the apartment," John told Andy walking to their cars. "I'm going to check with Missing Persons—there might be a name we can use.

"It won't be an easy ID without a face or fingers to print, and you have to open your mind to the possibility that he was killed somewhere else, John."

"There's nothing easy about this case. So far what do we know? An unidentified man is in the morgue without a face or hands, who was in an apartment that wasn't rented. I'll see you early Monday."

John walked to his car and called the number on the card he just received. The voicemail message announced that it was after business hours and they would open Monday morning at nine o'clock.

John left the property firm with his conviction that the body was in the one and only crime scene. There was no secondary crime scene; the killing took place in that apartment.

He drove away thinking about his children, knowing they would be as disappointed as he was for canceling his trip. He wanted to talk to them and hear their love.

His children were his daily blessing and he never lost sight of his role in their lives. He spoke with them daily and was always current with their activities.

He didn't want to resent his ex-wife, so he didn't. It wasn't about them. His relationship with his children was his. He discussed their welfare with their mother and made significant decisions together. He loved her for the children they produced together and the mother she is.

CHAPTER FOUR

Gary Sanford woke up later than he planned and had to rush to get to the golf course on time for their Saturday foursome. He drove into the parking lot and saw that he was the last to arrive.

Trey Peterson was the first to see Gary and waved yelling, "late night?"

"No, he answered smiling at his childhood friend, "good wine and the music of Mr. Parker".

Gary, Trey and Jeff Harrington had been best friends since kindergarten. He never imagined his life without them—he had no life without them.

John Garrison made the foursome. They met John in college and have been close friends since. John was a cop, and the others were all lawyers. They have been playing golf every Saturday morning since graduation.

Aren't you supposed to be in Seattle with your kids?" Gary asked surprised to see John.

"I caught a case that won't let me leave; my flight was changed so that Mrs. Garrison could keep a dental appointment she couldn't or wouldn't change. She didn't have time to get the kids to the airport to meet me for our trip to Vancouver and asked me to wait until today to give her more time to feed her narcissism and her well-nurtured ego. The kids and I talked, made future plans and here I am teaching you freshmen how to play golf, so you don't continue to embarrass yourselves."

"In your sick and twisted dreams—admit it, she owns you. You sold yourself to keep the peace instead of getting a piece." Trey said smiling, slapping John's shoulder.

"Be gentle," I'm vulnerable."

"Bull shit!" Trey shouted laughing. "Spell vulnerable and I'll kiss you on the lips and show you how gentle I can be to those I love."

They all laughed and felt the comfort in their relationship with each other, knowing it was a sanctuary from their worlds of chaos and frustration.

No one asked John about his case since it was their unwritten rule not to discuss business unless they needed each other's help within their specialties. They played golf with a passion and focus they reserved for this game.

After the game, they had breakfast at Katz' Deli, which had been their habit since the restaurant's opening. They arrived together and were greeted by Velvet, a rotund lesbian waitress who insisted that her wife was pleased with everything about her. She was loud, friendly, and attentive to annoyance.

Jeff, Trey and John ordered the strawberry pancakes as usual and Gary ordered an egg white omelet with a bagel. Gary gave Jeff his potato pancake, as was his habit—too many onions. He never told Velvet to hold the pancake because he knew Jeff loved it.

They talked about the women in their lives and lack thereof and made plans to celebrate Jeff's thirty sixth birthday next week with drinks and dinner at Delfresco's, which has become Jeff's favorite.

Jeff reminded his friends that he would be in Cincinnati Monday through Wednesday for depositions and planned to be back Thursday morning. They agreed to celebrate his birthday Friday evening and told Jeff to bring his wife. He declined the invitation for his wife, saying that the two of them would probably do something Thursday evening.

John took a rain check on a third cup of coffee, to spend the afternoon with a boy he mentored for the last two years.

Jeff was the next to leave the restaurant, planning to spend some quality time with his wife.

His friends knew that he was pre-occupied with his wife's distant behavior toward him in recent months. They were always weary of the pairing and subsequent quick wedding to a woman who was obviously not in love as much as she needed attention and a generous income. She was beautiful to distraction and was aware of the attention her appearance attracted. She was cold and aloof with her husband and his friends; notably Gary after he refused her flirtatious invitation for a drink and the desire to talk about her problems with her husband.

Those issues were off limits; they didn't involve each other in their personal relationships. They understood that their relationship was so bonded with time and experience that they couldn't be objective about each other.

CHAPTER FIVE

Jeff arrived home not knowing if he wanted to spend the remainder of his day with his wife. He married Cheryl Robbins six months after they met at a jazz concert he attended with Gary and Trey. Her beauty—the way she expressed her sexual appetite and it's potential, mesmerized them all. She had dark brown hair that flowed down her back like a delicate velvet scarf. Her eyes were deep, large almonds that invited you inside to be dominated by their never-ending depth. She was tall without intimidation. She didn't walk—hers was a glide beckoning admirers.

Jeff approached her like he had been waiting for her as long as he could remember. They left together and engaged in small talk over dinner and agreed to meet the following day for lunch. They spent the following day together and have been together since.

Cheryl had been a first-year law student when she met Jeff and decided to marry him. He had graduated the previous year, passed the bar and joined a prestigious firm. He was decent looking, seemed to be honest and honorable. He was easy prey.

She would marry him and create the life she planned ever since she knew she would not live like her mother who was and had nothing.

She waited a week before she slept with him performing a ritual that would leave him wanting more of the same as long as she wanted to use him.

She met his parents and knew immediately that they were not impressed with her performance. She also knew that they were devoted to their only son and wouldn't stand in his way when he married her. They would not be her problem. She saw no reason to spend casual time with them since they had nothing in common; especially since she was not in love with their son and would never give him the life, they felt he deserved. He did deserve a good life with a wife who loved him, but she wasn't attracted to him in that way. She didn't love him, and she knew she never would, but she could please him and nothing more was necessary for her.

Theirs was a small wedding, his parents and a few of his friends. There was no traditional reception because she couldn't bring herself to play the blushing bride opening wedding presents, sending thank you cards and hugging a bunch of people she didn't want to know.

Jeff bought the house before the wedding at her insistence that they would save money and should take advantage of the soft buyer's market.

She wanted four bedrooms so they would be prepared for the children he planned. She furnished every room before they moved in and announced that she would not return to law school because she didn't want to spend time away from him since he worked so hard. She wanted to be available for him when he came home. He fell for it like a boy opening Christmas presents.

Cheryl finally had what she wanted. What she worked for since she learned how easy it was managing men and she knew she had found the right man in Jeff.

The house was empty when Jeff arrived. He felt a sense of relief that his wife was nowhere to be found. He took a shower and dressed, expecting his wife's return any minute.

He called his parents to say hello and avoided his mother's questions about what was going on in his marriage. His mother meant only the best for him, but he would work out the issues that were tearing his marriage apart. His dilemma was that he didn't know what went wrong. He acknowledged his long hours working, but she had to accept that there was no other way at this juncture of his career. They agreed that he would work to insure their lifestyle and future. Still, it was no secret that his wife was unhappy. They have been married three years and she has taken no interest in their house, their friends or anything or anyone outside of their home. She continued taking birth control saying she was not ready to have a child.

Their lovemaking became less and less frequent and indifferent. Their first year was a marathon of gratuitous sex, but really nothing more.

Jeff became bored with his wife. There was nothing stimulating or challenging about their life together anymore. They argued about her inactivity to no avail. He offered to send her back to law school; she refused saying she had no interest or inclination, since they planned to have children soon, she wanted to stay at home to raise them.

He knew that children would be a mistake. He found himself working later hours and spending more time with his friends to avoid his wife and the possibility of children.

CHAPTER SIX

John Garrison didn't sleep well and finally stopped trying around five o'clock. He couldn't clear his mind of the body in the apartment or the condition of what he was sure was the crime scene. The killer would have no reason to clean so thoroughly if he just carried the body and placed it on the bed. If so, all he would have to do is wear gloves, cover his shoes before he walked in, leave the body, and walk out. He was had no doubt the killing took place in the apartment.

The killer wanted the body discovered exactly where it was. He had to know the routine of the manager's inspections, the activities of the maintenance crew and the layout of the complex.

How did he get a key? He wondered. Who was this victim and why did he deserve such special treatment?

John got out of bed without attempting meditation, which was part of his morning routine. He knew his head wouldn't clear enough to take him to the balanced state he wanted. He went into his kitchen and made coffee. He hated his coffee.

No matter what he did, he just couldn't make it right. He bought the best pots, ground the beans, used the best coffee and precision scoop and it turned out tasting like liquid shit. He tried again this morning and added a pinch of salt because someone told him that was the key. It turned out to be the key to salty liquid shit.

It was only six o'clock and too early to call anyone, so John decided to clean his apartment. He put on a pair of jeans and tee shirt and put his earphones in his ears to listen to music while and went to work.

He clean out the refrigerator first which was easy since it only contained beer, bottled water, two bottles of wine and some very old blue cheese that had been orange when new. As he cleaned the counter tops then mopped the floor, he pictured the killer doing the same.

He found himself enjoying himself, cleaning. He didn't realize how satisfying it could be cleaning where he knew his cleaning lady usually missed, however thorough she was.

He thought about the music he was listening to and liked the arrangement of Songs for my Father; Bony James was playing— Horace Silver would be pleased. When he was finished, he was aware of the peaceful ambiance of his home.

He left a note on the refrigerator for Marion, telling her that she only had to do the laundry because the apartment was clean. He would leave her usual fee in the usual place.

John had just turned off the shower when he heard the phone ring.

"My tea leaves told me you would be awake."

"Not only am I awake, but I have also made coffee, cleaned my apartment, including the refrigerator, changed the linens and have taken a shower." He reported to his grandmother.

"It is clear to me that something is weighing on your mind. If it's not the kids, I don't want to discuss it because it's your job and today is Sunday and we have plans for a good day. There is no time to include the darkness of your job. Are the kids ok?"

"The kids are fine as always, and you are right it's the job and we won't discuss it today."

"That's why I like you, my boy, you're so easy." I have decided to take you to dinner after the performance, so eat a light lunch and pick me up no later that one o'clock so we won't be late. Good-by Sweetheart."

He loved her more than she could conceive. His grandparents raised him and took him to every opera each season. He and his grandmother continued after his grandfather died while John was still in high school. It was his favorite thing to do—going to the opera with his grandmother. She taught him to appreciate and relate to the passion of the story, the music, and the performance. There was no other medium with more substance, none more earthy, impassioned, or tempestuous.

As a boy, they went to the Sunday matinees and sat in the Grand Tier, which were adequate seats, far better than balcony. After college, they started going to evening performances, however this season, his grandmother wanted to return to the matinees rather than being out so late, so he bought season tickets—side orchestra; that made the old lady feel on top of the world.

He opened his front door and picked up the large plastic bag that held the Sunday paper. His murder was on page two of the Metropolitan section. The article included nothing more than the fact that a man was found dead in an apartment and gave the section of town. There was no mention of the condition of the body or the apartment and names were not mentioned. It was as vague as he preferred so early in the investigation. He didn't have to concern himself with the usual crazy's confessions and blind leads.

He put the paper down; tired of reading and hearing about sharks attacking idiots daring to go into shark infested waters who were shocked that the sharks objected to the intrusion.

John called Katherine Whitney, an old friend who had no expectations of strings and usually made herself available when he needed a clear head.

"You're up early." She said answering and seeing his name on her caller ID.

"Breakfast?" He asked her.

"Your place or mine?"

"Mine. I'll cook breakfast."

"Before or after"

"Your choice," he said.

"Give me an hour."

He had nothing in his refrigerator to cook, so he made a dash for a store to buy eggs, bacon, cheese, and bagels.

It doesn't get much better, he thought walking to the super-market soaking up the quiet spring morning, a clean apartment, Katherine, Prince Igor, and dinner with his favorite lady.

The doorbell rang before he could put the grocery bags down.

Katherine was wearing a trench coat, high heels and carrying a large shoulder bag. She took off her coat, dropping it on the floor revealing only the shoes.

They had breakfast after.

He made a perfect omelet and more bad coffee. They ate and discussed the possibility of a long weekend in Cancun the following month if they could clear the time.

Katherine left by eleven o'clock, telling him she had to grade papers for school the next day.

He spent the next half hour talking to his kids and planning their vacation together mid- summer.

His oldest daughter, Jessica started her period the previous week and he made a mental note to send her flowers to celebrate this rite of passage. She wanted him to know that she was pre-pared and knew what it meant to have a period and what her body was doing. He admired her confidence and level headedness and always made sure she knew. His youngest, Sammy, was only inter-ested in her up coming dance recital and made him repeat several times that he would be there no matter what.

"It's on a Saturday, Daddy, you have to be here; no matter what."

"I'll be there no matter what, and I may bring you a surprise, but don't ask what it is, because I won't tell you."

He planned to take his grandmother with him, but he didn't want to disappoint the girls if she couldn't make the trip.

He said his good-bys to his girls and took his second shower and dressed for the performance of Prince Igor with his favorite date.

CHAPTER SEVEN

He read the newspaper and found nothing. They haven't identified him yet, he thought, putting the paper in the green recycle bin he kept in his garage.

He thought about his movements that night and day, scrutinizing every detail from approaching the victim at P&D's, to driving him to the apartment. He was right convincing him to leave his car at the club with a promise to return him after they satisfied their appetites for each other. That reminiscence repulsed him to nausea.

He knew he wasn't observed by anyone when he went to the apartment earlier that day to deposit the equipment he needed. The pills were easy to get and use, grinding them into power and mixed with the wine. Wrapping his hands was a nice touch with the explanation of an infection. Using blue Nitrile gloves made it more credible. The sorry son of a bitch bought all of it without question.

Waiting for him to die and bleed out was the worst part, boring at best.

He visualized all of his activity during his stay in the apartment. Everything was cleaned and the pertinent disposals were complete.

He had done his job well as planned. There was nothing left for him to do. It didn't involve him anymore since the entire situation had been handled in everyone's best interest.

The public has a short memory of sensational news that has nothing to do with them. After all it's not like the rising price of gasoline or lettuce, which would raise the ire of all good and *conscientious citizens.*

The death of a pedophile is just yesterday's birdcage carpet. The rape and abuse of young children is not enough of a concern when it's not personal. If it doesn't hit home, it's best left alone—it happens to other people.

Feel the passion!

CHAPTER EIGHT

ndy Becker was a weekend drinker and looked like it had been a good weekend when he arrived at Mama's Café for much anticipated good coffee and food. He ate three eggs over easy, ham, a side of bacon, grits, and biscuits. John ate toast and drank three cups of coffee, grateful for the taste of the real thing.

"This is the best food in the world. I mean it. You need to eat some of this. It doesn't get better."

John begged off, knowing that Andy believed what he was saying, since his idea of a great meal was dining in a booth at Denny's.

"We're going to meet with the maintenance supervisor this morning," John told his partner. "You can stop staring; it happened in the apartment."

"Where's the blood John? How could there be so much violence without blood or any trace evidence?

"He was dead before he was beaten and cut—a corpse won't bleed. He was probably beaten a day after he was killed." The coroner will have to tell us how he died. It could have been some kind of poison. I don't want to speculate; we just don't have enough. Maybe the janitor knows something, let's go."

Matt Porter was huge, they both observed. He was at least six feet six inches and weighed over three hundred pounds. He wore his blond hair the color of corn silk in a crew, and his aquamarine crystal eyes, small and staring, seemed detached. He looked like he was a member of the Sons of Freedom and had a small unkempt cabin in the woods of Idaho.

The maintenance man told the two detectives that he had been working for the building management company for six years. Prior to that he did odd jobs and had moved around from small town to small town. He married the girl he "knocked up in high school" in Diboll Texas, but left her there when he joined the army, from which he was dishonorably discharged six months later for smoking pot while on duty.

John was hoping Porter was from Idaho. It seemed a better fit. Maybe he had friends there and visited often in their unkempt cabins, he was thinking, and trying to picture this man beating the shit out of someone's face.

Andy asked him to tell them about finding the victim. After Andy explained what a victim was, Porter leaned against a wall looking toward his feet, and lit a cigarette butt.

"Me and Ms. Harding were inspecting empty apartments. She walked in the kitchen and I went to the bedroom and saw him layin' on the bed. She walked in behind me and just started screamin' and ran out the place to the office. You shoulda' seen it; face all smashed in and no hands. Can you believe it? No hands," he said looking up at John.

"I didn't know what to do, so I went to the office and she was callin' the cops. That's all I know."

"When was the last time you were in that apartment before you found the body?" John asked.

"A week or so ago."

"Why that apartment?"

"It was one of the empties, and we inspect them every week or two."

"Who was the man in that apartment?"

"How should I know? Hell, I don't know who they rent to."

"Was that apartment rented?"

"I wasn't told if it was. It was supposed to be empty."

"How long was that apartment vacant?"

"Two or three weeks, I think. I'll have to look at my logbook in my apartment."

"Mr. Porter, do you mind if we take a look at your apartment?"

"Hell, I don't care—I don't pay no rent here. Ain't nothin' in there except that logbook."

"We'd like to look around your apartment, Mr. Porter; there might be something in there that could help us." John told the man.

"It's just where I live. I don't know what your lookin' for, and I don't know nothin' about that man, but you can look all you want."

Matt Porter's apartment looked like an unkempt cabin in Idaho. It was sparsely furnished with a worn beige vinyl lounge chair that was pushed back with the footrest extended. It didn't look like it could return to its original position. The metal TV tray beside the chair was discolored and worn through the painted flowers that once covered the surface. The lamp sitting on the floor had no shade and was shaped like a small ginger jar that might have been in a child's room before the original owners threw it in the trash. The television was old with knobs instead of buttons and a hanger covered with aluminum foil replaced the broken antenna.

The kitchen stove had probably never been cleaned, the racks in the refrigerator were rusted and held the expected beer, bread, bologna, and a jar of mustard, most of which had dried on the rim and sides of the jar.

The bedroom consisted of a mattress on the floor with a pillow and blanket. His clothes were thrown in a large box on the floor in the bedroom closet.

"Do you have keys to all of the apartments? John asked.

"No, I have a master key that opens all of the doors."

"Where do you keep the master key?

"Right here," said the janitor, patting the key ring attached to his belt loop that must have contained at least a hundred keys.

"Have you ever lost your master key?"

"No. I keep it with me all the time."

"Where did you go after Ms. Harding called the police?"

"I had to see my parole officer. I can't afford to be late or not show up. That bastard hates me and would love to violate me, but I'll never give him a chance because I'm never going back."

"And what would you go back for?" Andy asked.

"Just a little drug charge a while back. Nothing much. I was just stupid and got caught."

"Is this your logbook?" John asked picking up a tablet that lacked a cover and was covered with coffee cup stains.

"Yeah, that's what I record the vacancies and what not."

"How would you describe what not?"

"Well, if they tell me the apartment is vacant, I mark it down and start getting it ready to rent again. I wrote down the date it becomes vacant and the date I finish the get ready, then I let the manager know the apartment is ready to rent again."

"Do you mind if I take your book so we can take time to examine it? I'll have a copy made and bring a copy to you. Would that be ok?" John asked him.

"Sure, help yourself; I can start another one."

"Thank you for your time, Mr. Porter. We'll be in touch soon." John said walking toward the door.

"Have you ever lived in Idaho?" John said turning back toward the maintenance man.

"Where is that, West Texas?

"No, closer to Dallas." John answered not surprised that the janitor was as dumb as a rock.

"What was that about Idaho?" Andy asked John.

"Nothing, I was just thinking out loud."

Andy knew not to push his partner for answers; sharing information was not his strong point.

John worked solo with a partner; Andy wasn't bothered by that arrangement at all, because that's who John Garrison was and he seldom missed a clue, so he was better off being left alone to do what he did best.

"He knows more than the nothing he offered," John said, someone had to let the victim in that apartment, and it wasn't to deliver his body."

"But why was he there, and how did he get so dead and not bleed?"

"*That* is the question, and that is why we call it an investigation, so let's investigate."

CHAPTER NINE

The detectives drove to the Galleria Area and parked in the garage that serviced the three identical office buildings on Post Oak Blvd that housed insurance companies, insurance brokers, accounting firms, mortgage and title companies and various and sundry other up scale organizations.

They determined that the Executive Suite Corp. office was in the building opposite their parking space, entered the building and took an elevator to the 34th floor. They opened one of the double glass doors and walked to the reception counter.

John asked to see the person whose name was on the card given to him by the apartment manager.

The receptionist smiled and called Brook Shafer, announced their arrival, and told them Ms. Shafer would be out in a few minutes inviting them to sit while they waited.

Brook Shafer walked through the door, greeted each of them with a gentle but firm hand and invited them to follow her to her office.

She wore a navy-blue suit with small round gold buttons down the front of her jacket and the bottom of her sleeves. Her navy-blue pumps were chic and small. Her black hair was pulled tight at the nape of her neck and tied with a black satin ribbon that was understated. Her earrings matched her buttons, small, round and gold. Her watch was small and gold. She wore no rings. Her eyes were deep blue, rimmed black that accentuated the contrast between her dark hair and blue eyes.

Brooke Shafer was stunning, John thought as he handed her

his card.

"We're investigating the homicide in the apartment your company leases and would appreciate your help with information about your clients," John explained, awestruck by her beauty.

"Yes, the manager called me right away. It was a terrible tragedy—it's still very hard to believe. How can I help you, Mr. Garrison?" she asked turning toward John, giving him her full attention.

"Ms. Harding said that the apartment had been vacant nearly to two weeks."

"That's correct."

"How do your guests get their keys?"

"Each guest has to come to our office to make payment and sign in. We then give them a key to the apartment and a card key to enter the property. We also give them the code to open the gate if a particular building does not use card keys: They have to pick up their keys by five o'clock if they have not paid in advance. If they pay in advance, and arrive after five o'clock, we will leave their key in a lock box." She explained.

"How do they get into the lock box?"

"We give them the combination."

"Do you have the names of your guests in that complex within the past twelve months?"

"Yes, I do. Please excuse me, and I'll get a copy for you."

When she left the room, Andy told him that he had that list from the apartment manager. John explained that he wanted to compare the two. He wanted to rule out either company leasing without the knowledge of the other.

Ms. Shafer returned with the list and offered any assistance they may require in the future.

"When will the apartment be available to us, Mr. Garrison?"

"Someone should be in touch with you about that within the week, Ms. Shafer."

John walked out of her office thinking only of the stunning Brook Shafer.

CHAPTER TEN

Gary Sanford regretted answering the phone immediately when he heard his mother's voice. Thanks to Caller ID, he avoided her calls as often as possible, but his bedroom was dark, and he answered without thought.

She was annoyed with him for not returning his calls for over two weeks, not knowing that he never listened to her messages.

"I've been busy at the office and haven't called anyone," he lied, feeling justified.

"Have you spoken with your father lately?" She asked with feigned concern, having no interest in his relationship with his father. She only wanted to know what he was doing and how he was living with Mrs. Sanford the second.

"Mother, I haven't had a chance to talk to anyone, so I obviously haven't talked to him. Why don't you call him? You're more interested in your ex-husband than I could ever be."

She resented the attack.

"I have no reason to call your father, Gary and you know that. I just wanted to know if you had spoken to him and when you are coming to terms with him to mend your relationship in some way."

"I don't have a relationship with him—I have no reason to call him, and you need to leave it alone, because I have."

"Can you have dinner with me this evening? We can eat early. It's been too long since we've seen each other."

It hasn't been long enough, he was thinking. Dinner meant hearing how difficult life has been for her since she is all alone now that she retired; arguing with him about his father—when he was going to settle down and get married.

He didn't want to hear her bullshit about not having grandchildren and being alone in the world. She couldn't fathom the world a better place as long as she was alone.

Does lightening have to strike her before she gets the message that she was a lousy mother, and she would be a worse grandmother? Gary thought—his mind screaming.

"Don't say no, Gary. I'll make your favorite smothered chicken and maybe a cherry pie."

What is it about food that makes my mother think all will be well once it's consumed? Is she that stupid, or desperate or just conniving? She was all that, and they both knew it.

"Ok, I'll be there by four o'clock, but I will not argue with you about anything or anyone. I'm walking out as soon as you mention your ex-husband, or what I should be doing with my life. Please understand the operative words here, Mother, *my life*," he replied, knowing his mother was beyond transformation and this visit would be good for several weeks.

Gary rolled over in his bed and thought about his parents. His father was aloof and worked more hours than a twenty-four-hour day accommodated. He was usually on his way out of the door when Gary woke up each morning and was seldom home before he went to bed at the end of his day for as long as he could remember.

His father was a successful personal injury lawyer, making his money on the asbestosis cases in the eighties. He was a shrewd and manipulative man who could justify his away a position satisfactorily for anyone including his wife and son. They didn't expect more from him because his mother defended every infraction, lie, absence and broken promise as if she agreed with him more than believing in him.

His mother taught high-school math and came home every day after school complaining about her no account, good for nothing, stupid students.

She thought every principal she worked for was incompetent

and less qualified than she. Her co-workers were trashy or worse, tacky; the same co-workers she socialized with often. Her relationship with his father gave her bragging rights to his success and money, to spend on anything that would pre-occupy her and distract her from her husband's lack of interest in their lives together. To his father, it was money well spent.

He never had a conversation with his father about anything while he was growing up, and after he was grown, he had no desire for a conversation with him because his father knew nothing of importance about him.

Gary didn't remember when he started hating his father or if he hated him. He resented feeling like an interloper in his own family, especially his father's life, in which he had no part.

He resented wasting time blaming his parents for the anger that he has come to treasure for its false sense of security.

He wanted to be rid of the feelings that haunted him relentlessly. He could rationalize to himself that neither of his parents were aware of how deep his pain dwelt. They were not affected in any way and would never be able to address it to a solution.

He turned on his back knowing neither of his parents was worthy of the time it would take to accept them both as they are.

He went back to sleep feeling safe in his own space, and content with the man he had become in spite of, not because of his parents.

He was seven years old in second grade at St. George's. Trey Peterson and Jeff Harrington were both in his class as they had been together since kindergarten and were best friends.

Father James Connor was the pastor of their parish and their soccer coach since first grade. The boys grew close to Father Connor and looked forward to being picked to do chores around the school and the church at the priest's request. The team went on field trips with the priest who often drove them home telling parents it was his pleasure to do so, giving him an opportunity to bond with the boys outside of school.

The parents felt fortunate knowing their sons were influenced and mentored by not only a priest, but also one who demonstrated sincere compassion and generosity. He tutored the boys when the need presented itself and monitored their progress in class seeing to it that their grades were consistent with their ability and potential.

A few weeks before the end of the term that promised summer vacation, Father Connor took Gary into his office and told him he needed help packing things away for the summer. He told the boy that he had a terrible headache and couldn't finish the packing without his help. Gary felt special because he was obviously the only one chosen for the privilege of assisting the priest.

After the boxes were packed and labeled, Fr. Conner sat down in his big chair and told Gary that his headache would feel better if Gary would help him by rubbing his head, which Gary obliged his mentor willingly. Fr. Connor said he was feeling better and took Gary's hands into his large hands and placed them between the priest's legs and instructed him to rub. Gary rubbed thighs for several minutes until the priest thanked him and told him that he would need his help the next day for more packing. He also told Gary that he didn't want anyone to know because the other kids may be jealous. He made the promise, and met his friends to walk home together, feeling empowered knowing he could help Father Connor feel good and they had a secret.

The following day, Gary went to Father Connor's office after school as planned and helped him clean out his desk and credenza. When they finished, Father asked Gary if he wanted to rub him again to make him feel better. Gary was grateful for the opportunity and began rubbing the priest's thighs with his small hands.

Father Connor moved Gary's hands between his legs and told him to rub his penis with both hands. The priest laid his head back against the back of his chair and held the boy's little hands in his own and masturbated until he ejaculated. Gary was frightened when he saw the priest sweating profusely, breathing heavily, in a fixed stare. He thought his friend peed on himself. Father Connor encircled the boy with his full-size arms, kissed and told him to always keep their secret. Gary had no doubt that he was the luckiest boy in the school because the priest who heard his first confession and gave him First Communion, a month earlier wanted him and only him to make him feel good and keep a secret.

Little Gary Sanford knew he couldn't tell his two best friends his secret because it involved a priest and priests could bless people and send them to heaven, where Gary knew he wanted to go when he was very old, like Trey's grandmother. She went to heaven to be with his grandfather who was very old too. He didn't like keeping secrets from them because they always shared their secrets and shoes since they were exactly the same size and they didn't want to get in trouble with their mothers if a shoe got lost. But this was different. He decided he could tell when they were very old and go to heaven together.

Gary, Trey and Jeff rode the bus together to Camp Timberlake in San Marcos, where they would spend most of the summer, as they did last year. They shared a cabin with a Bobby Prentiss, a boy from Albuquerque, who talked about snakes constantly. This summer seemed different than the last between the best friends--subdued. The friends didn't share any secrets like they always had. They remained close, but different.

They returned to Houston at July's end, tanned, and filled with stories about snakes, ribbons and trophies won and lost. In spite of the triumph of summer camp, they couldn't wait to start school in less than four weeks. They would be in the third grade and would train under Father Connor to be alter boys, learn multiplication, start Spanish classes and take part in the school trip to Austin if they had perfect attendance, never a problem, and maintained an A average, another no brainer for any of the three friends.

CHAPTER ELEVEN

John and Andy went to see the medical examiner for the results of his initial examination the body. They were told the Dr. Ellis was completing the autopsy. They waited in the doctor's office, because John respected his partner's reluctance to view the procedure since the death of his only son.

"Your victim had a fractured clavicle that had healed several years ago. He died prior to the beating and removal of his hands. His stomach was empty of food but did contain about ten ounces of red wine and 160 mg of Oxycondone. We should know more with the lab results, probably tomorrow afternoon." The medical examiner reported without looking up over his glasses.

"He was poisoned, and died in the early morning hours of Wednesday, perhaps between three and five o'clock.

His hair is dark brown hair, and his eyes were dark brown from what I could determine with the remains of his face.

He weighed approximately 170 pounds with his hands and was six feet two inches tall. He was probably thirty-six to forty years old. That's all I have for now—talk to me tomorrow; I should have more. You can read this in the meantime," the ME said handing his preliminary report to John.

"If you want to match him to a missing person, you'll have to wait for DNA and find something we can use for a match." Dr. Ellis said as he was walking out into the hallway— their signal to leave.

John went back to the Missing Person's Unit and requested a list of reports within the last fourteen days.

"We get dozens of reports per shift from parents; not nearly as many adults; perhaps three or four a week; sometimes less," the unit clerk told her favorite detective, the subject of her frequent, hopeless fantasizing.

There were seventy-seven male and female children under the age of eighteen. Most of the reported children just didn't arrive home from school on time and had hysterical mothers.

"We're not going to have a motive until we find out who this guy was," John said as he and Andy studied the list of missing persons that included six adult females and three adult males.

John called the first number on the list—the missing man answered the phone.

"Why the hell are you calling me?"

John identified himself and explained the follow-up.

"It's none of your god damn business where the hell I was, and why I didn't come home to the bitch who lives here."

John flinched as he heard the telephone bang in his ear.

"Ok, he probably still has his hands and face," Andy said while he was dialing the second number and saw the look on John's face.

A child answered John's next call to the home of the third missing man. He asked to speak with the little girl's mother. John identified himself and learned that her husband was still missing. She agreed to meet the detectives within an hour.

John could hear apprehension in the woman's voice when she said that she has had no word from her husband since Wednesday morning when he left for school. He was unwilling to discuss the possibility that the man lying in the morgue could be her missing husband, but he had to start with something, and they had so little.

It was after three o'clock and Andy complained that they worked through lunch and he had to get something to eat soon.

"Eat this," John responded offering him an Altoid.

"Thanks, and fuck you,"

John had never known anyone who appreciated food more than Andy Becker. He is never just hungry—his is a Zen-like devotion. His mantra is "I'm hungry".

"These taste like shit—I need food, Andy said sucking on the mint, I can't work like this every day."

"You don't work like this every day. I thought you ate for the day at breakfast." "Bite me, Garrison."

"No, *I'm* not hungry." John was deliberately sarcastic.

Traffic was crawling, but they arrived on time and were greeted by Helen Danford.

The house in West University was large and expensively furnished. She invited them into her living room, offering coffee and the cookies she baked earlier.

John watched his partner's insatiable preoccupation with the contents of the plate placed on the table in front of him.

While his partner imbibed, John asked Mrs. Danford if she knew of any reason why her husband would not return home or contact her.

"He has never done anything like this before. He teaches school and is usually home around five o'clock.

"Has he done anything like this before?"

"No, I told the other officers the same. His schedule is usually the same."

"And what would that be—his schedule?"

"He goes to his gym several mornings a week before school and is usually at home by six o'clock.

"Have there been problems in your marriage?"

"It's a marriage, Mr. Garrison—good and bad days. I'm not aware of a reason he would have to leave."

"Does your husband have any medical problems that you are aware of?" John asked her.

"No. He's in good health."

"Did you report any scarring or birthmarks on your husband?"

"I told them that my husband had a strawberry birthmark on his right leg; he fractured his shoulder; actually, his clavicle, from a fall off a ladder a few years ago. He was hanging Christmas lights and missed a step."

"What else did you tell the police officer taking the report?"

"I told him what my husband was wearing when he left home—his height, weight, hair and eye color."

"Do you have a photograph of your husband?"

"Excuse me while I get some for you."

John's partner drank three cups of coffee and finished the plate of cookies, without interaction with his host.

"Thank God she had food; I thought I was going to die."

You *are* going to die, John thought saying nothing to his partner, knowing his words would fall on resentful ears.

Mrs. Danford returned carrying a photo album containing pictures of her family. He chose a photo of her husband alone, and one with a man described as his father.

"Do you know the name of your husband's gym?" Andy asked her.

"Yes, it's Gold's on Richmond; usually three mornings a week before he goes to school."

John agreed to return the photos as soon as possible. She seemed more relaxed than when they arrived and offered a small bag of cookies to Andy, who accepted, beaming with appreciation.

"Why didn't you tell that woman we were trying to identify a murder victim?" Andy asked with his mouth full. "She thinks we're looking for her husband; why didn't you tell her?

"We still don't know enough yet. We'll give the information we have to Missing Persons and let them do the match."

"But it sounds like he's our guy." Andy said.

"It *is* our guy," John said, "but let Missing Persons do what they do, and make the facts known to the widow, while we find out why someone wanted the Reverend Darren Danford's son killed and mutilated."

"You've got to be shittin' me," Andy responded with surprise and looked at the photograph John handed to him.

CHAPTER TWELVE

Mrs. Danford seemed anxious about her husband's disappearance, John thought leaving her home, but she was controlled enough to make him pause before accepting her grief. She never mentioned their two children in any way. Their brief encounter seemed disingenuous in the least, but he wasn't able to see through her composure. There was more to the very attractive Mrs. Danford than a loving concerned wife, but she couldn't do this crime; it wasn't in her element.

John dropped Andy off at his car and went back to their office to finish his report, still thinking about what was behind the façade of Helen Danford. Before he left to meet his friends for a drink, he decided to look into the background of Darren Danford; the motive for his murder might be somewhere in his computer.

The database responded with more than he expected about the Danford's lifestyle. Dirty linen, he thought, sometime comes out gray.

He left his office with print outs documenting their victim's shortcomings, and was ready for happy hour, when his cell phone vibrated. He recognized the voice of Clay Woodward, in the Missing Person's Unit.

"It looks like your victim could be a match with Darren Danford—missing since Wednesday evening. The description of the fracture sounds the same as your dead guy, down to the birthmark. I'll feel better about it with DNA. Are there any children?"

"Two."

"I'll be in touch with results."

"Thanks, Clay."

John didn't need DNA for confirmation. He knew that Darren Danford's handless body was lying in the county morgue; he just didn't know why. He also knew that Danford wasn't the clean living, model citizen, described by his wife, who was his first suspect; not for the actual act, but she could have been directly involved.

I needed this happy hour, he thought, as he parked his car in the Kroger parking lot across the street from the popular club. He entered the office building and took the elevator to the top floor, where he immediately saw Trey Peterson talking with a beautiful woman who would share Trey's bed within hours.

Trey waved him over and led him to a table where he saw Gary talking to two men he didn't recognize. They waited for their much-deserved drinks, while Trey introduced his newest conquest—she smiled saying nothing. She lit a Newport, ignoring John lighting a match in front of her.

The crowd was light this early in the evening, and the buffet table was laden with toquitos, casadillas, miniature tacos, queso, chips, cheese, and fruit.

Dinner! They all seemed to think in unison.

Trey's friend excused herself to the ladies' room and traced her hand across the back of his neck.

"She has an impressive economy with words", Gary commented.

"I don't give a shit what she has to say; the less the better. I just want to fuck her, which is what I intend to do when I get rid of you children." Trey responded watching her disappear and looking around for more prey, just in case he needed a plan B.

"And what are your plans for later?" He asked the two men sitting with him.

"I think I'll hit a couple buckets of balls, then go home and sleep alone." Gary said. "Nothing for me," John added, "I have an early morning and some paper work to tackle before I go to sleep alone like my friend here."

"What do you know about the Reverend John Danford?" John asked both of them. "Nothing much—he has that monster church. The one with thousands of followers, satellite locations and a helicopter, and just in case you have a late Saturday night, you can hear his message every Sunday morning through the wonder and convenience of television." Gary responded.

"He must have a shit load of money judging from the size of his church, and his house." Trey added.

"What's your interest?" Gary asked.

"His name came up today, and I just wanted to get some feedback."

"You've been to his house?" Gary asked Trey.

"Yeah. It was a fundraiser for a political campaign. If you ever paid attention to me, you would remember that I invited you to go with me."

"Do either of you love birds know anything about his son?"

"The street says he likes boys and frequents P&D's. Could be just rumor, since he's married, has kids, is a teacher and his father is a prominent church leader, but who knows. He may be a freak in teacher's clothing and knows how to pull it off." Trey reported.

When Trey's girlfriend returned to the table, they stood, and she seemed caught off guard by the gesture.

"Are we leaving so soon?" She asked no one in particular.

They all sat down without response and shared the food on the several plates in front of them.

After another round of drinks, Trey stood and took the outstretched hand of his new playmate, bid them a good night, and left feeling good about the night that had just begun.

Gary left next saying he wanted to be able to see the balls he planned to hit.

John stayed alone over another drink and thought about

Darren Danford.

P&D's was one of the oldest gay bars in town and maybe the stomping ground of the missing Mr. Danford. He ate a few more tacos, paid the check and left to buy his next drink at old gay bar.

CHAPTER THIRTEEN

I t was seven forty-five when John parked into the crowded lot. He removed his tie and locked his gun in his glove compartment, making sure no one saw him before he got out of the car.

He entered the bar and saw only two women sitting at the bar; all the other patrons were men; most of which were in business attire and demonstrated no effeminate behavior, contrary to his expectations.

There were two bars inside. One was large in the front of the building facing several tables and five booths. The second was in a separate room in the rear; a smaller room without tables that led to a patio with small tables for two, cabaret style.

P&D's was frenzied; some patrons huddled in private conversation, others with voices maneuvering above the deafening sounds of Aerosmith, unaffected by the strain.

John sat at the end of the larger bar opposite the front door and ordered a beer. He spoke to no one, not wanting to draw attention to him that could raise suspicion from the very people he looked to for information about Darren Danford.

He sat wondering about how much Danford's wife knew about his alternate lifestyle, or if she was even aware.

The man on the stool next to him got up and walked away as another took his empty seat and ordered a Jack Daniels and water and waited for his order while casually greeting those he recognized.

"I'm a regular here and I don't recall seeing you before." He said to John before lifting his drink for a sip.

"I've never been here before." John told the man while he

stared ahead into the mirror behind the bar waiting for his drinking partner to become more inquisitive.

"I come in here every day after work. I plan to have my wake in this place. It's more like home than anywhere else, and I know all of the regulars. I guess you could call this my second home."

The man passed the sipping stage and moved onto two large gulps and ordered another.

"You know anyone here?

"I'm meeting a friend. I don't see him yet, but I'm early—he's on his way," John told the man and waited for the obvious question.

"So, what's his name? I may know him.

"Darren Danford"

"I know Darren, he's been coming here for a couple of years, but I haven't seen him for a week or so. He may be out of town, or maybe he's been sick, because he's usually in here two or three times a week, every week.

"I haven't talked to him for about two weeks, but we planned to meet here to celebrate my promotion." John said.

"The last time I saw him in here, he stayed for a short while and left with a guy I never saw before, but he looked good, so I can't blame him if he got lucky. Carpe diem, that's what I always say."

"Maybe I know the guy he left with, what did he look like?"

"Oh, he was about your height—dark hair, mustache, shaded glasses and a tight ass.

The man looked over John's shoulder, stood and gulped the last of his drink.

"Enjoyed talking to you, but my partner just came in and I'm not in the mood for his shit."

John watched his new friend walk to a man who immediately started an animated dialogue, that John could imagine involved their conversation.

He stayed and finished his beer while checking his watch, to support his growing impatience waiting for his imaginary friend to arrive.

"He was in here last Wednesday." He heard the bartender say. "I remember because a few minuets after he arrived, my ice machine shut off and I went to the other bar to see if the one back there was working. When I came back here, he was gone and he hasn't been back since, and it looks like he's not coming tonight."

"Thanks," John said getting off the stool, "I'm going to head out of here; if he comes in tonight, tell him I waited and to call me. My name is Chuck. Thanks again."

John walked across the street to his car knowing that Danford could have been looking for Mr. Goodbar and left the bar with the man who killed him.

He decided to pick up some groceries since he was facing the supermarket and an empty refrigerator at home.

He drove home picturing Theresa Dunn in Looking for Mr. Goodbar, sitting at a bar, reading The Godfather.

He went home and put a frozen pizza in the oven and read his notes on the case while he waited to eat.

He considered the note found on the victim's chest.

FEEL THE PASSION. THERE WILL BE NO MORE.

What passion drove anyone to this kind of violence, and did the writer mean; there would be no more killings, or what?

There was anger—rage; could it have been revenge?

He threw the burnt pizza in the garbage, went to bed, and fell asleep within minutes.

CHAPTER FOURTEEN

John and Gary Sanford met at the gym for their daily workout and pumped heavy iron after a half hour running on the treadmill. They sat in the steam, quiet and relaxing because no matter how often they performed this very early ritual, they still felt the burn.

"It's a shame you didn't get a chance to see your kids. Were they ok with it?" Gary asked.

"They're fine. I have good kids who have learned to accept what I do as one adventure after another. Their mother is good with them and is always ready to compensate when anything interferes with my plans for the girls. Our children have good parents whose priority is their welfare regardless of the relationship between the two of us. The kids are never a negative issue—we can't afford the potential damage."

"Do either of you consider moving so that your kids will have more of you?"

"I consider it every day. I grew up without parents. That's one of the reasons I talk to them every day, and see them at least monthly, thanks to Southwest Airlines, but it's not the same as being a full-time parent. They need me directly involved in their lives and I want them here. My family as well as Charlotte's family still lives here, and kids need their family. It *does* take a village to raise children, and my kid's village is here in Houston."

"Some villages aren't as supportive as you seem to think, John, there are too many kids out there who have parents and satellite families but fall through the cracks because the villages are shallow."

"I'm very much aware of my influence on my daughters—that every man they become involved with will be judged by them based on the kind of father I am, and the message of their value that I convey. I won't allow them to get lost in pursuit of a father figure. I will always be a positive father figure, and Charlotte and I have to make a firm decision on how they are raised to be productive well-adjusted women."

"Are you prepared to move to Seattle?"

"I will if it comes to that. Make no mistake, I don't want to leave Houston; I have a life here, as well as family. I respect Charlotte's right to live the life she chooses, and I'm confident it will work out while the girls are still so young."

"Fatherhood is a vague, if not foreign concept to many men." Gary said thinking of his father.

"I don't agree, I think every man knows the responsibilities and expectations; it's a matter of choice."

"If you're right, too many kids get lost if not destroyed by the choices of their fathers."

"But it's not about the kids, Gary, it's about the fathers. Somehow, we as a community have to make these kids understand that they didn't lose themselves, they just don't have participating fathers. I've got to get going, I'll see you in the morning."

Gary's resentment of his father controls everything he does and thinks, John thought about his friend as he drove to his office, grateful that his grandparents raised him without any more baggage other than who killed his parents.

He was finishing his report when Andy walked in carrying an open box of Danish in one hand and a bottle of milk in the other. He offered the last pastry to John who refused with the usual 'I already ate,' excuse.

"I came back to the office last night and found some interesting news on the missing Mr. Danford. There was a domestic violence report filed by his wife three years ago; she refused to press charges. When the uniforms showed up, she said they had an argument, and everything was settled. There were two more reports phoned in by neighbors, who were concerned about the fighting that apparently was frequent. Each time, his wife explained only arguing; nothing more."

"Did he ever beat her?"

"If he did, she never reported."

"I wonder if she ever beat *him*." Andy laughed.

"Now hold on to your Danish, John said looking up at his partner, "he was arrested for fondling one of his male students, but the charges were dropped when the parents came in with the boy and said their son lied because he was mad at his teacher for not letting him go on a field trip. They questioned the kid, and he confirmed his parent's account of what happened."

"Can you believe that shit?"

"This puts a whole new light on things. I think the kid lied for some reason and we need to know why."

"Danford probably paid the parents off and didn't give a flying fuck about their kid. This bastard should have had his balls cut off too." Andy shouted without knowing his voice was pitched.

It was obvious that his partner was angry, but he could be right about a payoff—it made sense, and would explain why the marriage was so volatile, and why Mrs. Danford gave the impression of a happy marriage when she probably knew that she was married to a freak.

They both went over their notes again before John finished their status report, while Andy sat at his desk angry and staring expressionlessly at nothing. John was sure his partner was thinking of his son, Tommy.

"It's lunchtime. Let's eat." Andy said, standing over his partner.

"You just ate a box of pastries."

"That was two hours ago and it's lunchtime; let's go."

"We need to talk to that kid's parents and find out what really happened with their son and his teacher." John said ignoring his partner's food issue.

"Before we meet the parents, I think we should confirm the identification to give us a starting point. It's too vague without knowing who he is, then we can find out why."

CHAPTER FIFTEEN

"If our victim is Danford, I don't think his wife's loss would be that great if she knows what we think she knows, and I wouldn't mind questioning her before he's buried without his face and hands." Andy finally spoke, finishing another cup of coffee with three sugars and flavored cream.

"I don't understand why you're not fat or dead; the way you eat." John said shaking his head.

"A good breakfast starts the day right. Didn't your grandmother tell you that? Besides, Beth knows how you feed me, so she gives me chicken, fish, and grass when I get home.

John laughed picturing Beth trying to keep her husband alive and well.

"You're right about Mrs. Danford. Let's see if we can wrap up the ID today, then we can express our sympathy and question the widow."

The ME was able to rush the confirmation that their victim was Darren Danford. He also confirmed that he was given a lethal dose of a synthetic derivative of codeine— Oxycondone mixed in three ounces of red wine.

"He didn't live long after he drank the wine. He was long gone before he was beaten and mutilated. Someone was very upset with your Mr. Danford, but at the same time, spared him from the torture of the beating and removal of his hands. Your killer had heart; crazy, but sensitive." Dr. Ellis said handing a copy of the report to Andy.

There were several cars in the Danford driveway and on the street in front of their home when the detectives arrived. John had spoken to Mrs. Danford earlier and she agreed to see them.

Reverend Danford opened the door, introduced himself with an open grin and led them to his daughter in law, and offered to stay with her during our visit. She dismissed him saying that she was comfortable and had spoken with both men previously. Rev. Danford walked toward the door and told the detectives he wanted to talk to them before they left.

"Mrs. Danford, we respect your time of grief, however, we have some questions that may disturb you, and I want to assure you that is not our intent. We want to find the person who killed your husband, and we need all the information you might have." John said. "We would rather wait, but there are some issues that need clarity, if you don't mind."

"Mr. Garrison, I am not embarrassed by my husband's deviant life, I was disgusted by it, and my family is disgraced," she said surprising them both.

"He liked young men and boys."

John watched her as she described her husband without emotion and wondered what why she remained in the marriage.

"Mrs. Danford, there are several reports of domestic violence involving you and your husband. Was he physically violent?"

"I don't think so."

"There's a record of domestic disturbance; could you describe the nature?

"I could, but I won't, Mr. Garrison. There has to be something sacrosanct about a marriage."

"With all due respect for your marriage as well as your loss, you may have information that will aid our investigation."

"Well then, I suggest you investigate without expecting me to do it for you."

Andy saw this woman as a certifiable bitch, who didn't give a damn about her husband or his death.

John chose to ignore her anger and sarcasm and chalk it up to grief or relief.

"Do you have any knowledge of the accusation of sexual abuse involving your husband and his students?"

"I only know of two minors with whom he had a relationship. My husband visited with the parents and the problem went away. I was told there were no other boys, but I never believed him when he told me he realized how he hurt those children. I really don't think my husband had any concern about either of those boys or their parents."

John was captivated by her calm discussing her husband's sexual proclivity.

"When my husband told me about the boys, he said they were no longer minors and there was no proof that he did anything wrong.

"Did you speak with the boys or their parents?"

"I had no reason to speak to anyone. The charges were unexpected and shocking. I chose to support my husband and sustained my support when the first boy recanted his charge."

"You said your father-in-law visited the parents of the students involved in the charges filed. Do you know why he made those visits?"

"I consider my father-in-law unconscionable. He condoned his son's sins and paid money for them while he stands in a pulpit every Sunday and denounces deviant behavior without compromise."

"How do you know that the parents were paid?" Andy asked.

"I wasn't involved; however, I know my father-in-law and I know how he protected his son."

"So, you have no proof that the parents were paid."

"I know that the children recanted after his visit with their parents."

"Did your husband ever mention the parents or why the charges were dropped?"

"No. Gentlemen, I don't think I have anything else to offer. What has happened is unfortunate. "I'm sorry for my children, as for myself, I am relieved and unburdened and will go on with my life raising my children, satisfied that their father will no longer share their space."

Andy realized his mouth was open and closed it when he saw John staring at him, frowning. He thought about the parents who accepted money for the rape of their sons. They sold their sons to this freak and benefited from the violation that changed their son's lives permanently.

Mrs. Danford told the two that she would answer any of their questions another time, but she had to spend time with her children and try to empty her house of family, friends and curiosity seekers with hidden agendas that weren't as hidden as they thought.

The Reverend Danford was in the kitchen consoling two women when he noticed the men he had asked to speak with earlier. He led them into the den, where they met with the victim's wife, and motioned for the two to be seated. He was tall, well dressed and in workout condition. He had a deep voice that resonated like that of a radio announcer or deejay.

"My family and I are overwhelmed and saddened by the death of my son and the circumstances surrounding his death. We want to cooperate with you in any we can to aid your investigation.

"Did your son discuss with you the sex abuse charge filed against him?" John asked.

"Did you have this discussion with my son's wife?"

"Will you answer my question Reverend Danford?"

"My daughter in law is overwrought and should have time to take this all in before you question her about details of her relation-ship with Darren. I don't see how she could possibly be objective knowing her husband, the father of her children was so brutally destroyed. You do understand what I'm saying, don't you?"

He never stopped smiling as he spoke and remained standing over the men until he presumed his message was received.

"Reverend Danford, we appreciate your concern for your family. It is important that you understand that it would be in no one's best interest to hinder or delay our investigation in any way. We plan to meet with Mrs. Danford again at her convenience; a decision best made by her without influence. John said to the minister eye to eye without expression and with complete conviction.

"Were you familiar with your son's alternate lifestyle, Rev Danford?" John asked him.

"I don't think I understand your question, sir."

"Your son was know to frequent gay bars and having sex with men, sir. Andy said emphasizing sir.

"I think you need to leave my son's house. I can't believe any-one could have said anything like that about my son. It's filth, and I won't allow you or anyone to impugn his reputation. He was a teacher for Christ sake. He was a husband and father and com-munity leader. I don't think you know just who you are talking to, gentlemen. I don't intend to threaten you, but I assure you that you will not continue on the path you have chosen for this investigation. You can count on that. Now if you'll excuse me, I'll show you out."

They walked to their car in silence, both smiling, trying to hold the laughter that exploded once in their car. "I assure you that you will not continue on the path you have chosen for this investiga-tion," Andy roared.

"It looks like a path well chosen, and I look forward to walking it with the Reverend Darren Danford.

"Before we talk to him or Mrs. Danford again, I want to talk to someone in the DA's office to see what we need to get bank records of the parents of the two boys who were molested, Mrs. Danford and Reverend Danford's. If we can show that the father paid off the parents in lieu of charges filed, The Reverend Danford may have some explaining to do. John told his partner.

"All we should need is the report on the charges filed and a statement from Mrs. Danford. I think his sex habits got him killed. We might want to look at the fathers of those two boys and find out if there any more kids out there who might have a score to settle that can't be settled with Danford money. Andy said.

"We may have a motive." John said to himself as he drove away.

CHAPTER SIXTEEN

Gary took a long hot shower and thought about his friend, John and how he had a good marriage even through divorce. His family was still a healthy unit. He and his children interacted with over a thousand miles between. He considered he and his father's distance with less than six miles between them.

He dressed and took his time driving to his office to meet with a client that didn't deserve the powder it would take to blow him up. His case seemed hopeless since his client was arrested with over three hundred 80 mg Oxycondone tablets in a bag on the front seat of his car and twenty-three hundred dollars in his pocket. His client's father was a successful dentist who seemed to tire of his son's lifestyle and didn't express any trepidation at the possibility of conviction and hard time.

The client's guilt was a given and not an issue for him, but he had to defend him and accept the fact that if acquitted, he would return to the streets to make his living to the detriment of the public welfare. He resolved never to represent this man again.

Defending street crimes was not Gary's preference. His few clients within that genre were usually as a result of favors to significant acquaintances. He had no sympathy for those clients who were clearly responsible for their crimes and demonstrated no intentions of ceasing their adverse behavior had they not been caught. He didn't feel accountable for their acquittals, but he did feel culpable in the sense that his skills as an attorney leant themselves to positive results. These feelings were not within his comfort zone with which he only had influence without control. He was not comfortable with anyone prevailing at the expense of the well being of innocence.

He didn't regret his choice of specialties in any way. He delighted in associating himself with clients accused of embezzlement, defending them to acquittal, or the insider trader, or even the claims adjuster who set up a dummy company, rented a post office box, created fraudulent claims and made payments to themselves. Gary rationalized that these clients were stealing from companies that were stealing from the public and deserved to be victimized. The public was innocent and did business in good faith. The same could describe the companies charging his clients.

Fuck them, Gary thought. Fuck them all. The big fish will always eat the little fish.

His practice prospered as a result of his success in the courtroom. He was sought after, and expensive. He made sure that everyone paid.

Gary was also pleased with himself that he managed to anger his father who planned a partnership with his son. Gary never understood how they could partner when they seldom spoke. He just assumed that his father worked out that detail to his own satisfaction. His mother didn't care as long as she could brag, bitch and moan. It made her happy. He was her successful, accomplished, well-paid son. It didn't get better for her in her vacuous shallow world in which she was queen and lived in it alone with her memories and misery. He knew his parents would never know him.

"How did you explain the pills and cash when you were arrested?" He asked his client.

"I didn't shit—it wasn't any of their god-damn business."

"What did they think you were doing?"

"Dealing."

"What were you really doing?"

"Dealing."

"What did you tell them?"

"To kiss my flat white ass."

"I'm going to assume that you expect to walk on this; what's your plan?"

"Those bastards can't prove anything. The cash I had was mine—my family has money. I don't know how those pills got in my car unless they put them there, and they can't prove they didn't."

"They don't have to; they just have to prove that you did with the intent to sell."

"I, or rather you rest my case."

"Do you know of any witnesses that could vouch for you?"

"All the witnesses will vouch for me."

"You know this for a fact?"

"I know this. Just tell me when and where, and I'll see you in court."

Gary knew his client would be acquitted because the state had no case, and he was good enough to convince the jury that his client was falsely accused because he was black, drove an expensive car and had a lot of cash. It works every time.

He called John to remind him of Jeff's birthday dinner on Friday.

"Is it just us, or are women involved."

"Just us; he's leaving his wife at home."

"I'll be there."

Gary noticed a brown envelope on the chair his client recently occupied, addressed to him. He opened it and pulled out a piece of paper with a note that read "a *little something to warm your nights.*" The envelope also contained a bottle of Oxycondone capsules.

"Sorry bastard." Gary said out loud, and left his office taking the package with him.

CHAPTER SEVENTEEN

John and Andy agreed that the more they knew about the victim, the closer they will be to catching his killer and motive. They were convinced the motive had something to do with the molestation of children, but who would know about it other those involved, specifically the parents, school officials, police department and the District Attorney's office.

While discussing those they assumed were involved, they realized there were more potential suspects than they cared to consider. The killer didn't have to have a direct involvement like that of the parents. He or she could have just been aware of Danford's taste for boys and acted to stop him or seek revenge.

John was sure they were looking for a man. A woman would have problems lifting a man the size of the victim. The forensic team determined that the victim was lifted onto the bed after the beating and mutilation.

Although a woman usually cleans more carefully than men, care and precision was key. It was if the cleanliness lent itself not only to erasing evidence, but purifying the circumstances surrounding the crimes of the victim.

Peter Altman was a prosecutor as long as John was on the job and they openly disliked each other without ever having been adversarial. Their vibes were not in sync and John never bought into Altman's ego screaming for acknowledgement of his genius that was never demonstrated.

"Why do you think seeing bank statements will help you solve this crime that you don't seem to have a handle?" Altman asked while reading their report. "Where's your evidence that those statements are germane to your case?"

"We have a statement from the wife of the victim that the parents of two boys were paid off by her husband to drop the charges and change their stories. One or more of the parents may be involved in this murder and we want to see if there's any unusual activity in their accounts that may confirm her statement prior to questioning them." Andy said." Without the bank statements we may not get evidence of a payoff unless they admit to it and I don't expect they would be so inclined." John added.

"How do you expect me to explain this supposition to a judge? After all, I have to consider my reputation. You wouldn't want to do anything that would taint my reputation and standing with the courts, now would you, either of you?"

"Aside from your reputation and good standing, this was a heinous murder. The molestation of these children could play a part in solving this crime. There is a possibility that Darren Danford molested the two boys, and the parents know it to be true. One or more of them my have enacted their revenge, in spite of a payoff for their silence."

"What if you find nothing in those accounts?"

"There's the possibility that Reverend Danford's church was the source of those funds because it may not appear that a church pastor is in the income bracket to make a payment of what could have been thousands of dollars. If that is the case, we have a responsibility to all of the families involved to follow through and I think you understand how a positive outcome would enhance your reputation." John declared, knowing the stroking would buy the warrants.

"I'll call you after lunch and let you know if the judge is as optimistic as you are."

"He's a card carrying, certified son of a bitch. Do you think anyone wonders why so many of the people he prosecutes walk out of the courthouse with him? Is he that incompetent, or does he have photos and tape on the DA?" Andy said talking to himself, walking with John to their office.

John smiled knowing his partner was on to something, but he wasn't concerned with the prosecutor's hubris; he was always useful.

They re-read the report and learned the boy's name and that of his parents. The child was eleven years old at the time of the alleged assault and a fifth grade student of Danford's. He stated that Danford kept him after school for talking during class. The teacher locked the door and used his erected penis to rub the boy's buttocks. The student alleged his teacher "did it to him in his car" once. He told his mother more than a month after the car incident and she reported to the police. Within a week, the parents retracted the statement. When questioned, the boy stated he lied because his teacher was always on his case. There was no report filed on the second boy reported by Mrs. Danford.

John called Helen Danford and asked if she remembered the name of the second child. She gave him the name and address of the boy and his parents. It had to be true, John thought. How else would she have detailed information about these people?

John called Altman and gave him the names of both families of the boys. He took the information and agreed to call back within the hour, in time before the banks closed for the day.

The news from Altman was a relief. The warrants covered the bank accounts of the Danford's, Reverend Danford, his church and the parents of the two boys; the teacher's credit union was also covered.

There were two banks and the credit union. The Danford's, the preacher, the church and Mr. and Mrs. Will Davis used the Union Trust Bank of Houston. Mr. and Mrs. Paul Hutchinson used the First National Bank of Texas.

John made an appointment with the manager of the downtown branch of the Union Trust Bank, advising him of the warrant. He left his partner to meet with the manager of First National. Andy

Becker called and spoke with the manager of the credit union and arranged to pick up the statement at six o'clock that evening.

He waited over an hour for the printouts of all of the statements requested. When they wheeled the boxes in his direction, any plans he had for that evening and maybe the next were dashed. He finished packing the boxes in the back of his car and called Katherine Whitney who taught accounting the University of Houston. She answered with her usual, "I've been thinking about you all day. I can't believe you called." He was flattered and explained what he was doing that evening and probably most of the night, and he needed her to help him go through the church's statements for possible discrepancies. She agreed to assist when he promised to provide dinner and she promised desert any way he liked.

He called his partner next and asked him if he would mind working together at his house and told Andy they would have the assist of a CPA. Andy said he picked up the statement from First National and was on his way to the credit union and would meet him after he went home to shower and changed and kiss his wife.

John stopped for Italian food to feed his accounting team for the night. One of his favorite Italian restaurants does not provide take out, however, the manager made an exception since he was a frequent patron and was sympathetic hearing John's dilemma. The full servings were made for two or more and he usually ordered half servings, but Andy ate for two, so he ordered full servings of spaghetti with meat sauce and meat balls that were the size of baseballs, mushroom stuffed ravioli, and lasagna and a loaf of bread. He sat at the bar and ordered a drink while he waited for his dinner and called Katherine and told her that his partner would be joining them and she might want to consider dressing for the occasion. She laughed and thanked him for the heads up.

CHAPTER EIGHTEEN

Andy went home to take a break before heading over to John's for the night. He was unable to rid his mind of parents who took money in lieu of charging their rapist. His thoughts drifted to his son, Tommy.

Andy's son was thirteen when he started cutting the neighbor's grass for spending money. He was proud of his growing business and the money he had saved. He was earning enough over the summer months to save most of it for a car he wanted to buy when he turned sixteen, which seemed forever but not hopeless.

Tommy Becker cut yards weekly during the summer and every two weeks into the fall at twenty-five dollars per yard. He was able to buy his own equipment and stop using his parent's mower, edger and weed eater. His father drove him on the weekends to his client's homes since he was underage. He knew his father was impressed with his enterprise and independence. He admired his father and pleasing him was a primary motive. He looked forward to his weekends with his father who sometimes talked about his work but never any revealing details about his current cases.

He was smaller than many of the boys in his class, but he was popular and confident and never intimidated by the size of his peers. He was well like by teachers and students alike and knew that being the son of a cop added to his popularity.

He asked his mother to drive him to one of his clients one Friday after school because his customer was going on vacation and wanted the grass cut before he left.

Tommy finished his work on the yard and rang the doorbell to collect his fee and to ask the resident if he wanted the grass cut the following weekend.

His neighbor was home alone and invited Tommy in for a glass of something cold while he wrote the check. He stepped in the house and noticed right away that the man's wife didn't spend as much time maintaining their house as his mother did theirs.

The man was friendly and told the boy to sit and started talking about the vacation he and his wife planned at Padre Island. Tommy thought the man wasn't really excited about Padre Island, but it was cheap and an easy drive.

Tommy was surprised when he started to feel sleepy and wondered what was keeping his mother; he was ready to end his visit with his boring neighbor and go home. He asked if he could use the phone to call his mother and was told that his mother called while he was cutting the yard and she said she would be a little late because she had to go to the cleaners before it closed. The man noticed Tommy's eyes drooping and told him to lie on the sofa while he did some work on his car in the garage. The man left the room and the boy passed out a few minutes later.

Tommy woke up when he felt his mother's pull on his shoulder. "Wake up, Tommy", he heard her say from somewhere, not close, "wake up, Tommy", he heard the familiar voice as he opened his eyes, feeling tired in a way that was strange and hazy. He sat up and saw his mother's worried look and his neighbor standing behind her without expression.

"There he is--too much sun I'll bet. He's seems ok now. You run along now with your mother and get some dinner, and you'll feel like your old self. I'll see you when the wife and I get back" he heard his neighbor say as they helped him from the couch. "I put all you stuff in the back your mother's truck and you're ready to go."

"I appreciate your call me Mr. Parker. I've never seen Tommy quite like this. I'd better get him home."

"Don't thank me and call me Herb, all my friends do, and I feel like we're old friends."

Tommy and his mother arrived home and saw his father drive up behind them. "What's wrong with you, Tommy? His father asked staring at his son and walking him inside.

"I fell asleep at Mr. Parker's house while I was waiting for Mom to pick me up."

"Why did it take so long to pick him up? It's just two blocks from here."

"Mr. Parker called me and told me he wanted Tommy to stay longer to help him do some work in the back yard. He said he had some mulch to spread and weeds to pull and he would pay extra. I told him it was ok and have Tommy call me when he was finished."

Andy's son was laying back and falling asleep when he heard what his mother said.

"Mr. Parker told me you called and said you would be late because you had to pick up the cleaning before it closed. There was no work in the backyard to do."

Andy was scared more than angry when he asked his son why he went into the man's house. He explained that he was waiting to get paid and the man offered him something cold to drink and started talking about his vacation.

"When I asked to call mom, he said I didn't have to and told me she called, and what she said, and that I should wait there for her. I started feeling sleepy and he told me to lie down because he had to work on his car; then mom came."

"What else happened," he tried not to shout at his son.

Tommy didn't answer. He was asleep.

Andy lowered his son's shorts and noticed the redness on his buttocks. He left the house after telling his wife to call the boy's doctor, asking him to meet them in the ER.

Herb Parker did not answer his doorbell. A neighbor next door walked across the lawn and said he saw Parker leave a few minutes earlier. Andy asked if Parker's wife was at home. The neighbor said Mrs. Parker moved out over a year ago.

"Do they have any children? Andy asked the neighbor.

"No. Just the two of them; we never saw much of her and they didn't seem to go anywhere together."

"Did you know much about him? Who did he work for?"

"They moved in about two years ago and never made friends with any of the neighbors. Several of us tried to make friends with them both, but they weren't interested and kept to themselves. She didn't work during the day. She may have worked at night, but I wouldn't know. I don't know what he did. I would see him leave early when I was leaving for work, but not always. My wife says he was home often during the day. He may have done shift work. I just don't know."

Andy was seething when he thanked the neighbor and drove home to pick up his wife and son.

"What's going on Andy? Why are we taking Tommy to the hospital? His wife asked, pleading with him for information.

"I think that bastard hurt Tommy, I think he raped our son."

"Don't say that, Tommy could hear you. "How could anyone do what you're saying? He's our neighbor for God's sake. This is ridiculous."

"Let's go Beth. We need to find out what's wrong with him right away."

"Not before he takes a shower. He been sweating from cutting grass and he needs a shower.

I'm not letting him go anywhere, dirty. Give us fifteen minutes, then we can go."

"Beth, didn't you hear me? He needs to be examined to rule in or out rape. He can't bathe first. Just get him and let's go."

Beth Becker would not allow herself to believe that anyone could violate her son.

She was in the man's house. She thanked him for calling her to pick him up. Tommy cut his grass all summer. The possibility of her husband's suspicion was ludicrous and evil. It didn't happen, not to her son. Not Tommy.

They met Tommy's doctor in the emergency room and Andy

explained his feelings about his neighbor and Tommy's physical condition.

Andy and his wife were sitting in a waiting room when he saw their doctor walking toward them saying he wanted to talk to them privately and let them into an office close by.

"Mr. Becker, it appears you were right. Tommy has GHB in his system and there has been rectal penetration." Andy heard his wife's scream as if in a vacuum as she slumped over the desk in front of her resting her head on her arm.

Andy's head, his whole being was awash with rage and hatred. He barely heard the doctor say, "I'm obligated to report this to the authorities."

"Do what you have to, I'm calling it in now, and I want that bastard found.

"Is Tommy alright?" Andy asked his doctor.

"Physically he'll be ok in a couple of days, however, because of the type of drug that was used, Tommy will have no memory of the rape. I strongly recommend he get counseling right away. I can make a referral, and you can take him home tonight. He'll need you to be levelheaded and as calm as possible to help him through the investigation and its aftermath. Keep in mind that this happened to him and he'll need your support and confidence."

They took Tommy home with very little to say. Beth Becker convinced her son that a hot bath would be better than a shower and left him soaking while she made sandwiches for all of them. When she went downstairs to prepare their supper, she heard her husband on the phone.

"I went over there, and he wasn't at home. I want someone here to take a statement from my wife and son right away, and I want a search warrant for his house tonight."

Beth didn't want to talk to anyone tonight and said the same to her husband when he walked into the kitchen.

"It will be tomorrow morning anyway since they have the rape kit in the hospital. Someone is going to pick it up tonight," he consoled his wife as he helped her make the sandwiches, he knew would go uneaten.

John was the first to arrive at the Becker home the following morning. He and Andy went into the den away from Beth who was ashen with fear and grief.

"Are you sure about this?"

"It happened and that bastard did it. I don't know what I'm going to do, John. I don't know what to say to Tommy. I'm more preoccupied with wanting to kill that freak, than I am with helping my son. You have no idea what I've been through just to keep myself from hunting him down and beating the shit out of him. I want him dead, John."

"I feel you partner. You know we'll get the guy, but you can't work this case. You have to support your family. Killing him is only going to send you away and they need you more than he needs killing. You know what happens up there to child rapists. It's worth keeping him safe to deliver him into the hands of men who have no collateral investment in their lives.

"The kit was delivered this morning and we talked a judge into a warrant as soon as we get the statements from Beth and Tommy. It's happening Andy. Stay home with your family and let us handle this. You know I'll let you know what's going on every step of the way. You can't contact this Parker guy; it could hurt the case. Give me your word you won't try to contact him. We need you to do nothing Andy."

Andy Becker was encouraged with his partner being the lead on this case, even though it was not their department. The exception was obvious due to the circumstances of their partnership.

Andy sat with Tommy for hours explaining what they thought happened to him and trying to make him understand how the process would develop. Tommy couldn't understand how anything could happen like his father described and have no memory. He trusted his father and believed that he would be safe because his father told him so.

John took the statement from Beth and Tommy separately and they were consistent. He was sickened thinking what had happened to a child he knew since he was a baby, who called him Uncle John. He couldn't help thinking about his daughters and tried to know how Andy felt; he would want the same kind of swift justice because nothing else would do.

He left the Becker's assuring them they would get the warrants for the house search and DNA sample.

CHAPTER NINETEEN

Herb Parker was at home when they arrived with the search warrant. He was immediately belligerent and sarcastic as he read the papers handed to him by John Garrison. The officers spread out through the house and commenced the hunt for evidence. John sat in front of the computer and asked for Parker's username and password.

"Don't think ill of me, Detective, I'm a normal man who likes to look at pretty things."

John was looking at the web page on the screen in front of him that made his stomach feel empty and sick. A man and a woman engaged in oral sex with a young boy; a man and a boy engaged in oral sex. John clicked on links that were similar to the web page and some that were more deviant.

He turned off the computer and told its owner that he would have to take it for further inspection and possible evidence.

"I think it's time to call a lawyer," Parker said to John.

"Tell him to meet us downtown and I'm placing you under arrest for the possession of child pornography. You have the right to remain silent. Anything you say may be held against you in a court of law. You have the right to an attorney, if you can't afford an attorney one will be provided for you. Do you understand these rights as read to you?"

"Yeah, I understand what you're trying to do, and it's bullshit."

An officer locked handcuffs around the man's wrists behind his back and walked him to a patrol car.

John stayed in the house until he was satisfied that they had everything they could find including a glass on a table beside the couch, that still contained liquid. John hoped that was the glass Tommy used. He called Andy and gave him a status telling him the forensic team was examining the sofa for semen as well as the bed.

Judy Hayes, had worked sex crimes for as long as John was a homicide detective, working each case as subjective as she could without losing her focus. She walked out of the bedroom toward John, her face squinting with confusion.

"Tell me exactly what you are looking for and why."

"My partner, Andy Becker's son was in this house yesterday and there's evidence of his being raped. We think it happened here by the owner. The boy was drugged with GHB and semen was found in him."

"Follow me, I think you might be interested in what we found," she said leading him back to Parker's bedroom.

The closet door was opened, and a thick electrical cord was running out of the closet, plugged into an outlet on the bedroom wall. The forensic team stepped aside to allow John inside where he saw a small refrigerator covered by an afghan against the back wall of the closet. Judy opened the small door of the refrigerator and revealed the head of a woman.

Herb Parker was tried and convicted by two separate juries for the murder of his wife, and the rape of Tommy Becker. The lesser charge of providing GHB to a minor was dropped because there was no evidence of the drug in the house. The glass contained only water, only Parker's fingerprints on the glass.

Tommy was fifteen years old before the trials were concluded and his life had changed irreparably two years earlier as he came to accept what happened to him on that day, he went into his neighbors to get paid for cutting his grass.

He was drinking his parent's vodka at night to help him sleep without the having to think about anything. School became a chore he never experienced before he was raped and. He was quiet and stayed in his room most of the time he was in his house and had little to talk about with his parents. His psychiatrist assured his parents that he would work his way through, and out of his depression with the medication prescribed, but Tommy didn't take his medication because he didn't want to feel better. Feeling better in his mind would mean accepting what happened to him and he couldn't allow his rapist that privilege.

He managed to graduate from high school with average grades and no plans for college or anything productive. He moved out of his parent's house and moved into a small efficiency, worked odd jobs to pay his rent and support his mind-altering habits that sheltered him from a reality that included the life he planned when he was young and innocent, trusting the world provided for him.

His mother brought groceries to his apartment every week and talked about their lives as she would have preferred and avoided the truth about her son's lifestyle choices and her shattered dreams for him. She had denial down to a science and it suited her well.

His father visited him and tried to get him into a rehabilitation program and assured him that he understood what his son was going through, and that he would always have his support. Andy Becker talked to his son about Herbert Parker and his conviction that would end with a lethal injection. He wanted his son to be assured that his crime had been avenged; he shouldn't give Parker the prospect of destroying his son's life.

"He has taken enough from you; don't give him all of you. You have value and promise, you are capable of loving and giving of yourself in a way that makes you a compete man. Share and live your life again. Please don't give my son away to that man or anyone. I love being your father, Tommy. I am honored to have raised you and shared in your dreams. I don't want to be the man I have become without you in my life. I need you to be the essence of who you are, and I need you to be the man I know you want to be."

He loved his father for his honesty and consistent support. He never felt that he disappointed his father; he knew however that he would never fulfill his father's expectations that he worked so hard for, and that he regretted more than the rape.

Tommy Becker celebrated his nineteenth birthday at his parent's house and went to his apartment and drank himself to sleep, the night that Herbert Parker was executed for the murder of his wife.

The following morning Andy went to his son's apartment to give him the birthday gift he left behind the night before. When there was no answer, he opened the door with the key his son gave to him and found Tommy laying on his bed bleeding from his right temple, no longer afraid of his life, no longer in pain.

Andy sat next to his son and loved him as he read Tommy's letter to his parents.

Dear Mom and Dad,

I have no reason to be here any longer. Please don't ever think that you didn't do everything possible to help me. I know that you have. You couldn't have been better parents. I couldn't love you more for all that you are.

Mom live your life again and be the mother that I always remembered and loved. Thank you for loving me and always making sure that I knew I was loved. This is not about either of you.

Dad be the man you were. The man I wanted to be like. Don't give him the privilege of taking your life.

This is my decision. It's about me.

I know that you will always remember me, but don't think of me as lost or wasted. Think of me as Andy and Beth Becker's son. Life couldn't have given me a better gift.
Love, Tommy

Andy made the necessary calls and waited for the medical examiner to take the body and police officers to leave his son's apartment. He gathered his son's personal property that he knew his mother would want and went home to tell his wife her son was dead.

Beth Becker held her husband tightly and sobbed in a way he had never heard.

"I can't handle this," she cried to her husband. "That man destroyed our son, and we couldn't save him. I can't believe he's gone. What does that mean, Andy? What does it mean? Does it mean we aren't parents any longer?"

"We are the parents of Tommy Becker. Our son lives in our hearts and our loving memories. We are the parents of Tommy Becker who was a wonderful son, Andy told his wife.

She read her son's letter and cried holding on the letter when her husband put her to bed.

He hurried to open the front door so the doorbell wouldn't disturb Beth and saw John standing there. Andy held on to his friend and cried for the first time since he was a boy.

Andy and Beth buried their son knowing that his death would not destroy them, or their marriage. Tommy was right, they had to live on in spite of this tragedy. They had to honor of their son. They knew that the alternative would mean the destruction of their family, which is what Tommy, didn't want and led to his decision to leave this world.

Beth always said that everything happens for a reason and in its own time. They didn't always understand, but they were determined to live their lives loving each other and their son.

CHAPTER TWENTY

J eff Harrington arrived at Hobby airport and called his wife while he waited for the van to take him to his car. When she answered, he told her he would be home within the hour and asked her to have dinner with him. He said he hadn't eaten all day and thought she might like a night out. She agreed and said she would be ready when he got there.

Maybe we can make a night of it, he thought, while driving out of the garage. It had been weeks since they went anywhere together. She seemed willing and he wanted to take advantage of the time and try to refuel their relationship that had cooled long ago without him noticing.

He was exhausted and wanted a drink and made a mental note not to drink too much while they were together. He gave her everything she said she wanted. He tried spending more time with her, but she was so seldom available. He didn't know how else to salvage his marriage and wasn't sure he wanted to continue trying, but failure was never an option for him, and he wondered if that was the reason, he tried so hard. Did it have anything to do with his wife or loving her if he loved her? He wondered.

Cheryl Harrington seemed happy to see her husband when she hugged him and kissed him softly with passion.

"You look tired," she said, "we can stay home if you like and I'll make something for dinner."

"You look to good. Let's show you off and to Delfresco's and then to a club for music and drinks. Just give me twenty minutes and we're off." He said running up the stairs to change.

Jeff felt like they had gone back in time. They were actually enjoying themselves for the first time in months. He didn't wonder why. He didn't want to question the gods. They went to the club and ran into Trey and Gary who were without women and didn't seem to mind. Jeff relaxed and felt better than he had for too long. He was with the people he cared about most in the world and all was well.

They went home and made love like before they were married.

CHAPTER TWENTY-ONE

John arrived home in time to take a shower before his guests arrived for dinner and a night of auditing. He called his daughters and listened to them recite the grades on each report card, and both asked their father what he was going to send them for all of their A's. He told them he wasn't going to pay them for doing what they were supposed to do, but he would send them something just because he loved them.

He called his grandmother who chastised him for being too busy to check on her earlier in the week. She said she didn't have any more time to talk because she was getting ready for a wild night of sex with a young man, she met at the gas station that day. He wished her a wonderful night of pleasure and told her he would see her on Sunday for dinner. She reminded him that he only loved her for her food; he agreed and hung up feeling better as always after talking to her.

Andy was the first to arrive. He delivered the statements of Darren Danford from the teacher's credit union and that of the Hutchinson's.

"A friend of mind will be here soon," John told him, "she's a CPA and teaches accounting, so I thought she would be a great help especially on the church. She should be here any minute. I have dinner; we can eat first then get down to work. You won't believe how much paper I picked up from Union Trust. Follow me."

"Jesus Christ," Andy said whistling, "we'll be here for the rest of the week."

"This is the rest of the week. It's Friday."

"Ah shit," John shouted, "I'm supposed to be meeting friends for dinner tonight for a birthday celebration."

He excused himself and called Gary Sanford's cell and begged off the birthday dinner, telling him that work demanded his attention for the night. He would see them all on the golf course the next morning.

It was a birthday celebration with friends who spent most of their birthdays together and he didn't need to be there unable to join in the remember old times repartee.

CHAPTER TWENTY-TWO

Delfresco's was crowded as it usually was on a Friday evening. Gary could see why Jeff favored the palace. It's seductive, yet the subdued ambiance was plush without pretension. The colors—that of a peacock, were warm and rich. The décor was imaginative art deco, with massive, rounded booths, torchier lighting in shades of green along the wall and carpeting in shades of purple and green with a circular print consistent with shapes of the booths and lamps.

Gary arrived with Jeff. Before they were served their first drink, they watched Trey walking toward them smiling.

"Happy birthday, my brother. You're finally as old as we are. You're a man now and I love you." Trey said pulling his friend from his chair and hugging him with sincerity.

"Thanks man. I love you and you know it."

They waited for Trey's drink and toasted Jeff and themselves—their bond.

They each ordered salmon and tuna tartare with caviar as an appetizer.

"I wonder if this caviar is the real thing," Trey said chewing his food.

"Like you would know." Gary teased.

"Everyone knows I'm a bon vivant." "Everyone knows you're a player and have never had a playmate who could spell caviar." Jeff said slapping his friend on the back of his head and laughed.

"You have pierced my heart with your caustic tongue, but I'm a man and I forgive you."

"You're a true friend, now shut up and eat your fake caviar." Gary chided.

"The two of you looked like newly weds last night," said Gary. "What's up in the Harrington household"?

"The usual with a slight twist that passes with time. This is not the night or the occasion to discuss anything that might become thought provoking. It's my birthday and I'm not leaving here until I am very drunk and satisfied that the two of you will have an exorbitant check to pay for this auspicious celebration."

CHAPTER TWENTY-THREE

Darren Danford Sr. sat in the study of his home considering the path he chose to this day of possible reckoning. Always gregarious, even as a boy, he knew early on that he wanted to be rich, famous, and powerful. He received an undergraduate degree in economics from Stanford, and a law degree from Yale, and was a successful attorney until he realized that he was getting rich, but fame and power eluded him.

The church leaders of his youth became his role model for success and power. They had power over their flock and if they had a television ministry, their flock could encompass the world and number infinitely. He enrolled in Divinity school with an agenda that was not intended to be hidden. It was never discussed. He graduated with honors as planned and networked his way into the echelon of influence that afforded him the opportunity to take over a fledgling inner-city church with an active membership of less than two hundred members. The church building was more than forty years old and had fallen in disrepair along with the lethargy of its members.

Reverend Danford had no intention of building his career as leader of a rundown church with a handful of the faithful from the immediate neighborhood.

Repairing the church was not an option he considered. He utilized his gift of enterprise and rhetoric to induce his members into a fund-raising frenzy to build a new church. He started by selling the existing church and leased a larger facility that had been an abandoned warehouse. The proceeds from the sale of the old church purchased land in an area that would be more conducive to the membership he envisioned. Sunday after Sunday, he preached messages that fed the egos and sympathies of his flock. He developed community-based services that included various classes, seminars, AA, Al-Anon, singles and senior citizens groups and crated a board of directors that was responsible for the rules and direction of the ministry. He would always have a seat on the board. They broke ground for the building of the new church within five years and the Reverend Darren Danford ingratiated himself with the city's moneyed movers and shakers that were flattered by the handsome young preacher that could provide them with a worthy cause, political issues and constituents.

The weeklong celebration of the opening of Grace Memorial Church was phase one of his master plan to build the largest church in Texas or perhaps beyond.

CHAPTER TWENTY-FOUR

John opened the door for Katherine who stood there wearing a trench coat and high heels, carrying a large shoulder bag, causing him to regret her next move that he would have to explain to Andy Becker for the rest of his life. He realized his eyes were closed when he heard her roar of laughter and his partner was asking him if he was ok. He opened his eyes and embraced the wave of relief as she removed her coat to reveal a white button-down shirt and khaki skirt. She reached into her large bag and removed a pair of brown clogs, laughing the entire time. He smiled at his friend, taking her coat and bag and introducing her to Andy.

Katherine lifted her bag from a chair and removed a box containing the most mouth-watering tiramisu he remembers ever seeing.

They ate until they were stuffed, leaving dessert for later if not another day. Katherine started work on the church's bank records after John explain what they were looking for and elicited her confidence about anything discussed among them or anything she overhears between he and his partner about the case. Andy called Beth to check on her and told her that he may be all night, then started working on the records from the credit union.

It didn't take John long to learn that the credit union account was used for direct deposit of the murder victim's payroll check, and a payment deducted monthly for a car payment. There were several overdrafts within the last three years. The account was in Darren Danford's name only. There was no record of an account owned by his wife.

Andy started auditing the First National Bank of Houston account belonging to Paul and Denise Hutchinson. Paul Hutchinson worked as a truck mechanic for the City of Houston; the father of two teenaged boys, and his wife worked as an office assistant at a local title company. There was no record of a savings account with the bank or any kind of an account beyond their checking that had a balance of three hundred forty-seven dollars. A direct deposit was made bi-monthly in the amount of one thousand ten dollars by the City and bi-monthly check cashed in the amount of five hundred ninety-two dollars that appeared to be the payroll check of Denise Hutchinson. Monthly checks were written for rent, car payments, household utilities and grocery stores in addition to several checks for cash. There were no checks payable to any credit card companies. The Hutchinson's spent their income as they earned it, with no evidence of savings. Andy scrutinized the records that were consistent with deposits and withdrawals that gave an overview of the family's lifestyle.

"Bingo." Andy said in a monotone that caused John to look up from his own audit.

"A deposit for sixty thousand dollars was made on February 3rd 2018. This has got to be it. Where else would they get that kind of money? It's the payoff. Every penny of it." Andy stood up stretching his arms and walked to the kitchen.

"Check that date in the other accounts," Andy said to the other two auditing, as he walked back into the room carrying a plate with a large piece of tiramisu.

John had been working on the victim's account and didn't find a deposit or withdrawal in that amount that day or the week before or after. There was a direct deposit from the school district once a month.

"This is interesting," he said to his partner, "three years ago, the account was a joint account with his wife, then changed to his name only. There is a check written to his wife for thirteen hundred dollars a month on the day of his payroll deposit." John continued to study the account looking for activity that might lead to an explanation of the Hutchinson's deposit, but found nothing that would explain their windfall.

Katherine was in another room working alone and had not been heard from since they started. John and Andy took a break with a beer while Andy ate another serving of the rich dessert. John answered his phone on the first ring and recognized the voice of Beth Becker.

"I just wanted to remind you that I know that my husband is having a food orgy and I hold you responsible because he can't help himself." "I cannot tell a lie." John made his confession, smiling. "Tell him I'm going to bed with the neighbor and I love you both; oh, one more thing, send him home for breakfast. Bye."

"You know your married to a physic. She's going to bed with your neighbor and you have to have breakfast at home." He reported.

"You did well, my friend. Continue to forget tonight's menu and I won't have to shoot you."

"Have you wondered why no one has mentioned the wife of the Reverend?" He asked John.

"Yeah, I've been thinking about that. No one gave us any indication that she was in the house the day we met the father, and he and Mrs. Danford made no reference to her.

Just then, Katherine walked into the room looking at the papers in her hand, placed them on the table where John was working and said, "You need to look at this."

"There was a withdrawal on February 2, 2018, and April 10th; both checks made payable to Reverend Danford and signed by him and a Mavis Foster. Those two apparently sign all of the checks." Katherine said.

They were staring at the checks in the amount of sixty thousand dollars and fifty-five thousand dollars. The checks were cashed at the same bank the day it was written.

"There's more. Notice how much money is deposited each Monday. Obviously from Sunday plate collections," she said.

"Whoa, Andy said and whistled. "It's a fucking fortune."

"Ok, now look at these withdrawals on the fifteenth and thirtieth of each month; check made payable to the preacher. I would have to verify it with their accounting records, but those checks are probably payroll just for him. There are other consistent checks written on those days to a few others who probably work for the church. Do you think we're in the wrong business? This preacher earns big bank every month," she continued to report her findings.

"I need a bathroom break and a drink," she told John.

Andy watched her walk away and turned toward John, tilted his head, and winked. "Say nothing. We friends."

"I understand," Andy said. "Beth is my best friend."

Andy went through the statements of the Davis' and found a deposit of fifty-five thousand dollars.

"I'm the man. Here it is, the other payoff. It's just like the Mrs. said, there were two boys, and this is not a coincidence."

What do you think they did with the money?" John asked rhetorically.

"I'm still looking."

John went back to the victim's statement. Katherine returned to her assignment without a word.

Andy looked up and stared at John saying, "it looks like the Davis' used some of the money for a mortgage down payment. Here's a check for thirty thousand made payable to a title company. Everything else looks like day-to-day living. The Hutchinson's nickel and dimed their winnings down to their current balance.

"I can't find anything unusual about the victim's activity other than the payments to his wife that may easily be explained, John announced looking up from his stack of paper.

"I wish I could say the same for the father," Katherine said walking toward them. "He's dirty; I'm sure of it, but I'll have to see more before I can put it together for you and I need sleep. I'll work on it while you're away and we can get together Monday." She was gone and the house felt empty hearing Andy leaving and saying something about having a good weekend.

John went to bed alone and thought about Darren Danford and his father.

CHAPTER TWENTY-FIVE

Denise Hutchinson was surprised to see Reverend Danford when she answered the bell, opening her front door. She recognized him from his television broadcasts and frequent photos in the paper. She was awestruck by his good looks and demeanor when he told her who he was and asked to speak with her and her husband. She led him to her living room and pointed to a chair that embarrassed her with it's faded fraying from age and neglect. She told him that her husband was on his way home from work and was expected any minute. She excused herself, explaining that she had just walked in shortly before she arrived and wanted to freshen up. He refused her offer of water. There was no liquor in the house except some beer in the refrigerator, but she didn't think it would be appropriate to offer alcohol to this man of God.

Paul Hutchinson walked into his house wearing his oily jumpsuit that was his uniform and called for his wife who ran to the door whispering to him that they had a guest who was waiting to speak to both of them and arrived unannounced.

"What's he doing here?" He asked his wife, frowning.

"Shh. He'll hear you. I don't know. He just showed up and wants to talk to us," she said and walked with her husband to the living room, where Reverend Danford stood smiling extending his hand to Paul.

"I hope I haven't inconvenienced you much, but I wanted to speak with the two you about my son. I realize that your relationship with my son was nothing more that a brief business venture, and that was of a personal nature that only involved my son and your family. I trust you will continue to keep that information private. I'm sure you understand my meaning. There is no reason why your family should be involved is such an unpleasant matter. I can't tell you how much my family and I appreciate your discretion and your kind and sincere sympathy. It sustains me. I also want you to know that you will always be welcome as visitors and hopefully members of our church. People such as yourselves are the backbone and strongest support of our ministry, and I am grateful to have had the opportunity to visit with you and appreciate your fine demonstration of friendship.

The Hutchinson's listened to this man of the cloth who graced their living room. Darren Danford stood and held out his hand and told the couple to call him at any time if they ever had a need, walked to the door thanking them again and was gone.

CHAPTER TWENTY-SIX

John called his grandmother before he got in the shower to see if she was getting ready. She told him that she was packed and dressed and was waiting for him to get the lead out. She said she didn't wrap the gifts she had for the girls. She didn't want those airport people tearing them apart, so she packed them in her suitcase.

They had an eleven thirty flight to Seattle to spend the weekend with his children. The girls had no idea that their great grandmother was coming to see them. He couldn't wait to see their faces. He used frequent flyer miles and savings to upgrade to business class to make the old lady comfortable. He set his alarm to wake him early so he could take time to meditate, go to the gym, work out and steam to calm him self and clear his mind for this weekend with his family.

He drove up his grandmother's driveway when he saw her open the door carrying her suitcase toward the car.

"Don't get out little boy, I can do this."

"Give it to me and get in the car." He said as he opened the door for her.

"I thought you changed your mind; it took you long enough. You look like you've been up all night. Did you have breakfast?"

"I did." He lied.

"Well let's go then and don't drive too fast, I want us to get there in one piece."

He loved her.

They arrived on time, rented a car, and drove to the girl's school, the site of Sammy's recital. He stopped on the way to buy flowers for his talented daughter. They arrived just as the program began and took seats in the rear.

Sammy was seated on the stage looking anxious and beautiful. He felt the pain of missing them.

When his daughter walked to the piano, he was startled by her confidence. She was in control and had no awareness of anyone but herself and what she was about to do. She was perfect and she finished her piece, paused, stood, and bowed.

Her face lit up as she saw her father stand clapping his hands and whistling his pride. Before anyone could stop her, she jumped from the stage and ran to her father's arms and hugged him unaware that the audience was still applauding her performance. Jessica ran down the aisle to her father and screamed when she saw her grandmother. It didn't get better than this, he thought.

John and his grandmother waved one last time before they entered the plane that would take them home, away from his children and he kept his shades on to shield from curious eyes.

"You'll never know how wonderful this weekend was for me, John. You couldn't give me a better gift; thank you sweetheart, I love you. And I love those girls," she said to her grandson after she was belted in her seat. Charlotte is raising them well and I'm proud of the way you get along with her since the divorce."

"You did your part," Mrs. Garrison. He said winking at her. "She's a good mother. That was never a problem; we were the problem." He told her.

He leaned his head back and started thinking about what was waiting for him in Houston.

Who killed Darren Danford and why? The motive was buried in family secrets, but whose family.

He drove his grandmother home and made sure she and her house was secure before he went home and to bed early. He wanted to be fit to take on this case alone while the Becker's were on the vacation they had planned over a year. He turned down an offer to have a substitute in his partner's absence, because he didn't want to have to bring a stranger up to speed and he trusted Andy's instincts and intuition. He knew he was better off working alone for two weeks and didn't think there would be a problem bringing Andy status quo, and the rate things were going Andy might not miss anything.

CHAPTER TWENTY-SEVEN

Helen Danford stood over her kitchen sink washing breakfast dishes after sending her children to school; their first day back to school since the discovery of their father. She had the presence of mind to ask for the help of a childhood friend, a practicing clinical psychologist for advice regarding her children and the way they process the loss of their father as well as the publicity that will be inescapable. Her friend's partner agreed to treat she and her children until they were able to live their lives as she always planned before she learned to despise her husband, for what he had become, and for the way he almost destroyed their family.

She started separating her life from his when she learned about his pedophilia. They would no longer share their bed, table, bank account or conversation other than light chatter. She attended church services with him to lend some civility to the pretense of the family he abandoned, and to give her children exposure to families that formed the village she fashioned to augment their self esteem and sense of value and purpose.

She made a fresh pot of coffee and put warm muffins on a plate preparing for her father in law's visit. His telephone call to her earlier was anything but his feeble attempt to comfort her. He needed the alliance he assumed she would afford him under the circumstances.

He would not know of her absolute disgust with the way he protected and controlled his son. Reverend Darren Danford functioned as a control addict that would not allow room for independence for anyone within his realm of influence. She was under his influence as long as she was married to his son, but she was never within his realm of control.

He was distant from his grandchildren, but they loved being celebrities when involved in the church and activities. The children advanced his image of family commitment and marriage values. He encourages heterosexual relationships exclusively at the same time accepting membership of homosexuals but preaching that their behavior was counterproductive and opposed to the teaching of the church and all Christians. The family was the keystone in society, and anything that demeans that community could not be tolerated according to the gospel of Reverend Danford.

He arrived on time and held his daughter in law close while he told her how proud he was of the way she was handling their loss.

They sat in her kitchen drinking coffee and made idle conversation about the wake and funeral service that brought mourners from all over the city.

"You know that Darren had a generous insurance policy that will take care of you and the children comfortably and the church has created a trust for the education. Money will not be a problem, Helen." Her father-in-law told her, while touching her hand across the table.

"He didn't save much, but I made sure that he paid his premiums, of course never dreaming that I would have this conversation. My son should have buried me. That's the way things should be, but God has his own plan, and we have to accept that. Do you understand what I mean?

"I understand and I have no concern about money. We're going to be all right. There is no reason for your concern."

"Of course, I'm concerned. I'll always be concerned about my family. I want them to know that I'll be here for them and will stand in for their father whenever they want."

This man was pathetic, she was thinking as she listened to him talking about a man who abused boys and had frequent gratuitous sex with other men with no concern whatsoever about his wife and children.

"Have you met with the police again? He asked.

"I agreed to meet with them tomorrow morning." She answered.

"What could they possibly want with you? Haven't you told them everything they wanted to know? What more can you tell them?

"I have no idea. They just told me that they had a few more questions. I'll tell them whatever I can." She answered him knowing he was uncomfortable.

"Now Helen, we don't want their investigation to dishonor Darren or this family in any way. You understand what I'm trying to say don't you?"

"Of course, I do. You don't want them to know those dirty little secrets." She said staring at him.

"Don't be disrespectful, Helen. We put all that business behind us. No reason to rehash all that again." He preached.

"I don't want to rehash anything. I don't even want to think about the freak that you think should be respected. He had no respect for himself or anyone. Why should I be concerned with respecting his memory? His memory is strewn with the most despicable, disgusting lifestyle that destroyed the possibility of respect or honor. Your son was a predator. He deserves nothing from us. He'll get nothing from me. I don't intend to tell the police or anyone anything that will hurt my children. There is nothing I can do about the choices your son made other than protect his children from the memory they have of his ignoring them most of their lives. Your son didn't live the life you preach. He did not build family values. He was aloof and uninvolved. He used us to present an image of stability, but the only stability in this house was and remains my love and commitment to my children." She asserted with simplicity.

"Helen! I never heard you talk like this. Don't you and the children know how much you mean to me and how important you are in my life and that of the church?

"Of course, I do and we will always be together," she lied. "The church is important to me and the children. They have had enough disruption in their lives, and I intend to continue our involvement. You will always be their grandfather and they need your support and involvement," she lied again.

"Well," he said, "I just want to make sure that the police don't do anything that may drive a wedge between us. After all, their investment is so minimal compared to ours. And I want you to know that Darren loved you and the children in his own way. He couldn't help himself with those men. Something took control of him that was evil. It was the enemy. Of that I have no doubt. My son didn't have any control over the enemy. That kind of behavior is the work of the enemy. The devil, you know that, don't you? If he were able, he would have been able to rebuke that evil and be the man that I raised him to be. You have to find a way to forgive him and to forgive yourself for anything you may have done to make him do those things. I know that you probably didn't know he may have been turned away from his home, but I don't think you should blame yourself for what my son did to himself." He pleaded with her.

The saddest thing about this man, she thought was that he sincerely believed every word that came out of his mouth. He believed that she probably drove his son to abuse boys and make love to men in cars, and bathrooms because he couldn't have possibly raised a child who would act in that manner on his own. He was unable to accept the man his son became which was not consistent with his design of perfection. She was fully aware that this was all about her father-in-law and that suited her just fine because she wanted to be healthy, whole and unencumbered when his empire unravels and destroys him.

CHAPTER TWENTY-EIGHT

John was at his desk early going over the reports he gathered from the Medical Examiner's office, Crime Scene Unit and Missing Persons, when Andy walked in carrying two cups of coffee and a bag from Shipley's Donuts.

"I see breakfast was light this morning." John said looking inside the donut bag.

"I haven't eaten a decent meal since you left. She's a hawk, John. She watched me every second. I ate grapefruit and salad and peed day and night."

"And you look wonderful." John smiled.

"That's because you have never seen a dying man. This is it. I know I can't last much longer, and we'll be away for two weeks and who knows what kind of food I'll have to eat in Spain?" He pleaded with his partner.

"You are one pathetic human being. You and Beth have been dreaming about this trip for as long as I've known you and what don't you know about the country? You'll eat paella, real sardines, like we don't see in cans, olives to die for, fresh sea bass and the pastries will take your taste buds to dimensions only imagined. Now eat your greasy donuts, bring me up to date, then get the hell out of here." John said pushing the bag toward Andy.

Andy Becker went over the bank statements with his partner. With the exception of the large deposits into the accounts of Hutchinson and Davis, nothing incriminating was found. The Davis family purchased their house two months after that deposit. They have a joint savings account with a balance of seven thousand three hundred sixty-two dollars and accounts for each of their two sons with balances of ten thousand dollars each. The two accounts were opened with ten thousand each the same day they deposited the sixty thousand. They also have a safety deposit box in that bank, but we didn't have a warrant to see the contents.

"It looks like they used that money to provide security for their family. On the other hand, the Hutchinson's provided instant gratification for them. We may want to see what's in that box." He said looking at Andy.

"Since the warrants covered Mrs. Danford, I went back to the bank yesterday and found an account for the victim's wife and one for the wife of Reverend Danford." Andy said raising his eyebrows.

"No shit, John said surprised. "The daughter in law used her maiden name hyphenated, Allen-Danford, which is why it didn't come up the first time, but I remembered seeing a piece of mail in her house addressed to Helen Allen-Danford and I played a hunch and voila! Now it was the reverend's wife that caught me by surprise. No one has mentioned her, but there she is, big as life with a substantial bank account and a more substantial address in Memorial. There is over six hundred thousand in her account and the daughter in law has a balance of four hundred fifty-eight thousand dollars. Where did all that money come from, you wonder? I met with your girlfriend, Katherine. I think I'm in love," he grinned. "She had baked fish and grass with Beth and me and we spent the night going over the church statement. It looks like the wives are being paid for services unknown at this time from the church coffers."

"No shit!" John said looking up in amazement. "Andy, I'm buying you the biggest, the best lunch you've ever had, and your secret will be safe with me from Beth. You're a god and I love you."

They spent the rest of the morning going over the statements and John put their findings in a report, primarily for his own reference.

They ate a long lunch and Andy left saying he wouldn't forget to buy a fan for John's grandmother.

"Don't forget to look into the preacher's wife," Andy said, "there's a story there and I can't wait to hear it.

"I'll have it all wrapped up before you get back just have the time of your lives and be safe."

CHAPTER TWENTY-NINE

Richard Peterson sat in the courtroom listening to the opening statement of the plaintiff who alleged permanent injury resulting from a gunshot wound in his thigh. The injury was a minor flesh wound that didn't involve bones or tendons and healed within a few weeks. The plaintiff was employed as a security guard for a small neighbor grocery store. The plaintiff argued that he would never be able to walk properly and his bladder fails hourly on the half hour. He suffered from migraines and constant back pain. He is unable to leave his house for fear of another attack, and as a result of that fear will not be able to work in his chosen field. The plaintiff sat at the table opposite Trey wearing a Thomas collar and holding the cane he used to walk into the courtroom. He was five feet six inches tall and weighed three hundred sixty pounds. He looked like Jabba the Hut.

Intricate contracts between major oil companies and their sub contractors became Trey's forte, since joining the firm, but from time to time he took cases like this one so he could demonstrate his prowess to judges whose endorsement he wanted if he chose to run for political office; an idea he has thrown around since working on a local political campaign while in law school.

He was looking forward to presenting his evidence and demonstrating to his client, why he recommended they not settle.

He loved trying cases and was conflicted with his curiosity with public office. He considered a judgeship, but thought he was too young and would be bored. City or state office was more to his liking and inclination and would be a forum for his views on public education that was failing in his state.

He started making the rounds at various political fundraisers and large social functions two years ago. He networked with the corporate officers of the companies he represented, owned season tickets to the symphony, opera and performing arts theater, most of which he never used but gave to friends and made himself known in the most populous churches in the city.

Trey worked with schools, providing after school tutoring, and mentoring to children considered at risk who would benefit from such a program because the system failed them very early in their lives. He was aware of his largess from his parents who provided the best of everything. He was always encouraged and directed by his parents and exposed to a world foreign to the children he wanted to save. He knew early on that his goals and objectives were not as lofty as one would expect from him, but he felt it was his responsibility to make available to children the opportunity for the exposure that would prepare them to be productive adults. There were just too many children who were in a system without direction or purpose other than use them as the numbers required to provide schools with funds. It was all about the money.

He heard the judge call his name and he stood and asked that his opening statement be delayed until later in the trial.

The plaintiff called as witnesses, his wife, who told the jury that her husband was unable to perform sex, a doctor who testified that his patient would never be able to walk without a cane, and the man who shot him. He testified that the plaintiff was sitting on a chair away from the front door behind the magazine rack and had dozed off, when a young man came in and demanded money. The storeowner tried to get the attention of the security guard to no avail. The man raised his gun, pointing it at the owner's face. The owner grabbed the man's wrist of the hand holding the gun pushing him to his right side; when the gun went off in the direction of the guard, hitting him in his thigh.

Trey elected not to cross-examine any of the plaintiff's witnesses, appreciative for the testimony of the shooter, that clearly ruled out the gross negligence in the pleadings.

He called to the stand a private investigator, hired by his client for a background check and surveillance. The plaintiff's background included a felony drug conviction for which he served four years in the state penitentiary, from where he was released on parole for the remainder of his sentence; under those circumstances, gun possession was not an option for the plaintiff. Finally, the investigator provided a video of the surveillance, that showed the plaintiff walking in and out of his house several times per day over a three-day period, without the aid of a cane or any prostheses. He carried large garbage bags to the trash container and pushed it to the curb. He drove to a new job with a roofing company, where he loaded roofing tiles onto trucks and finally, he was taped, breaking into a house and carrying two televisions and a microwave oven to his car.

The plaintiff's attorney conferred with his client, than stood agreed to dismissal that was accepted. The case was dismissed, and the judge had the plaintiff held pending charges filed for the alleged break in and parole violation.

Trey didn't consider those types of outcomes victories; they were reminders of what to avoid and how to avoid making fools of themselves and their chosen profession. These were the cases that made the law and lawyers the butt of jokes and he hated that because nothing about the law was a joke.

He answered his cell phone and heard the voice of Reverend Darren Danford inviting him to lunch. Trey was surprised and hungry and agreed to meet with the minister of the church he usually attended when he wanted to impress one of the female members.

When he arrived at the restaurant chosen by the pastor, Reverend Danford was seated at a table that gave him a view of the front door. This man likes to be in control, Trey thought when he saw that his host had been seated long enough to have finished his iced tea, however he lied and said he had just arrived. Trey was curious and hungry.

"I'm sure you've read about my son and the terrible tragedy surrounding his untimely death?" He confronted Trey. "The police are questioning my family and I'm not sure our best interest is protected, if you know what I mean, Richard. I'd like for you to speak with my daughter in law and see how you may be of assistance."

"I don't handle those kinds of cases," Reverend Danford, "however, I'll call you with a referral who would better suit your family's needs." He offered the minister and ordered his lunch.

"Richard, I want you to understand that my family must be protected at any cost and I want the best you have."

"As I explained, I will be glad to call you tomorrow with the name of a lawyer. The police routinely question the families of victims as part of their investigation; perhaps you have misunderstood the process and will find that there is no need for further concern for your family in that regard." Trey told the minister.

"No, I think I'd better have someone with my daughter in law when she talks to them again, after all, she has been through too much alone and she has to think about the welfare of her children." He told Trey and asked for the check before Trey was finished eating.

What was that about, Trey thought while he ate his lunch and watched his host leave the restaurant.

CHAPTER THIRTY

John Garrison planned his day working solo and intended to speak with Mrs. Danford about her husband and perhaps get something on her mother-in-law.

He was in the shower when he thought he heard his phone ringing but decided not to answer. He dressed and decided to call the victim's wife later in the morning when he heard the phone again. The voice on the other end was that of another detective who was at the scene of what looked like a murder.

"I think you should be here," his colleague said. "There's a note that matches the one your victim was wearing. How long will it take you to get here? The ME is ready to release the body, but we want you to see it first; the scene is a bit unusual."

"What's unusual about it?" John asked.

"Just get here ASAP."

John stopped him from hanging up when he asked, "how long have you been there and why didn't you call me earlier?" We took the call at three ten and we've been here since three forty. No one thought about calling you until we found the note and realized that this could be the second victim of your killer, so I called."

John took down the address, finished dressing and drove to the murder scene that turned out to be a rather large house in an upscale neighborhood. He parked his car away from the house and studied the onlookers hoping to see someone who stood out among the yuppie neighbors whose curiosity interrupted their usual morning routine.

He walked toward the house wondering if any of the people he was passing were potential witnesses.

He walked into the house that was filled with various investigators scurrying around looking for different kinds of evidence for the same results.

"Where's the body", he asked anyone listening.

"It's upstairw, follow me." replied a uniformed officer. He followed the officer to an upstairs bathroom that was considered part of the massive master suite and saw the nude body standing in the shower with his back to the faucet, a necktie around his neck tied around the shower head. He was leaning forward and dead.

It looked like the man had been masturbating when something went wrong. The scene had the same clean neat look as the apartment only this man was whole. He still had his hands and face, but why consider this murder, he was thinking without having said a word since he entered the room.

"Auto erotic asphyxiation", he heard the ME's voice. "Ever heard of it?

"He's a choker? What's with the lemon in his mouth?" John asked, staring at the naked man.

"I'm glad you asked." Dr. Ellis responded. "Some of these people and apparently this one use a lemon wedge to bite on to wake them up when they start passing out. This one however was a different sort of lemon wedge. It was poisoned. Doesn't that beat all? It looks like he tied himself up on the shower head, put the lemon wedge on the soap dish, right there in the wall, started loving himself, picked up his lemon, put it in his mouth and lights out. That was all she wrote. He was out like a light before he even got it off. We're going to take him now. He's been hanging there long enough."

"How long has he been there?"

"He died sometime between eleven and one."

"How do you know the lemon was in the soap dish?"

"Smell the almonds."

"Where was the note?" John continued to question the doctor.

"Under a folded towel on the vanity; very neat. Now if there is nothing else, I need to take body before he starts to smell up the place." Dr. Ellis said and walked away.

"Why do you think the note was hidden?" asked Chad Bailey walking toward John.

"Whoever ever did this, probably wanted the full attention of whoever found the body. This guy likes the shock value." John speculated. "Who called this in?"

"Anonymous male"

"Are there anymore lemons in the kitchen or anywhere in the house?" John asked.

"No lemons anywhere, not even the other part of the poisoned piece. But there are fingerprints everywhere, but we don't know who they belong to yet. The place is clean but not sterile like the last place." Chad said.

"Did you get photos of the carpet? Look at those marks" John said to Chad pointing to the floor at lines in the carpet. This doesn't look like a vacuum cleaner; more like some kind of rake." He added. "The lines lead out of the bedroom down the stairs and out of the house. There might be something in the carpet we could use."

John saw Jim Spenser, the detective who called him earlier walking toward him.

"Tell me about the victim. Who is he?" John asked Spenser.

"Dr. Brian Hargrave. Single, lives alone, and has a practice in the Medical Professional building on Fannin."

"High rent district."

"Real high. We found a phone number for his parents in Beaumont and called them to meet us here. We're still waiting for them. I thought you might want to talk to them before they go downtown to ID the body." He reported.

"Thanks for your help on this. I would rather talk to them here first."

"We found these in boxes in a bedroom closet." Spenser said showing John two large boxes containing dozens of videotapes.

"I watched one. You'll want to see this." He said turning on the machine that was already queued for showing. John and Jim Spenser watched sex acts between young and very young boys.

"Are they all like this one?"

"Six so far." I haven't had time to see the others and I didn't want to take the chance of his parents walking in on it without knowing their son's unusual habits."

"I'm beginning to wonder if it is as unusual, we thought." John said feeling disgusted.

"Would you mind packing those up and taking them in and I'll look at them after I've had a chance to visit with the family? There might be some fingerprints on those tapes we need."

John went back to the bedroom and opened the dresser drawers of the homeowner and saw the usual contents that were all folded neatly and in order. The walk-in closet was custom made for a man with an inordinate amount of clothing. There were sections for slacks, and jackets that were shorter than the section for longer items. There were bins for sweaters and shoes and drawers for socks. On the floor in the middle of the closet sat a bench. I like this closet, thought John. I may have to look in to one of these, he said to himself. He pulled sweaters from the bins and placed them on the bench. One of the bins contained two sweatshirts. He removed the shirts and saw a brown envelope. He opened it and saw that it contained videotape and a small envelope containing notepaper with the words, *I thought you would like a copy. I have the original.* It was signed, *a parent.* He put the note back in its envelope and but that back in the manila envelope along with the tape and put it a plastic bag. He walked out of the closet and handed the plastic bag to Chad Bailey for possible prints.

"Wait a minute, Chad. Let look at some of the tape before you take it. Close the door in case the parents show up." John said.

Chad watched. "Holy shit, it's him with a kid." Chad said and left his mouth open.

John rewound the tape and put it back in the bag, giving it to Chad. John wasn't in the mood to explain his reasoning for another warrant to examine bank records, so he looked for statements the victim probably had in the house. The note may have suggested blackmail.

He looked through desk draws in what appeared to be the victim's office and found a metal box that was unlocked and contained several envelopes from a bank. An examination of the contents of the envelopes revealed bank statements for the year. John gave the box to Chad.

They heard unfamiliar voices downstairs and realized the parents had arrived, when he heard a woman scream.

"Where is my son? What is going on here? I want to know who's in charge now."

"I'm Detective John Garrison and I'm in charge of this investigation." John said to the woman.

"What investigation? Where is my son? She screamed.

"I'm so sorry to tell you that a man was found dead earlier in an upstairs bathroom, and we believe he may be your son."

Mrs. Hargrave leaned into her husband's arms and sobbed in disbelief. They both sat on a sofa in the living room, distraught and confused.

"Mr. Garrison, please tell me what is going on here. We just spoke with our son last evening, and there was no indication that anything was wrong. How can anything like this happen?" The victim's father appealed to John. There has to be some kind of mistake. Just explain to me what happened here."

"Mr. Hargrave, the body was just discovered a few hours ago and our investigation has revealed very little so far." John responded.

"How did he die?"

"We'll have to wait for the Medical Examiner's report to make that determination. We will need you to make a formal identification. I can arrange transportation for you."

Mr. Hargrave, can you answer a few questions, or would you rather wait until another time? I realize this is very difficult for both you and your wife and I don't want to add to your distress, but it would be in everyone's best interest to have as much information as soon as possible." John said the father.

"It's Doctor."

"Excuse me?"

"It's Doctor Hargrave, not Mr."

"I apologize, sir. I had no idea."

"Don't worry about it. How would you have known? Now, what kind of information do you need from us?"

"Are you aware of any problems your son may have recently experienced that would cause depression or a change in his attitude in any way?"

"Not that I know of. He seemed the same to me as he always was."

"Was he in good health that you know of?" John questioned the father.

"He was in excellent health. He took very good care of himself. He ate healthy and worked out regularly."

"Do you know if he had a problem with money?"

"Mr. Garrison, our son was well paid for what he did for a living. He was successful and his potential had not been realized. He had a very bright future. I can assure you; money was not an issue for my son.

"Are his friends known to you and your wife; and did either of you know of any problems he may have had with anyone?"

"Mr. Garrison let me explain something to you. My wife and I are not aware of any difficulties my son may have had. He had a successful practice. He was healthy and well adjusted. As far as we are concerned, he lived a normal healthy life, and I don't see what more I can tell you."

"One last thing, what was his specialty?"

"Pediatrics, his father said with pride."

John finished with his questioning of the Hargrave's and watched as they left the house to go to the morgue to confirm the identification of their son's body while still in disbelief.

He wondered if these were revenge killings; was there a vigilante out there annihilating pedophiles. He thought about Andy Becker and how he was handling the investigation and if it would be possible for him to be objective, especially now that the crime has doubled.

Andy and Beth seemed to have handled their loss without losing themselves in the process. They talked about Tommy often since he was the son they loved, instead of burying his memory in fear that the mere mention of him would ignite fires of pain that would not quench.

Andy was a good cop who lived two entirely different lives. Tommy and Beth lived in the other. He was hoping that these cases would be solved before Andy returned because, regardless of how he felt about these murders professionally, the painful memories were not completely buried. They won't get over it; they'll just keep getting on with it.

John met with the Medical Examiner early and went over the preliminary report that revealed cyanide poisoning in the lemon wedge and on the victim's right fingers. There were no lacerations, abrasions or bruising anywhere on his body other than ligature marks on his neck from the tie he used to strangle himself for pleasure.

"Wouldn't he have smelled the poison?" John asked the doctor.

"He may have, however, why would he suspect poisoning if he had been alone and had no intentions of killing himself. The odor, if he were even aware of any, wouldn't have been an issue in the throws of passion." There were some ligature scars that were not new. This wasn't his first excursion to his glass enclosed passion cove." Dr. Ellis responded. "He did it often. He also liked a little toot now and then." The doctor continued.

"Are you saying what I think?" John asked.

"Only if you're thinking cocaine. Found some. There was still a bit in his nostrils, so he snorted shortly before he tied himself up. There was no damage as with a consistent user. This was recreational use, maybe just when he took a shower." The doctor said winking. "That's all I have so far, Sonny. If there is anything else significant, I know your number and you know mine. The report should be finished in a week."

Dr. Hargrave was a homosexual, a pedophile, a recreational drug user and a pediatrician, John thought and left the morgue.

CHAPTER THIRTY-ONE

John drove back to Dr. Hargrave's house to talk to the house-keeper who agreed to meet him there. When he arrived, she was standing in the driveway.

"Thank you for coming Miss Flores. Have you've been inside yet?" He asked, greeting the victim's housekeeper.

"No, I don't want to go in there alone after what happened. I can't believe it. I cleaned the house all day yesterday. Dr. Hargrave came in before I was finished and paid me, then he changed his clothes and left before I did.

"What time was that? He asked.

"Around three thirty."

"What time did he leave?"

"Oh, maybe four o'clock. I never saw him again."

They went into the house and he watched her look of disgust when she saw the disruption of her labor of the previous day.

"I don't understand, she said. What is all that stuff all over everything? I just cleaned everything yesterday. What happened here? She said, while holding the sides of her face. Mrs. Hargrave called me this morning and asked me to come over to clean today. I told her I finished everything yesterday, but she said that she just wanted me to straighten up a little. I can't believe this."

"Was that Dr. Hargrave's mother who called you?" John asked the housekeeper. "Yes."

"How did she know how to reach you?"

"She has my number. She's called me before. Sometimes when the doctor is out of town for a while, she'll call me to make sure the house is clean." Miss Flores explained.

"How did you get my number?" She asked the detective. I saw your number in the doctor's organizer and your name written on certain days on his calendar. His mother told me who you were." He told her, impressed with her command.

"What is this stuff on everything?" she asked again.

"It's used to find fingerprints. It will clean off of everything." He explained to her.

"I'd like you to wait until we release the house before you clean it again. I'll speak with Mrs. Hargrave and let her know when you can come back." He told her.

"But I gave up another job today to come here for Mrs. Hargrave. I don't want to upset her and how am I going to get paid for today? I can't afford to lose eighty dollars, just like that. And how am I going to get home? My son drove me, and he's gone to work." She pleaded with him.

"I understand, Mrs. Flores. Please let me pay you and I'll drive you home if you let me." He told her.

"Can we go into the kitchen, Mrs. Flores?" He said as they walked in the large room. "With the exception of the dust, can you tell me if anything is out of place? He watched her as she inspected the kitchen with a keen eye.

"Everything is here. I can't believe the dirt."

"Are all the knives kept in this holder?" John asked pointing to the holder on the countertop.

"No, there are some other knives in this drawer." She said pulling a drawer. "All of the knives are here."

"How can you be so sure, Mrs. Flores."

"Because I clean this house every week. I'm the only one who puts them away. Dr. Hargrave didn't eat here too much. When he did, he just rinsed the dishes and I washed them whenever I came."

"Is all the food in the refrigerator the way you left it yesterday?"

She opened the refrigerator frowning. "No. Who took the lemons?" There were three lemons in the bin yesterday. There are always two or three lemons. I could never figure it out because he didn't eat fruit."

There was no fruit or fresh vegetables in the refrigerator. There was just flavored cream for coffee, skim milk, several cheeses, a jar of orange marmalade, and a bag of English muffins, bottled water and two bottles of wine.

"Will you look in the cabinet and tell me if everything is in place."

He watched the woman open each cabinet and inspect the contents slowly and with care. She checked the pantry that contained mostly cleaning products and some can and dry goods.

She finished her inspection and said, "everything's here."

"Do you mind going through the rest of the house with me to see if anything is out of place or missing?" He prodded her.

"Where did it happen?" She asked.

"Upstairs in the bathroom."

She led him on her lengthy tour and inspection of Dr. Hargrave's home. She said nothing while she looked in every drawer and closet throughout the house with the same scrutiny as her kitchen inspection.

After what seemed like an hour later, she finally announced that everything was as she left it the day before except the bar of soap, she left in the shower was now on the vanity.

"Do you usually put folded towels on the sink? He asked. "Yes, always. He likes extra towels, so I put them on the sink for him. "Can we go downstairs now? I don't like being up here."

They walked downstairs and back into the living room, where the housekeeper sat down.

"Mrs. Flores, how long have you worked for Dr. Hargrave?"

"Well, let's see." She said. I started working for him when he lived in the other house for about three years and he moved in this house the weekend before my daughter's fifteenth birthday. I remember that because we were getting ready for her Quinceanera. It was a wonderful day for my daughter. Her padrino and madrina paid for her dress that was pink, and Dr. Hargrave paid for the entire fiesta; the room in a big hotel, food, liquor, and the biggest cake you ever saw. It was pink to match her dress. All the damas wore pink and all the chambelanes wore pink, but kind of a different pink. He even paid for the bolas her cousins gave everyone after the Misa de accion de gracias. It was a beautiful day, and my daughter was so beautiful. My family couldn't have afforded a very big fiesta."

"I'm familiar with the Quinceanera, however, I've never been to one. I'm not familiar with all the traditions and the words." He said. "Well, she had six damas; they're like the bridesmaids in a wedding and the chambelanes are like hostesses, we had twelve of them. The Misa de accion de gracias is the Thanksgiving Mass and the fiesta is the party after the mass. The bolas are gifts given to everyone after mass. It's a very old tradition in our culture when our girls turn fifteen." She was happy to explain the tradition to this gringo.

"That sounds really nice." He said gaining her confidence.

"So how long did he live in this house."

"Six years." She said.

"So, you've been working for him about nine years."

"Yeah, that's about right." She answered.

"Did Dr. Hargrave usually come home while you were here?"

"No, I didn't see him very much. He worked all day and I'm usually finished by noon. Yesterday, was my heavy cleaning day, so it took longer." She explained. "I guess I won't be coming here after I clean up this mess. He was a good man, and I'll miss him." She said with tears.

"Mrs. Flores, did you ever see any of his friends or anyone who visited him? John asked.

"No, I never saw anyone except his parents. I never saw any friends."

"Did he act any different when you saw him yesterday?" "No, he was just the same as always. Just a nice man."

When he finished his interview with the housekeeper, he gave her eighty dollars as promised and drove her home. He watched her walk away and felt sorrow for her loss of a friend, and a job.

CHAPTER THIRTY-TWO

He drove away thinking about what the two victims had in common. They both liked boys. Did they know their killer, or was it random, he wondered? They were both professional and lived in two worlds: the public persona, and the dark side. The Danford's were aware of the dark world that may have been the reason for the murder, but it doesn't look like the Hargrave's knew about their son's secret.

Did they know each other and frequent the same bars, parties, or what?

He planned to speak with Hargrave's parents later in the day. Perhaps they would know friends or acquaintances.

He also planned to meet with Mrs. Danford without her father-in-law. Reverend Danford was another matter altogether; perhaps he should be put on the back burner for a while until they had enough to give to the Fraud Unit.

John met next with Chad Bailey at the Crime Scene Unit lab.

"Your crime scenes are the cleanest in my experience." Chad said. "The hairs and skin in the carpet and upholstery were the victims and his cleaning lady who combed her hair a lot. We found her hair in carpet fibers, the sofa in the living room and on his bed. I can't imagine what that was about." He offered.

John pictured the housekeeper's head full of curly hair that didn't look like she combed it much at all, but it did move every time she moved her head, and she ran her hand through her hair often.

"How else could her hair be all over the place?' John asked Chad.

"If it's very dry, hairs will fall out, if she rubs her hands through it, or if she is sitting against upholstory, she could leave a few hairs." Bailey explained.

"There was one more thing," Bailey said turning toward John, "there were pieces of bamboo in the carpet; thin pieces like splinters." There was nothing in the house that was made of bamboo, John was thinking. Why would there be bamboo in the carpet or anywhere in the house?

"What about the kitchen," John asked, "any indication of where the lemon was cut?" There were no knives missing from the kitchen according to the housekeeper. Where did the killer cut the lemon?"

"Nothing in the kitchen was out of place." No sign of lemon juice anywhere. I can't explain that one, other than the killer cleaned up or the victim cut the lemon and cleaned up himself." Bailey said.

Cleaned up with what? John wondered. There were no paper towels in the trash container, and there was no dishcloth in the sink. The killer cleaned up again.

Before he left his office, John copied all the investigation material on each of the murders to take home with him, where he would be able to spend more time going over the information. He also had copies of all of the photographs of the crime scenes.

He made a telephone call to both the Hutchinson's and the Davis'. There was no answer at either house, but he left a message identifying himself and telling them he wanted to meet with them the next day.

He ran a criminal and civil check on both couples and learned that Will Davis was arrested twice for drunk and disorderly and once for domestic disturbance. His wife reported him for abuse but refused to press charges. He was arrested and convicted for assault and battery when he admitted to beating a classmate when he was seventeen years old. He pleaded no contest and was given two years probation. There has been no activity in the last three years. Tanya Davis was arrested twice on bad check charges.

There was no criminal activity with the Hutchinson's; but they liked to sue. They sued Metro, the bus company, because Denise Hutchinson slipped backwards down one step on the bus. They sued the electric company because lightening stuck a tree in their back yard breaking a branch causing it to fall on a lawn chair. They sued an Indian restaurant when Denise broke out in a rash from the curry. One suit was tried, and they lost; the other two were dismissed within weeks of filing.

John called Gary Sanford and invited him to happy hour. He needed to step out of the darkness these cases had created and into which he was drawn. He turned on Diana Krall's Cd and languished in her sexy dulcet interpretation of I'll Remember You.

He thought about Gary, Jeff and Trey and the friendship they shared. There was a sadness that dwelt deep inside each of them that didn't give the impression of being addressed. Their bond was apparent, but they were more clannish than close. They shielded themselves from substantive relationships with women and men as if they wore an invisible do not touch sign that was apparent to anyone who was willing to look close enough. He enjoyed their acquaintance but was always aware that he was a spectator only.

CHAPTER THIRTY-THREE

He arrived at the Hargrave's hotel and called them on the house phone. Dr. Hargrave greeted him with a warm handshake and Mrs. Hargrave appeared more willing to talk to him than she was the day before.

"I didn't realize that I shouldn't have asked Brian's housekeeper to clean up so soon. I'm really very sorry for that."

"Oh, it's no problem Mrs. Hargrave. She was very helpful to me and I appreciate her cooperation.

"She's been with Brian for several years and we trust her. She took good care of our son. We've decided to move into the house and retain her. We lived in Houston until we retired to Beaumont, and we've been talking about moving back for a while now. We just didn't expect to move under these circumstances." She said with warmth he hadn't seen before.

"Please sit down, Mr. Garrison. I've ordered lunch; I hope you haven't eaten."

"No Ma'am, I haven't eaten. It's been a full day for me, and I appreciate you're thinking of me." John said.

"It's the least I can do to apologize for my behavior."

"Your apology is not necessary, but I am hungry." He said and felt comfortable with this grieving couple that didn't seem to be aware of the heartache they will encounter as their son's lifestyle was revealed.

They lunched on shrimp au gratin in puff pastry and Caesar salad. John didn't realize how hungry he was and was grateful for his host's forward thinking. Their luncheon conversation was light and included their travels during retirement.

When they finished, John was surprised with Dr. Hargrave's abrupt, "now, let's talk about our son and who killed him."

"You don't have to protect us, Mr. Garrison, although we appreciate your attempts. We know our son was gay and we accepted it. He was our son, and his sexual orientation was just that. It had nothing to do with the way he practiced medicine, paid his taxes, voted, and treated his parents and colleagues or the kind of man he was. He was a good man; kind and generous with himself and his money. Regardless of what he may have done or how he lived, he didn't deserve to be murdered." The victim's father said to John with a parent's pride.

"I don't know how we can help you," Mrs. Hargrave said, "but we'll do anything we can."

"Do you know any of his friends or acquaintances?" John asked both of them.

"He was never close to anyone outside of the family. He didn't have childhood friends, although he participated in school activities when he was young as well as in college. He was a loner, and he didn't seem to be affected by that in a negative way." His mother answered.

"Did he practice alone?" Asked John.

"No," his father answered, "he had two partners. Dr. Robert Evans and Dr. Patricia Wright. All pediatricians. He met Robert in medical school and reacquainted after their residency. They opened the practice together and recruited Patricia. They worked well together and had a casual social relationship. Both Robert and Patricia are married with children. Both of them knew Brian was gay. It was never an adverse concern among them. Their relationship was productive and pleasant at best. They were successful and they credited each other for that success." His mother and I aren't aware of any personal relationships. He was single and never had a lasting sexual relationship that we know of. We don't know if he was attracted to young boys. If he was, I don't believe he compromised any of his patients." His father continued.

"Did your son have any financial difficulty?" John asked them both.

"As I said, he was successful and was financially secure. I'm not aware of any problems he had with money. He was always very astute with his investments and spending." His father answered.

"Who are his heirs?"

"We are, along with his sister."

"I didn't realize he had a sister." John said surprised.

"His twin. She is traveling in India. We spoke with her this morning and she is on her way." His mother said.

"Does she live in Houston?" "No, she and her family live in Baltimore, where she practices medicine with her husband."

"How would you describe their relationship?" John asked.

"Close, all of their lives. They spoke at least once a day. She also accepted his homosexuality. Needless to say, she is devastated by what has happened to her brother. It pains me to imagine how she is getting along on her trip home alone. She was traveling with a group, but there was no one to travel home with her. She's going to meet her husband in New York this evening. I'll be so glad when she gets there so she can have someone to fly to Houston with." His mother said through tears.

"Mr. and Mrs. Hargrave, I'm not going to keep you any longer. Thank you for lunch, it was very thoughtful of you, especially under the circumstances. I'm very sorry for your loss. I'll call you tomorrow about releasing the house. Thanks again and good-bye." John said and left the two of them to deal with their family tragedy.

John called Mrs. Danford and asked if she would be available to meet with him in the morning. She agreed.

After his meeting with the Hargrave's, he wasn't in any shape to talk with anyone else about these murders. He drove to his gym for a swim and a steam. He had time to go home and change clothes after he left the gym and before he met Gary. Diana Krall sang to him all the way home and he was glad he took off early to sweat out some of the crap he dealt with all day long.

He was frustrated that nothing he learned was leading him closer to the killer.

CHAPTER THIRTY-THREE

Gary Sanford and Trey Peterson didn't see John when he walked in. He went directly to the buffet, filled two plates with the bill a fare and placed them on the table in front of the two friends.

"Hey, where did you come from?" Gary asked.

"You two were so engrossed with each other, I thought you were in love and I didn't want to disturb you." John said.

"Shut up and sit down," Trey said, "you know you're the only one for me."

"That's what I always thought, but you do have a reputation." John said laughing.

"I have a plan," John told them, "let's get drunk and get a cab home."   "Sounds like a plan." Don't wait for us, we're past the starting gate and running." Gary said raising his glass.

John ordered a double scotch on the rocks with a splash.

"One more thing; lets engage in debauchery and hit on everything that's not nailed down." John said.

"Bad day?" Gary asked John.

"Bad week," he answered, bad murders, real bad killer and no answers." John said sipping his drink.

The club was crowded with many more woman than men, many of whom were staring at them and John thought he would have to get drunk before he gave any of them an inclination that he might be interested in the night only. He realized that he just wasn't in the mood. Not so for Trey, he was now sitting at the bar very close to an attractive young thing that had her hand on his thigh and seemed to be soaking up all of his bullshit.

"What's Jeff doing tonight?" John asked Gary.

"Probably sitting at home alone, sippin' and waiting for his wife or wondering where she is, or not giving a flying fuck about either. I'm getting sick of Jeff and his wife. It's time for him to kick her to the curb and move on. He's drinking more and enjoying it less, and still trying to work out an unworkable marriage that will remain unworkable because the bitch has her own agenda and it doesn't include her husband, but it may include someone else's husband, if you get my drift." Gary said, pissed off at his boyhood friend.

Trey never got drunk when he was on the prowl. He needed control. He drove Gary home since they came to the club together and John drove himself because he felt he was sober enough to drive the short distance. He took a hot shower and made coffee hoping it would lift him out of that sinkhole he felt when he pulled into his garage.

It was still early, and he was wide-awake and alert after drinking three cups of his foul coffee. He answered the phone on the first ring.

"Just checking to see if you made it home." He heard Gary's voice and Charlie Parker in the background.

"I'm here, and sober from some shit coffee I made. Do you have any other music besides Parker?" He asked his caller.

"Of course. Miles. What else is there? See you in the morning at the gym. Be early and you can buy my breakfast." He hung up and John wondered what Gary did while listening to Charlie Parker day and night. There was no question that he was obsessed with the saxophone player. He owned every piece of music Parker and Miles Davis ever recorded and had five copies of Birth of the Cool, which he explained that he couldn't take the chance of being robbed, so he placed the albums and CD's in various places in his house. It was a real obsession. There was no other music in his possession.

John took his working file from his car and spread the contents on his kitchen table and studied the photos of each murder scene.

The killer had to know his victims in order to gain access to the apartment and the house without force or suspicion. Both locations were spotless but for different reasons. The killer cleaned the apartment. The housekeeper cleaned the house and the killer left traces of the poison in the soap dish as if he wasn't concerned about its detection. Both scenes and killings had an essence of arrogance like that of a preppy in one of those very private schools off limits to common folk, even those whose academic prowess gave them access via scholarship through the benevolence of affirmative action. His followed his thoughts to Gary, Jeff, and Trey; they each had that same kind of arrogance; that stride, that unawareness that another class existed among them. They were organized, precise, focused and determined men. There was no room in their lives for anything less than what they expected for themselves. Exactly like the killer of these corrupted men.

John came back to the contents on his table and smiled at the thought that his friends exhibited traits of this ferocious killer, but he had to accept the fact that their characteristics were a model that begged consideration.

The condition of the first victim exhibited fierce rage that was personal. The manner of the killing of the second was more casual—relaxed, but deliberate. The killer was at ease in both locations, more so in the second that was more his turf, but a preppy wouldn't say turf. He was in his element. He thought about the three friends again. Both victims engaged in homosexual behavior, but the second was flaming and the first was a switch hitter that apparently didn't matter to their killer. It was about the boys, so there had to be a boy or boys in the life of Dr. Brian Hargrave that may not have been a patient as his father assured. Dr. Hargrave probably wouldn't have compromised his practice or his standing as a physician, but that's what he did. The boys were who he was.

His phone rang again, and he looked at the clock that told him it was eleven forty-five and he was concerned when he saw his grandmother's name on the caller ID.

"What's wrong?"

"I couldn't sleep so I thought I would bore you for awhile. Why would you think something was wrong? Can't an old lady call you at this hour? My lover just left, and I didn't want to go back to bed."

"You need to get a new lover; one who would wear you out." He said laughing with his grandmother.

"I've been thinking about kicking him to the curb. Do you have any friends? She asked laughing.

"Really," he said, "are you ok?"

"Actually, I'm just fine. I had my check up today. I'm perfect. Then I pulled those weeds my grandson didn't pull, and then I cleaned the house; took a bath and napped. I slept longer than I intended, so now I'm awake and talking to you."

"I was talking to a lady today that I'm going to hire to do your house cleaning once a week."

"I don't need any help."

"It has nothing to do with need," he chided her, "I've already decided and that's it. I'll bring her over one day next week."

She surprised him when she said, "you know, I wouldn't mind having some help around here. This house is big. Bring her over; it will give me more time to play bridge. You're a good kid, little boy. I think I'll bake you a pie on Sunday. Well, this scotch and milk is doing the trick; I think I can sleep now." She said and he followed with "love you much", they both said good night.

He remembered his grandmother telling him that she went to New York for her twenty first birthday, and she went to a party where most of the guests were drinking scotch and milk, and she thought that was so sophisticated, and she's been drinking it ever since. He never knew anyone else who drank the concoction; he couldn't even imagine the taste that had to be worse than his coffee.

He was looking at the photographs of the carpeting in the Hargrave house and tried to imagine what made the strange tracks that went from the upstairs bedroom, down the stairs.

He saw that it was well past midnight, and he didn't expect to be up that late. He gathered the photos and reports and placed them back in the folder and went to bed and for reasons he didn't know, Jeff Harrington came to mind. He seldom saw Gary and Trey together without Jeff and wasn't aware that his marriage was in the kind of trouble Gary eluded to tonight. Jeff didn't strike him as someone in a bad anything, let alone a marriage. He guessed his marriage was as well put together as Jeff seemed. John met Cheryl Harrington. She was very attractive; yet always pre-occupied with herself. Thinking back on their meeting, he could see now that the couple was a bit odd. She lacked Jeff's discretion and sense of style and aloofness. She was more like someone Trey took home for a temporary conquest. She lacked staying power. Why did he care, he thought as he felt himself dozing? At least his mind was clearing itself of the carnage in the file that sat on his kitchen table.

He made a mental note of calling Mrs. Flores to discuss working for his grandmother, hoping she wasn't too booked to accommodate her. He fell asleep thinking about his grandmother having a housekeeper.

CHAPTER THIRTY-FOUR

"Mr. Davis don't misunderstand my visit," Reverend Danford was saying to the boy's father, "my concern is for your family." "My family and I wouldn't want any of you involved in a situation that could only cause you discomfort".

"When did you start giving a damn about my family? What is your real reason for coming to my house?" Will Davis shouted at the minister. "My wife and I haven't had anything to do with your family since we met your son for the first and last time. We want all this put behind us and I don't think I like what I think you want us to do."

"Mr. and Mrs. Davis, I don't want you to do anything. I am only suggesting that you do not discuss the business between you and my son, if asked. It's only a suggestion. I wouldn't ask for more."

The Reverend Danford kept his composure to control the room. They were intimidated more than angry, and he needed their alliance more than the resentment they exhibited.

"Please accept my apology if I offended you in any way. It was certainly not my intent to do anything but relieve you of any concern you may have that might expose the privacy you now enjoy. I will make sure in every way possible to shield you from any encroachment into your personal affairs." The minister assured them.

He drove away from their house knowing that their anger was a threat to his vision, and they would have to be managed and monitored. He would speak with them again soon and convince them that their silence was in their best interest. He knew if the police found them and questioned them about their knowledge of his son, Will Davis just might decide he has nothing to lose if he revealed their secret. Mr. Davis you have much to lose and I hope you figure that out soon, he thought as he entered the freeway on his way to his office, confident that these two families would never have the wherewithal to destroy what he spent his professional lifetime building for himself.

CHAPTER THIRTY-FIVE

Trey Peterson knew that he wanted to be in a position to use Reverend Danford's clout is he should decide to run for office. The Good Reverend knew a lot of people and most of the movers and shakers he needed to endorse his bid, so he didn't want to disappoint him. He called a friend of his who could give the Danford's advice if it were required. He couldn't understand why Reverend Danford was hell bent on protecting his family when it appeared the police were only interested in routine information about the death of his son. Unless there was more to it than the minister let on, which may impugn his standing in the community and that would not bode well for his bid.

He called the church and asked to speak with the pastor.

"I'm so glad you were able to call me Richard." Reverend Danford said when he picked up the phone. "Will you be able to assist my family after all?"

Trey gave him the name and telephone number of his friend and said that he had spoken to his friend and he is waiting for a call from the family.

"You didn't mention my name, did you Richard?"

"No sir; it was not my place to do so. You'll have to tell him yourself." He answered.

"I told you that I wanted you to handle it for me, I don't think anyone else will do under the circumstances."

What circumstances, Trey thought.

"This is a criminal matter, Reverend Danford; I don't practice criminal law and I would not be your best choice." He tried to convince the minister.

"Richard, there's nothing criminal here, I just want you to offer your services to my daughter in law and advise her on what she should tell the police if asked.

"Reverend Danford, I would be happy to assist you and your family, however, under the circumstances you would be better served with someone who specialized in these types of cases.

"Alright Richard, I'm going to take your advice with some reservation and call your friend, but I want you to be available if I'm not pleased.

"I'll do whatever I can Reverend."

"Thank you, Richard, you'll be hearing from me in a couple of days. Thank you for calling." The Reverend Danford ended the call.

Trey sat at his desk and thought about Reverend Danford and the news he was reading about the death of his son and wondered what was really going on. He felt the church pastor was dragging him into a situation where he didn't belong. He referred them to Gary because it was right up his alley, but now he wondered if he made the right choice. He didn't trust the pastor and after speaking with him on both occasions, he was convince to this than just making Mrs. Danford more comfortable talking to the police.

Gary was right for the job; however, they were well known in the community, and apparently had some money. Gary could handle it. It shouldn't require more than one visit.

He picked up the phone and Gary was on the other end.

"Why didn't you tell me it was the Danford's?

"He asked me not to." Trey said.

"What's going on with these people? Why does Mrs. Danford need representation? Is she a suspect or what? Gary said without taking a breath.

"All I know is the Reverend called me for lunch and asked me to give some assist to his daughter in law because the police are still talking to her. I told him that it wasn't my bailiwick, so I turned him on to you. And I might add that I don't expect a finder's fee."

"Your baili what?" Gary asked, sarcastically. "I always wanted to use that word. Good use, wasn't it? Trey was laughing.

"What's the big deal?" Trey asked him. "Just go see the woman tell her what she needs to know and meet me for a drink. Better yet, you can buy my dinner and a shirt I saw today."

"Kiss my ass and buy your own clothes. Did you know that John is the lead detective on this case?

"Yeah. So, did you. Remember the last time we went to happy hour? He mentioned it then. Maybe you need to cut back on the booze and pay attention." Trey chided him.

"I guess I wasn't paying attention. I really didn't care. I don't know what they want me to do. The preacher sounded like his son's wife was on her way to death row. Did you hear if there were any suspects?

"I have no clue." Trey said.

"I have an appointment to meet with both of them in the morning at her house. Reverend Danford said that John would be there. He also said that he wanted you to be involved just in case they needed you. What is that about?" Gary asked.

"He kept insisting that I handle this for them, and I insisted I couldn't. He's a control freak and he thought I could be controlled. I think he's obsessive." Trey said.

"Well, I'm a control freak and obsessive." Gary said.

"And that's why I referred you because you're the best freak I know. Call me and let me know how it turns out. I'll talk to you later."

Trey hung up the phone still wondering why Reverend Danford was so driven about representation for his daughter in law. If he were trying to hide something, would she go along with him or are they both hiding something. It wasn't his intent to get Gary involved in a lot of drama from an overbearing control freak. He knew that Gary wouldn't allow himself to be a part of a cover up. If there were something to hide, that would be between the Danford's and John Garrison.

Trey put it out of his mind and thought about his potential run for office. He had made the decision to go for it, but hadn't shared his decision with anyone, not even his closest friends because he wanted to wait and see what the field looked like before he threw his hat in a ring. He was close to deciding on state office because of the influence the office would afford him for his education projects.

Trey's thoughts filtered back to the Danford's, and he wondered why the man was murdered, and left in an unoccupied apartment. Why not just leave him where he was killed or was there more to what the papers reported? He remembered seeing Mrs. Danford at the church and commenting on how attractive she was. He made a note to himself to get acquainted with the widow; she may need comforting; the kind he was so good at. His secretary walked in his office and wrenched him back to the now, announcing his next appointment he was preparing for testimony the following day in a case involving his client's truck overturning on the freeway onto a van carrying a family of four, killing all. His client was drunk.

CHAPTER THIRTY-SIX

John and Gary met at the gym at six o'clock and worked out for an hour, finishing in the steam room. They showered and dressed for work and drove to Mama's Café for breakfast.

"I received a call from Reverend Darren Danford asking me to meet with his daughter in law to represent her when you question her this morning. Why do you think she needs representation?" Gary asked his friend.

"That's very interesting but not surprising coming from the Reverend. He is aware that we have uncovered information about his son that could, and probably will damage his reputation, and he probably wants some damage control. I'm only surmising here." John answered.

"What kind of information?"

"Are you going to represent her?"

"Is she a suspect?" Gary asked.

"Not at this time. I don't think she killed him.

"Was she involved?

"I really don't know. I don't see it. If you're going to represent her, I'll tell you what we have."

"If she's not a suspect, I'll represent her. If she is, I don't want to get involved." "This morning, she's not a suspect, however we need some information from her. If your in, your in, so what's it going to be?"

"Alright, I'll go the meeting and we'll see what happens."

"Darren Danford was accused of sexual misconduct with two boys. The parents of one of the boys filed a report; we haven't found anything on the other. The charges were dropped, when the boy recanted, and it seems that Reverend Danford made a large payment to the parents of each of the boys. Mrs. Danford is aware of both incidents and was very cooperative with the information. Their marriage was affected and apparently after she found out, she separated herself from him, but they both remained in the house.

Reverend Danford on the other hand is not too happy about discussing his son's activities involving the boys and that is probably why he called you." John explained.

"Why did Reverend Danford make the payment?" Gary asked.

"I don't know. We pulled his bank records, and it showed the withdrawals that matched deposits of the two families. Before we go into anything more, let's go and meet with them."

"This seems pretty convoluted and it looks like the preacher is going to try to make things messy." Gary said paying the check.

"Reverend Danford greeted them at the door of Mrs. Danford's home and led them inside to the living room.

"Reverend Danford, I'm Gary Sanford, we spoke yesterday, you wanted me to represent Mrs. Danford." Gary said to the minister, while shaking his hand.

"Yes, I thought we would all be more comfortable with you here in case something came up that we weren't sure of." The pastor said smiling at John."

They all stood as Mrs. Danford walked into the room carrying a tray with coffee, cups, and saucers, placing it on the coffee table with grace and calm that spoke volumes of the woman.

"Mrs. Danford, my name is Gary Sanford. I'm an attorney, and at your service should you have a need today."

"Mr. Sanford, thank you so much for coming, but I have no need for an attorney. My father-in-law has apparently misunderstood my needs at this time. You are however welcome to stay, but I have no intention of retaining you." She said smiling warmly.

"Now wait," Reverend Danford said standing up, "let's not be too hasty. I think you need an attorney, and I think we need Mr. Sanford involved."

"Darren, I will explain this to you only once," she said, "my husband has been murdered and for that I am sorry for my children. I intend to do anything that is expected of me to help the police find his killer. Since I didn't kill him and I don't know who did, I have no need for an attorney, and I will not have an attorney."

"Helen, I would like to speak with you alone, if you don't mind." Her father-in-law told her, still standing.

"I'll be happy to speak with you, but now I'm going to talk to Mr. Garrison as we planned, and I think he and I will talk alone." She said.

"I won't have it." He told her.

"Darren, you're not listening to me; you don't have a choice."

Gary stood and said, "Mrs. Danford, Reverend Danford, I'm going to leave as there is nothing more for me here. Thank you for the coffee, and it was a pleasure meeting you both." He walked toward the door, followed by Helen Danford.

"Thank you for coming, Mr. Sanford, I won't apologize for my father-in-law; he has control issues, and I am impressed how well you handled the situation. She closed the door behind Gary and returned to the living room.

Gary walked to his car thinking about Helen Danford. He was struck by her control of her father-in-law and her father-in-law allowing her control. Their relationship was dark but not mysterious, he knew. There was more to Mrs. Danford, but it wasn't worth his speculation. He would send his bill and it was finished.

CHAPTER THIRTY-SEVEN

"Helen, you are not yourself and I want you to postpone this interview until you are feeling better." Reverend Danford said.

"Thank you for your concern, but I feel better than I have in many months and I'm looking forward to talking with Mr. Garrison. Please ask me anything." She said, looking at John.

"Mrs. Danford, I'd like to talk to you about the parents of the boys that accused your husband of sexual misconduct." John said and was interrupted by the minister.

"That's it. This will stop now. You don't know what you are talking about. My son was a teacher, husband, and father; he would never behave in that way. I will not sit here and listen to this, or let you continue destroying my son's memory."

"Then I suggest you either leave the room or leave the house." She said. "Your son was bi-sexual but preferred men to women, and abused boys. Too many people know what you think is our dirty little secret, but it's dirty, it's not little and it's no longer a secret."

"I don't intend to go anywhere, Helen."

"Then you will respect my home and my guest if you intend to stay."

John watched the exchange and admired the widow who stood her ground with this larger-than-life public figure.

"Mr. Garrison, I never met either family, I didn't know anything about the boys until I saw two large checks on my husband's nightstand one morning. I asked him about it, and he was hesitant until he said the boys accused him if fondling them and their parents agreed to a settlement in lieu of filing charges. Also, at the time, I didn't know that charges had been filed."

"Did your husband tell you why he elected to make the payments if he was innocent?"

"He was innocent!" The pastor emphasized.

John watched Mrs. Danford's glare.

"He paid them because he wasn't innocent", she said. Let me take you back to an earlier time. It was about five years ago, when I received a letter in the mail that said my husband was homosexual." She reached into her jacket pocket and pulled out an envelope handing it to John.

"I didn't believe it at first. I thought it could have been one of his students who had a grudge. The following week, I received another letter with a photograph enclosed." She said while handing John the second letter.

John looked at the two letters and the printing looked familiar. It looked like the notes found on the two bodies. The photograph was of Darren Danford standing in front of a man who was on his knees, engaged in oral sex.

"I want to see those," the pastor said to John, reaching for the letters.

"No Darren, you'll destroy them, and I won't let you."

"Helen, please; you must stop this now. Don't you see what you're doing to all of us? Think of the children. Danford said.

"I am thinking about my children. I am the only one thinking about my children, unlike their father who never considered the damage his behavior would do to his children. I want this out in the open, and to put it behind us, and I intend to disclose anything I know."

"Mr. Garrison, I apologize for the disruption."

"It's ok, please go on." John told her.

"I confronted my husband with the letters and photograph; since he couldn't deny a photograph of himself; he admitted that it happened only once. I was more furious than hurt, or even shocked.

I was sickened by his behavior and even more so by his begging me not to leave him. He begged me to stay without telling his father what I knew. He told me that his father couldn't handle it, so I never told him until today."

"I don't believe a word of this trash. I don't know why you are trying to tarnish your own husband's name." Reverend Danford shouted standing over her.

"Mr. Garrison, please have a copy of that photograph made for my father-in-law." She said and excused herself.

"You can't possibly believe what Helen has told you."

"Reverend Danford, I'm here to talk with Mrs. Danford. She is obviously willing to talk about her husband in way that is personal, but the information is germane to our investigation. It's difficult to deny the obvious, that your son was charged with sexual misconduct and the photograph speaks for itself." John said.

"Do you have any idea; any concept of what this kind of information will do to our good name, and what about the church? He was my son for God sake! This will all fall on my church and me. Don't you understand what's at stake here?"

"Reverend Danford, I don't think you understand. I'm investigating the murder of your son. This is not about your standing in your church. With all due respect sir, I can't allow you to interfere with this investigation. I hope you are not suggesting that we disregard the information that Mrs. Danford has given. Reverend Danford, I have been patient while listening to your point of view, but if it becomes necessary, I will continue my interview with Mrs. Danford in my office." John told the minister.

"That won't be necessary Mr. Garrison. My father-in-law is leaving now and we can continue." He heard her say walking back into the room.

"I want you to leave now Darren. It's obvious that you won't stop interfering and this is what I want to do, now please leave and you can call when you are feeling better."

"Mr. Garrison, I don't think you know who I am and more

important, who I know." The pastor shouted, "you will hear from me about this, and Helen I am ashamed of you, and how you insist on destroying our family; you're not the woman I knew."

John watched the man stomp out of the house after glaring at Helen Danford enraged that he could not dissuade a woman he considered nothing more than a helpmate to her husband and now him.

"My father-in-law was wrong when he assumed that I would support his intentions of a conspiracy to deny my husband's deviant penchant for males of any age. My children are young enough to work through any fall out that might harm them. I have lived with this deception longer than I can tolerate. Since I learned about my husband's secret as well as his crimes, I have had to watch my children constantly. I would never allow them to be alone with their father under any circumstance." John watched her relieving the pain and anger that prompted her to remain in the farce that was her family.

"I could have walked away at any time," she went on, but I seldom saw Darren; we had nothing whatsoever to do with each other and, I didn't have the emotional energy to fight his father and the church with a divorce, so denial was my refuge." She told him.

"Mrs. Danford, you don't have to talk about this aspect of your marriage; no one is judging you; I am only interested in any information you may have consistent with the investigation of your husband's murder." John said, embarrassed at hearing her re-live an intimate period in her life.

"I don't mind", Mr. Garrison, I have never discussed this with anyone. As far as any more information, I don't think I know any more." She said.

"Where did your husband get the money, he used to pay the parents of the boys?" He asked. "Oh, his father gave it to him."

"Was that unusual, I mean did he often give large sums of money to your husband?" "Often enough," she replied, "he gave us the down payment on this house. This is not the house we chose, however my father-in-law felt that we should have a larger and more expensive house than we could afford, that would be more fitting for his son. The down payment he gave us was more than the value of the house we planned to buy. At the time, I had no problem with his generosity because I loved the house. The amount was large enough to assure affordable monthly payments. He paid to furnish several rooms in the house and often gave my husband money for reasons I never knew."

"According to your husband's bank statement, he gave you a monthly stipend, can you clarify that?" He asked her.

"When I learned about my husband's habits, I agreed to stay in the house if he signed it over to me and took out an insurance policy that would pay off the mortgage should he die. The amount he gave me was for the mortgage payments. My husband lived in my house for the last five years." She said with contentment. "I work three day a week and pay all of the household bills and my expenses. I took nothing else from my husband. I wanted nothing else from him."

"Did your husband ever mention being threatened by the fathers of the boys who accused him?"

"If there were threats, he would never tell me."

"Did you notice a change in his behavior at any time before was killed?"

"No. He would sometimes have breakfast with the children and he usually came home after dinner; I didn't see any change, whenever I did see him.

"What kind of work do you do, Mrs. Danford?" He was curious.

"I'm a clinical psychologist. I worked full time before the children were born, then I cut back to part time.

"Do you have a relationship with Reverend Danford's wife? He could see her look of shock at the question.

"I would really be surprised if Darren discussed his wife with you. To answer your question, I never met the senior Mrs. Danford. Darren and his father told me that she didn't want any involvement with the church, and he refused her demand for a divorce, so she moved to another state, and is not involved with her family. I was very curious for a long time, however, after I became more acquainted with her son and her husband, I understood her absence. I consider her one very smart woman, wherever she is."

"But, what about her son? Did she ever have any contact with him? Was she contacted when he died?"

"Darren never talked about her, and I don't know if his father called her when Darren was killed."

CHAPTER THIRTY-EIGHT

John drove away feeling like he spent the morning in a jungle watching and listening to the father and widow Danford fight like guerrillas protecting their territory.

The preacher's dismay with his daughter in law was not convincing. She existed for him not only to exhibit as his son's wife and grieving widow; there was more he was not the bane of her fragile existence. What was life like in that house for the victim these last five years, he wondered, trying the imagine their lack of family values and substance.

There is more going in that family than he could see clearly, and the Reverend Danford is prepared to protect himself. How far would he go and what was he capable of doing to anyone who threatened him and his domain, John wondered.

John called Gary and told him it didn't matter if she had an attorney, no one would have been able to stop her from telling everything she knew regarding her husband and their marriage. Gary said he received a call from Reverend Danford telling him that he wanted representation for himself.

"I turned him down because I have this feeling that he's one fucked up individual and, in all probability, he needs a doctor more than an attorney. He never said why he thought she needed a lawyer, and I didn't want to know. Thanks to caller ID and secretaries, I'm not taking any more of his calls."

"There's a lot involved here, I think, and he just might need an attorney before this is all said and done. John said before ending the call.

John called his daughters feeling the need to hear their voices to bring him back from the total dysfunction he witnessed earlier in the day. The girls were their usual effervescent selves vying for their father's undivided attention to bring him status quo with the day's activities.

He said good-bye to his daughters grateful for their glow that lights his day. He wondered about the widow Danford; was she capable of contracting her husband's killing. Did her loathing of her husband include destroying him in order for her to permanently rid herself and her family of his very being? She has proven herself to be calculating and methodical in her cunning; but is she a killer? If so, why kill Brian Hargrave? Maybe the two victims were lovers, and she knew. What more did she know and what if anything did, she do about it?

She is very much a suspect, John acknowledged, although he hoped she would not be, but she had a motive. She hated the man and she hated what he did to her as a woman. He preferred a man. That was motive in her mind. She didn't take the news of her husband's sexual penchant as well as she demonstrated today. The thought of him enraged her enough to destroy him; and he was destroyed. He thought it strange that neither the widow nor the father ever mentioned how the killing took place. The mere ferociousness of the act would give way to curiosity at least. Perhaps neither one was surprised or didn't care.

Reverend Darren Danford was also a suspect. He had much to lose should his son's activities become public fodder creating adverse judgment of his leadership. John considered the church pastor willing to do whatever was necessary to maintain his position. Would that include the death of his son? He seems more interested in protecting his son's name than his son. No one seems to be grieving for the man. No one seems to feel a loss of any kind, more of a relief.

He drove to P&D's Club and talked to a bartender who was different from the last he spoke with. He identified himself and explained that he was investigating the murders. He showed a picture of Danford and the bartender recognized him immediately.

"He came in here several times a week. I didn't know he was a teacher until I read about it in the paper." The bartender said. "Did you know that the doctor that was killed came in here too, and was a friend of the teacher?"

"No, I didn't." John responded, sitting down and ordered a cup of coffee.

"Yeah, they came in here a lot together. They were pretty good friends." The bartender went on.

"How could you tell?" John asked him.

"They met here for lunch often. Did you know we're open for lunch? Not dinner though. We can make more money on the liquor, so we remove some of tables after four o'clock and just serve a buffet of hors d'oeuvres; you know, finger food for happy hour. The kitchen's still open, why don't I get you a sandwich or something. We have great sandwiches here." He said to John, while handing him a menu from behind the bar. John ordered a chicken salad sandwich and coleslaw.

"Good choice," the bartender said, "we make the best sandwiches around here; you'll see."

The bartender walked into the kitchen, leaving John to his thoughts. The club was empty except for what seemed to be a few neighborhood regulars, watching television and a couple reading newspapers.

The bartender returned with John's lunch and stood over him waiting for his reaction. John didn't realize how hungry he was and told the man what he wanted to hear. "This really is good."

"Sure, it is. Just like I told you. You know you don't have to be a brother to come in here. We welcome everyone." The bartender told John. "You can come and bring your friends. We have straights in here all the time. In fact, there's a straight guy who had lunch with those two a couples of times." The bartender said.

"Excuse me?" John said, looking up at the man.

"The two dead guys. He had lunch with them."

"Do you remember when that was?" John asked.

"Well, about a week before the teacher got it. We decided to serve seafood every Friday for lunch and that was the first time. They were here and they all ate boiled crawfish. We serve it with potatoes and corn on the cob with newspaper on the table, just like it should be served, and they really liked it. I remember because they were regulars and I really wanted to know what they thought about the food." He said grinning.

"Have you seen the straight man since that day?"

"No, haven't seen him since. It could have been some kind of business meeting and since they're both dead, I guess the man didn't have a reason to come back.

"Do you remember what he looked like?"

"No, his back was always to me, but I could tell he was straight. He dressed like one of those guys in a magazine though, you know, real expensive everything.

"If you saw him again would you recognize him?"

"I never saw his face, but I remember that body; perfect in every way, if you know what I mean."

CHAPTER THIRTY-NINE

Jeff Harrington was in Chicago visiting with a client and planned to be there until Wednesday of that week, although he told his wife he would be returning on Thursday. He called his wife several times since he left home, but she either didn't answer or she wasn't at home. He was now convinced that his wife was involved with another man. She had no interest in Jeff's attention whatsoever. Since his birthday, she was cold and distant, and seldom at home until very late without explanation. When she did come home, she was wide-awake and stayed up for hours and was always sleeping when he left for his office. One morning, he saw a bottle of Xanax on the table beside their bed. The medication was prescribed to her and on examination of the bottle; he noticed that it was the second refill. He might have asked her about her absences, if he were interested, which he wasn't, but if she was involved with someone else, she had to go. He did however, wonder why she had problems sleeping, she did nothing all day except shop. They now had a full-time housekeeper because Jeff couldn't stand the clutter.

He finished with his business late Wednesday morning and was able to get a flight back to Houston early afternoon. He didn't bother calling his wife; he left his car at the airport and would drive himself home. When he arrived in Houston, he called Gary to meet him for a drink. Gary asked him to pick him up because his car was being serviced.

When he saw Gary, he noticed him carrying an overnight bag. Gary explained that his house was being fumigated and he was going to stay overnight at a hotel.

"Why don't you stay at Trey's?

"He's out of town and I didn't know in time to tell him about my house to get his key." Gary replied.

"Then stay at my house and save your money."

"Cool," Gary said, "but will it be ok with Cheryl?"

"She probably won't even be there for most of the time." He said.

They stopped and had a drink, talked about Chicago, and what went on at the Danford house.

When they arrived at Jeff's house, there was a car in the driveway next to his wife's car, blocking Jeff from the garage.

Gary and Jeff entered the house through the front door. The house looked empty and was quiet. Jeff was concerned because of the unfamiliar car in front and the fact that the house seemed lifeless.

He walked toward the bedroom, Gary behind him, also concerned. The bedroom was dark; drapes drawn and quiet.

Jeff walked into the room and turned on the light and froze, losing feeling. Gary saw the two people sleeping in Jeff's bed and pulled Jeff out of the room. Gary couldn't understand why the sleeping couple didn't stir. He could hear them breathing, but there was no movement.

They both walked back in the bedroom and discovered the reason for the undisturbed sleep. On a nightstand was a small mirror with two and a half lines of white power, obviously cocaine. Beside the mirror was a bottle labeled Xanax. Gary knew that they could be out for a while.

Gary walked out of the room and noticed that Jeff was not with him. He saw Jeff in the hallway sitting on the floor with his face in his hands.

"Let's go downstairs." Gary said, pulling his friend to his feet.

"I need a drink." Jeff said.

"Not now, you don't. Let's talk about this and what you can do." Gary said, walking with Jeff to his kitchen. Gary poured his friend a glass of orange juice and saw the tears in his eyes and felt his anger and humiliation.

"Jeff, I want you to listen to me carefully because there's no way of knowing when they will wake up, and you are going to have to make a quick decision about this." Gary pleaded.

"What are you talking about Gary, decision about what? I want them both out of my house, and her out of my life. She's never going to have a chance to use me again. The whore is doing drugs and fucking who knows who in my house. I just want her out now." Jeff shouted.

"So, you just plan to wake them up and put them out, to what end? You want this woman out of your life by giving her half of everything you've worked for and income? Just consider this. Drop a dime on her and let her beg you for a settlement. We can call John and let him take care of the rest. Just let me handle this; you're too angry and you're not thinking." Gary said.

Jeff straightened himself and said, "I'm not too angry, just disgusted. Make the call. I like it."

Gary called John Garrison on his cell and reached him as he was driving away from P&D's. John listened to Gary describe what was going on and what they wanted to do about it. After John spoke with Jeff and was assured that he wanted to proceed, he phoned in a report and met the two uniformed police officers at Jeff's house.

Jeff answered the door and showed policemen to the bedroom where the couple lay sleeping, then joined Gary and John in his living room. They all heard the couple shouting at the policemen; then quiet. Then they heard one of the officers reading them their legal rights and placing them under arrest. Cheryl Harrington screamed that she wanted a lawyer and that her husband was a lawyer, and she didn't know whose cocaine was in her room.

Jeff saw his wife walk into the living room with her guest and the two officers and started screaming at him.

"Jeff tell them who I am and that they are making a mistake. Gary, I need you to handle this now. They want to take me to jail."

She didn't express any knowledge the presence of the man who had slept with her hours before. Jeff looked at his wife and said nothing.

"I can't represent you, Cheryl. I'm a witness." Gary told his friend's wife.

"Witness to what, you bastard? She shouted at him.

"Jeff, you know this is bull shit." She pleaded to her husband. "I'm a witness too Cheryl. I let the police in the house after Gary called to report you and your friend. Oh, one more thing, I'm filing for divorce." He told his wife.

CHAPTER FORTY

John knew it was time to talk to the parents of the boys who accused their teacher, and he needed to find a link between the two victims.

Paul Hutchinson agreed to meet with John before he went to work because he didn't want his boss to ask questions if the police showed up on his job. His wife took the day off and joined them at her house after taking the children to the bus stop.

"Mr. Hutchinson, your son accused Darren Danford of molesting him, but the charges were dropped when he recanted. Why did he change his story? John asked the man.

The Hutchinson's looked at each other and appeared uncomfortable saying nothing for at least a minute. John watched and waited for the answer from either of them.

"It was all a mistake. My son was sorry for saying those things. Nothing happened. It's over and we don't talk about it anymore. Why are you questioning us about this now? That happened a long-time age." Paul Hutchinson said.

"Did you take money from Mr. Danford after your son changed his story? There was another look at each other and a longer silence.

"Mr. Garrison, that isn't any of your business, and I don't see why we have to tell you anything more. I want you to leave now." The man said.

"Thank you, Mr. and Mrs. Hutchinson, I'll be in touch." John told the couple and left their home.

He drove away and wondered if he looked as stupid and they thought he was. Another suspect to add to his growing list, and he was no closer than he was when Andy left. He would question them again separately at the station when his partner returned the following week.

He thought about the Davis family and decided not to visit with them in their home, not wanting the same result as with the Hutchinson's. He'd wait for Andy and bring them downtown.

CHAPTER FORTY-ONE

Jeff didn't want any involvement in the adjudication of his wife's criminal predicament. Gary recommended an attorney to represent her and told Jeff that she would probably get probation that would include drug testing, since it was her first offense. Jeff was pouring his third drink saying nothing.

Gary drove Jeff to his parent's house since he didn't want to stay in his. Jeff needed to tell his parents what was going on in his marriage. They would spend the night with his parents and Jeff agreed to move in with Gary until he made some decisions about where he wanted to live.

Gary called Trey and left a message to call him at Jeff's parents. He left Jeff alone to talk to his parents and was worried that Jeff might be drunk and not able to make himself clear to them. He sat in the adjoining room and listened to his friend talk to his mother and father in a relaxed, and deliberate manner with clarity and determination not to allow them to bring their own way of thinking or judgment into an already resolved situation. Gary was impressed and proud of his friend for the way he was handling himself with what could have been more unpleasant than Jeff was prepared.

Mr. and Mrs. Harrington always supported their son's decision, and this was no exception. After they were told about the arrest, they were more relieved than condemning. They agreed with their son, not to have any contact with his wife.

Gary answered Trey's call and told him what was going on. You've got to be shittin' me," he said. I'm in Austin and on the next plane.

Trey arrived at the Harrington's and told Jeff he would handle the divorce.

"I want you to file it right away. The house is in my name; however, I'll offer her twenty five percent of the proceeds of the sale and nothing more. I want you to get her to relinquish all rights she has to everything else." Jeff told his lawyer.

"Are you prepared to fight her on this?' Trey asked.

"I'm prepared to fight her and win. She's not prepared to fight at all. Just explain to her that she could lose everything, and I won't back down." Jeff told him.

"Just leave it to me, and it's done." Trey said.

Trey regretted being there when his friends found Cheryl and her bed partner. I'd kill or die to see that woman naked, he was thinking, but quickly squelch the thought choosing instead, to sympathize with his best friend.

He found Cheryl Harrington living in a motel that she moved into after being released on bail. Trey presented the offer her husband made and told her that it was final.

"Trey why is he doing this to me. I've been charged with possession of cocaine and my life is ruined. Why would he do that?"

"Cheryl, I'm representing Jeff in his divorce, I can't comment about your criminal situation. I strongly suggest you take the offer and sign off on the divorce and just move on. It's not going to get any better." He said to the distraught woman.

"But I really didn't mean for anything like this to happen. It was just one of those things that people go through. We could have worked through it if he would have just given me another chance and trusted me."

Is she for real, Trey thought?

"Cheryl, I really can't talk to you about this; I represent your husband, and this is inappropriate.

"Why don't you look these papers over and call me in a day or two." He told her.

"I'll sign them now. Let's just get this over and tell Jeff to send me the check. I need to find an apartment soon because this room is getting expensive." She said.

Trey was surprised watching her sign the papers. He expected her to hold out for more and try to delay the divorce to persuade Jeff to take her back. For the first time since he met Cheryl, he felt sorry for her seeing her living in a motel after her life as an attorney's wife, living in grand style in her mini mansion. The pity faded when he realized that she would land on her feet with another man footing the bills.

He left his client's wife and was satisfied with a job well done. Jeff was free to be Jeff again.

"Have you ever considered anyone in addition to Bird and Miles? Jeff asked Gary while he listened to more Charlie Parker music. "This is ridiculous, Gary, how can you stand listening to the same music day in and day out? There is more music out there in the same genre as these two. Don't you ever get tired of them?

"Are you acting stupid just to piss me off, or are you really that stupid? There is no other jazz but this. There have been attempts, but never the real thing. You should know that by now Jeff. How can you stand listening to anything else? Gary said.

"Well put your earphones on then because I can't take it anymore. It's really driving me crazy." Jeff told his new roommate.

"I can do better than that, let's go out and do some clubs. I'll drive because you've already had too much to drink." Gary said. "No, you go on with out me. I'm going to stay here and drink some more. I'm not in the mood for people and you need to spend some time away from me because all I'm going to do tonight is bitch about your music."

"You've got a point; I'll be back much later. Don't fall asleep on the couch, go to bed first, and I'll see you in the morning." Gary said, and left Jeff with his liquor and his memories of his marriage.

Jeff was sober enough to know that he was drinking more than was safe for him to function, as he knew he should. He's been drinking more and more since his marriage and he didn't like the feeling of needing anything. Need was never in his repertoire of the man he thought he was meant to be. He sat wondering who expected him to be who be had become or even who he should be. He didn't recall ever having any input in his lifetime about his life.

He knew that his life changed the moment he entered his bedroom and saw his wife sleeping with a man whose name he still didn't know. He had lived his entire life without himself; life just happened. He never had to work for anything, need anything or want anything he couldn't have. The plans he made were always based on his friend's plans or his parent's plans that just happened to include him. He was on his own for the first time in his life and he felt the strains of responsibility to other people peeling away, and liquor seeped into that self he wanted to explore sober and on his own terms.

He had to find a place to live soon he thought; it was too crowded here with Bird, Miles, and Gary.

CHAPTER FORTY-TWO

*H*e lay back on his bed listening to his favorite musician through earphones feeling satisfied with how his plan was working.

The doctor was finally exposed as he was with his choice of movies and photographs. Brian Hargrave lived a life of contentment as an openly gay physician, well respected in his field and community. He was a good friend and associate to his partners. He was not inclined to stop using the children he found; some homeless, all afraid and all needing the attention of someone they would trust.

He fed them and loved them and then he destroyed their lives, confident that they would never expose him as their abuser. Their fear of his abandonment overwhelmed their self worth. They had none, and he depended on their desire to belong to this nice man who said he loved them and took care of them. He would never stop so I stopped him. He thought about the boys out there waiting for him, feeling abandoned and alone.

He thought about the doctor hanging from his showerhead, naked with that lemon wedge in his mouth, looking like the freak he was for his entire world to see. He needed not only to be exposed, but also humiliated.

Darren was weak and pathetic. He used and abused his students then threatened their parents if they didn't agree to protect him and change their stories. He told the boys who his father was and his father would make God kill their mothers if they told. He took his victims to his father's church and let them hear the preacher's power over the people and the children feared him and were compliant. He demonstrated a harsh physical control over the boys, giving them no way to escape his grip. He laughed at them when they cried and slapped them when their crying seemed out of control. He taped his attacks and watched them with pleasure once more, feeling the only thing over which, he had any power. He used his hands to hold them and abuse them; he used his face to ridicule their fear. He would never make another boy cry and feel helpless and confuse his masculinity.

He would stop the next ones and leave the rest to those who are charged with protecting our children.

CHAPTER FORTY-THREE

Gary took his mother's call without hesitation since it had been over a week since they last spoke. He knew she wanted to know what had happened to Jeff and his wife only out of curiosity without any real interest, since she was not involved.

"You haven't returned any of my calls Gary, I've been worried about you. Just call me and let me know everything is ok." She told her son.

"Everything is just fine. I've been working a lot of hours and getting home late. I've been in court three days this week and I just haven't had the time to call."

"Is Jeff still staying with you? I just can't believe what I heard about him and his wife, Jeff of all people. Is she going to jail? Can you believe it, Jeffrey Harrington's wife in jail? It's amazing; I'm still shocked."

His mother was enjoying this, he thought. She always resented the family Jeff had. His parents were still married, and their ties strong, something his mother felt cheated without.

"Jeff is fine, and I doubt if his wife goes to jail. Everything will work out as it should." He told his mother.

"How many tickets are you going to buy for the Anniversary Gala? She asked.

"Gala for what, and why should I buy any tickets at all?"

"Gary, your mother is the chairperson of the fiftieth Anniversary Gala for Father Connor. Aren't you proud of me? It will be a dinner at the Wortham; live band, sit down dinner, and of course an award presentation. The Bishop will be there along with the Mayor, City

Council and three County Commissioners. You won't believe the corporate sponsorship I have, almost complete underwriting. This is going to be fabulous. You and your friends have to be there, after all, he taught you, Trey and Jeff. How many tickets should I put you down for? They are two hundred fifty dollars each or, twenty-five hundred per table. I'm sure you can get enough of your friends together and get a table. You don't want to make your mother look bad, and it's Father Connor."

Gary had no intention of making his mother look bad. He remembered Father Connor. He would always remember Father Connor.

"Put me down for a table and be sure it's a good one. Of course, I remember Father Connor; I wouldn't miss it. I'll bring Jeff and Trey. I'll put a check in the mail to you today."

"Oh, Gary, a table; that's wonderful. Don't worry; it will be a very good table. Why not bring the check by tonight and I'll cook dinner?"

"I wish I could, but I'll be here very late, and I have to meet with a client tonight so just give me a rain check and we'll do something soon." He lied.

Gary hadn't seen Father Connor since grade school and never thought they would meet again. Everything happens for a reason, he could hear John's grandmother say, and wondered what the reason could be. He would never put the priest out of his mind, but he thought he was out of his life. He was sickened by his mother's involvement and enthusiasm with the man responsible for changing his life, as well as the estrangement in his relationship with his parents. On second thought, he told himself, his parents were responsible for their relationship. They both failed to accept the responsibility of taking care of their son's emotional welfare. They expected him to accept their denial and live with it as if it were a favorite old shirt.

He called Trey and Jeff and invited them to dinner at his house. He wanted to tell them that they would be celebrating the anniversary of Father O'Connor and it would be a good time to spend with Jeff since they have all been too involved with their practices to consider their friend's divorce and his willingness to move beyond his wife and her own problems that have nothing to do with him.

Gary thought about Jeff's inability to accept failure since he didn't think it was an option for him. Well, it was time he realized that even he can, and will have failures without losing anything significant, and if he really opened himself to the possibility, he might learn from the experience.

He left his office to pick up the dinner he invited his friends to share.

CHAPTER FORTY-FOUR

The man was lying on his left side with his hands tied then hogtied to his ankles. He was still wearing his glasses, which seemed odd for his condition. He was fully clothed in a light blue oxford cloth shirt and khaki slacks. He was wearing brown loafers and no socks. His wallet was in his pocket containing sixty-seven dollars, driver's license, three credit cards, a Kroger card and a Sam's Club card. Another pocket contained a dollar and fifteen cents in change and a roll of mints. Spread under the man was a plastic tarp with blood pooled from the gunshot through his left temple. His hands held an envelope that contained a piece of stationary on which was block printed. HE EARNED THIS. THERE WILL BE NO MORE.

The woman was in a bedroom lying face down on a plastic tarp. She was naked. There was a gunshot in each knee and the back of her head. Placed on the small of her back was a photograph clipped to piece of stationary with the same words as the note in the man's hands. The photograph depicted the woman, nude, lying on a bed with two young boys who were also nude.

The house was large, expensive, and well kept. As with the others, nothing looked out of place; nothing looked disturbed, except the bodies of the homeowners who were James and Barbara Evans.

There was quiet in the house; the quiet that follows the terrifying violence that the couple lived in their last minutes at the hands of their executioner.

Dr. Ellis was bent over the man, while Chad Bailey was directing the photographer through the crime scenes.

"Hola, mi amigo!" John heard Andy who was walking into the house.

"I leave you for just two weeks expecting you to clean things up and I come home to three more bodies, John." Is there an epidemic or are we talking serial?" Andy said shaking his partner's hand.

"Can you believe this? You should have seen the last one. What are you doing here, he asked, I didn't expect you until Monday?"

"We got back earlier this evening, and I called in to see what was going on and here I am."

"The jet lag must be dragging you. You look like shit. Go home and I'll bring you up to date in the morning." John said.

"On one condition, crisp bacon".

"Crisp what?"

"Bacon—I haven't had crisp bacon in two weeks. Those people over there expect their bacon to walk toward them. I could stay and work this, you know."

"No, you can't. You're not thinking. You're obsessing. Go home while you can still drive. I can't use you 'til you're awake, which is not what you are now."

These are not senseless killings, John thought walking through the house as if now by habit, hearing the same chatter about bodies, blood, wounds and who. There had to be a pattern, some common thread woven through each of these victims and their killer. He was telling us something about himself, John thought about the man who committed these horrendous crimes. It was more than the content of the notes, left with each body. This was the end of what, he wondered. Whatever these people were doing he ended it. It came back to the children. This killer was a vigilante hunting pedophiles. In his mind, he was saving children, and at the same time the killer knew he couldn't save them all; he was in pain, the kind of pain that would not heal, so he's going to save all the children he can. This man had been abused by someone he trusted; someone who took his childhood, and he had no one to help him retrieve it.

Where are you, John wondered finding himself feeling sorry for the man he sought; thinking about Tommy Becker and the pain he could no longer handle and killed himself?

We haven't made the world safe for our children by any means. We just try to give them everything we didn't have to feed our own egos, John told himself. We spend more time hunting and convicting those who harm our children than we do creating and maintaining an environment that allows our children to be who they are meant to be, safe and secure, knowing trust would never be an issue because someone would take care of them. John felt the pain of losing the children we all hold dear. This killer would be caught and punished, and there would be no difference. This will only be viewed as senseless killings. We just don't get it.

CHAPTER FORTY-FIVE

"If Will Davis or Paul Hutchinson is the killer, what connects them to Dr. Hargrave and the Evans?" Andy asked his partner over breakfast.

"They both had sound motive to kill Danford, but why kill the others unless one of them decided to stop the madness."

"I don't know", John, said, "I was waiting for you to talk to Davis and Hutchinson, but that was before the population at the morgue multiplied."

"Who were the Evan's?" Andy asked while chewing home fries.

"They're both psychologists; practicing together, specializing in sexual dysfunction and pedophilia. They both work for defense attorneys as expert witnesses and apparently make a lot of money doing it. Danford's wife is also a psychologist, working part time with at risk adolescents."

"Each of the victims was killed in a different way. The methods could identify the underlying lesson the killer was demonstrating to them, or us, or both." They were all involved with child pornography, all were involved in sex with boys, all at the top of their professions, and somehow, they are all connected to each other as well as to their killer. If we find that Dr. Hargrave treated the Davis or Hutchinson boy, we have a thread." John said.

"I'll get a list of the Evans' clients and patients, and you get a list of Dr. Hargrave's patients, and will meet and go over the lists this afternoon. I promised Raymond I would go his school's father son luncheon today, so I'll see you later." John told Andy.

John mentored Raymond Morris through Big Brothers and

Sisters. Raymond's mother works as their apartment complex manager and supports four children, while her husband serves time for selling cocaine. She had the presence of mind to find a mentor for her son before she lost him to the street, since she couldn't spend the time, she felt all of her children required to stabilize after the most wrenching life change when their father was imprisoned for a crime no one would have dreamed committed by a PhD in Chemical Engineering. They lived well, six-bedroom house, swimming pool, private schools, and a stay-at-home soccer mom. The children knew no other way of life when they moved from their larger home, into a two-bedroom apartment in a part of town, they had never had a reason to know. They entered public school for the first time and were all completely overwhelmed by the chaos and indifference they experienced by the new scholastic environment.

Jill Morris was determined to maintain her family's values, and to have a home for her husband when he returned. She talked to her children daily about the importance of taking advantage of their school without resenting the loss of their previous privilege. She made them accept the responsibility for their place on earth and taught them how their choices will dictate their future. Each of the children had mentors and she insisted that all of the children along with their mentors meet with her once per month to discuss their good and bad times, their ups and down and concerns. As a result, all of the children were honor students. Their relationship with their father was conflicted. They had not seen him during the two years he had been away. They loved their father, but their shame and disappointment too often overshadowed his place in their lives. They each received a weekly letter from him. He had long since apologized for his crime and accepted the responsibility of his choices. He refused to allow their resentment to deter him from communicating with them and encouraging them as he did before he went away. After he made it clear to his children how wrong he was for hurting and displacing them, he fathered them as he did when they lived together as a family. He would not allow visits from his children, because he did not expect them to do any-thing to put them in a prison for any reason.

Jill Morris taped their monthly meetings and sends the tapes to her husband. She long ago came to terms with her husband and his incarceration after directing her anger and resentment to a com-mitment of solidifying her family unit for better or worse as she vowed a lifetime ago. She loved her husband and intended to pre-serve her marriage not only for she and her husband, but to dem-onstrate to her children that their family was the foundation from which they will build their lives.

John met with Raymond and stood proud of him as he watched the boy receive an award for his outstanding math and science scores. John took photographs of the events to send to Raymond's father.

CHAPTER FORTY-SIX

Andy was sitting at his desk going over the list of Dr. Hargrave's patients when he saw John walk in wearing a three-piece suit.

"Did you say you were going to a school lunch or a funeral?"

"I look good, don't I?" John replied.

"I met Dr. and Mrs. Hargrave. Nice people: they gave me access to anything I wanted, so now you can ask me what I found while you were giving personal appearance lessons to children. William Davis Jr. son of William Sr. and Tanya Davis has been a patient of Dr. Hargrave since he was born. We need a medical authorization from the parents or a warrant to get a copy of the file, but we hit pay dirt." Andy said.

"We sure did, John said. I went to the Evans' house and found their files. They worked out of a home office. All of their clients were defense attorney's including the firm where a friend of mine is a partner," referring to Gary Sanford, "these people made bucks; thirty-five thousand for court testimony, a thousand dollars for consultation, in addition to their private practice." John said reading from his notes.

"Let's see what we have; the Davis boy was taught by Danford and treated by Hargrave. Nothing on the Hutchinson kid; let's pick up Will Davis and hear what he has to say" John said.

"It's not quite five o'clock yet", Andy said, "let's wait for him in front of his house, that way his wife won't have a chance to call him and scare him off."

John and Andy sat in John's car in front of a house half a block away from their suspect's house, but close enough to see him when he arrived home. It was after six thirty and there was no sign of Davis when they saw Tanya Davis drive out of their garage. John got out of the car and told Andy to follow her while he waited for Will Davis. Andy saw John talking to a neighbor when he followed Mrs. Davis back to her house.

"She just went to the store; I followed her inside, but she only bought a few groceries and came back."

"Davis hasn't shown up yet; the neighbor says he stays out late often and the couple fight like cats and dogs most of the time. We'll wait." John said.

Andy called Beth to tell her he would be late.

They were both dozing at two fifteen when their suspect's headlights woke them. They got out of the car and walked to the house and arrived just as Will Davis was getting out of his car. They approached him and explained that they wanted to ask him some questions about his son's allegations and the murders. The man became belligerent saying he would speak with them without a lawyer, at which time; they presented a warrant for his arrest, read him his rights, handcuffed him, and walked him to their car. When they arrived at the police station, Davis was given an opportunity to call an attorney, however, he didn't know of any and asked for a public defender. John and Andy left the suspect to be locked up until his attorney arrived and went over the information, they had to prepare questions in the event Davis agreed to talk to them.

It was seven thirty in the morning when they met with the suspect's attorney, Herman Walker.

"Mr. Davis is willing to answer your questions as long as I am in the room." The attorney spoke.

"I have no problem with that." John said. They waited for Davis to be brought from the holding cell where he spent the last several hours waiting.

"Mr. Davis tell us about your son's sexual abuse by his teacher." John asked.

"What do you know? My son never reported anything like that to the police. I want to know who told you that shit. My son ain't no faggot. Nobody touched him, I don't care who you talked to."

"Mr. Davis no one is accusing your son of anything. You received a large sum of money from Darren Danford to compensate for his touching your son. We have your bank records as well as Mr. Danford's records; we know he gave you the money and we know why. We have the check with your signature" John said.

They watched Will Davis sit with his eyes lowered saying nothing for several minutes. Finally, he said, "I didn't do anything wrong taking that money. He owed it to us and more; that freak son of a bitch."

"Why did he owe you?"

"You know what he did. Don't play games with me. I don't care what anybody says, my son ain't no faggot."

"Mr. Davis, no one is saying anything about your son."

"Yeah, I know what people will think."

"How many times did you see Mr. Danford?" John asked.

"Two or three, then he gave us the money and that was it. I didn't want to see that low life bastard again."

"When did you learn of the death of Mr. Danford?"

"When I read it in the paper."

"Can you account for your whereabouts the Wednesday night before you read about it in the paper?"

"Hell, I don't know. I was probably at home or at work."

"Where do you usually go after work, Mr. Davis? We waited for you until two fifteen this morning."

"Oh, that was nothing, I was just out chillin' with some friends."

"Where were you?"

"Just a couple of clubs, I can't remember the names."

"What are the names of the people you were with last night?"

"I don't remember their names. Who cares; it's just some guys I know and drink with."

Andy stood up and walked over to toward the man and said,

"don't play us for fools, where were you and who were you with last night? Tell us now, so we can move on." Andy walked back to his chair and stared at the suspect.

"Look, there's this woman that's not involved in this. You don't need to know anything about that. We don't need to bring all that up."

"We need her name, Mr. Davis. John said.

"Fuck you!"

"Mr. Davis, you have a history of violence with your wife, as well as others. You were acquainted with two murdered people, one of which sexually abused your son and gave you a considerable amount of money, so we're going to sit here and listen to you answer our questions or you can go back to a cell and fuck any one you like. Do you know where I'm coming from, Mr. Davis?" John shouted at the man.

"I want to talk to my lawyer alone."

John and Andy left their suspect alone with his attorney and sat silent for a while drinking coffee.

"He's not our man." Andy spoke first.

"I know, John said, the man who we're looking for is compulsive, obsessive, intelligent, organized, deliberate and has a personal vendetta. Vengeance is always personal as it should be. He doesn't hate the people he kills; he probably doesn't know them well enough; he hates what they do and what they represent when they do it. This man is also patient. He waits. He plans. He carries out his mission, and for him it is a mission."

They drank more coffee and waited and thought about the man they were looking for.

Who are you, John thought, *and what makes you hurt so badly?*

CHAPTER FORTY-SEVEN

Trey was the first to arrive and heard Charlie Parker playing Night in Tunisia and knew the music would go on and on.

"Do you think shrimp fried rice and spring rolls would be spoiled if I left them in a hot car for three hours?" Trey asked Gary.

"There's something very wrong with you, Trey. Why did you bring that garbage in my house?

"I ate the fried rice on the way over here; it was great, but I don't know about the spring rolls yet."

"Why would you leave it in the car so long or at all? Why not put it in the refrigerator in your office?"

"Because one of the clerks said she would throw up if she smelled food in the office and I was trying to be nice."

"Oh, this is about fucking. Have you fucked her yet?"

"She's new; I haven't gotten around to it yet."

"You're a sick man, Trey. Give me your rancid food, so I can dispose of it now."

"What's in the other bag?" Gary asked his friend.

"I found this for you and thought you might like to have it." Gary opened the bag and pulled out the Charlie Parker, Bird at St. Nick's album and was stunned to see it in his hand.

"Man, are you serious? Where did you find it?"

"I've been looking for it since you said you couldn't find an original, and I knew you didn't like the birthday gift I gave you, so I thought this would do better. And besides, I hate your music, but I love you, happy birthday." Trey said and hugged his childhood friend.

"Thanks, Trey, this is fabulous, and you're right, that was the ugliest shirt I ever saw in my life. I've been using it for an oil rag to polish the furniture."

"That's a good thing; it didn't go to waste. I wouldn't have worn it, which is why I gave it to you after some chic gave it to me, and I gave her the boot."

"Where's Jeffrey Harrington and why are we here." Trey asked, opening a bottle of beer.

"He called a few minutes ago; he's on his way. Better yet, he's at the door." John said when he heard Jeff's key in his front door.

"What's that smell, Jeff said; I hope you don't expect us to eat that shit. I could smell it outside."

They ate ribs, chicken, potato salad and beans from Burns, the best Q in town. The three friends listened to Gary's new album, and his telling them everything about how and when it was recorded. Gary was in his element when talking about Bird.

He started listening to his music in high school when he had to do a class project on 40's and 50's jazz pioneers and has been hooked on Charlie Parker and Miles Davis ever since. He now owns every piece of music they ever recorded including original albums and every compact disc issued. It was an accepted fact that Gary Sanford listened to no other music, in his house or his car, and didn't give a shit who complained.

"Ok, we have eaten, now why are we here?" Jeff spoke.

"My mother is chairing a anniversary banquet for none other than our former teacher, Father Connor and I told her we would be there."

"Speak for yourself, I won't." Trey said.

"You can count me out too." Jeff followed. "We haven't seen him since we were kids, why do we care, and why can't we just give your mother the money for the tickets and not go. What is this all about?" Jeff asked Gary.

Gary looked at his two friends, stood up and cleared the dishes saying nothing. He walked out of the kitchen carrying three bottles of beer and gave one to each of his friends and sat down again.

"Remember that summer at camp when we bunked with that whiny kid who talked about snakes all the time?"

"Yeah," Trey said, puzzled, "I'm not following."

"I know it's been a long time, but do you remember how we never talked about school that summer; about nothing that happened the entire school year, or anything that was important to us, like we use to? We just talked about what was going on at camp and that bastard with the snakes? John asked them.

"I remember." Jeff said.

"And you know why we didn't talk about anything else don't you."

Both of his friends looked away and said nothing. They had never lied to each other about anything and their feeling of discomfort was foreign to them.

"He did it to you too, didn't he? Trey was the first to speak to Gary.

"He did it to me too." Jeff said, unable to raise his head.

They looked at Jeff who was laughing uncontrollably and shouting, "you expect us to celebrate that bastard?"

"I don't want to celebrate anything; I want to confront that bastard. It's time we confront him about this thing we've carried around for thirty years. This thing that drove a wedge between us all and fucked up our lives. Can't you see that?" Gary shouted to both of them.

"I've never talked about this to anyone ever." Trey said. I couldn't tell my parents or even you, who would have believed me. I've been running scared ever since he first touched me and made me feel ashamed to be myself; afraid that no one would want me because I didn't want me, and didn't know what to do about who or what I am. I let this man take control of the way I think about me, so I fuck every woman who sits next to me for more than five minutes, so I don't have to stop long enough to even consider a relationship. I trust two people in my entire world beside myself and the two of you are as fucked up as I am." Trey said with anger he didn't even know he harbored.

"I can't believe we're talking about this after all these years. I thought it was just me." Jeff said.

"No, you didn't, Jeff. You just didn't want to know; you didn't want to think we all went through it and didn't handle it like you." Gary said.

"What's that supposed to mean?"

"Jeff look at you; you're perfect in every way except you drink too much, and that's because you don't want to hear those things that go bump in the night. Everything you do is controlled and staged to be safe and confined to keep the world at arm's length. You've never lived your life on your terms; you let it be orchestrated for you, and when you got the sheet music, you followed it note for note and it's never been off key. The man tried to fuck us; rape us, and we've let that fester for thirty years, and dictate to us the kind of men we think we should be. That's what I mean." Gary was yelling. "We all live in fear of living without each other because we have this thing between us. I'm not discounting the time we've had together, it means everything to me, but let's face it; anything could happen to any of us, and we function only because we know we are together in this world. We have to face the fact that we are men and we really do want wives and children and a piece of apple pie. Why let that bastard take that away from us? Why give it to him?"

"You mean no one of ever told anyone? Jeff asked.

"I told my mother in a round about way." Gary said.

"You've got to be kidding; you told your mother? What did she do about it?" Trey asked him.

"One day, she told me my father was in bed with a bad headache and I told her to rub his penis to make it feel better." Trey laughed so hard, he fell off his chair and lay there out of control. They all laughed when they thought about how naïve they were as children trusting their priest and teacher; the father of their church who could not harm them.

"What did she say?" Trey asked, still lying on the floor.

"She told me not to ever say anything like that again about Father Connor. Then she told my father and he threatened to kick my ass, and he and I haven't had a decent conversation since. They didn't believe me; they were content in their faith in the priest and their lack of any loyalty toward me." Gary told his friends.

"That's fucked up." Trey said.

"I wonder how many more of us there are out there. There's no way I'll believe we're the only ones." That bastard probably did dozens and dozens of boys in the last thirty years, and if we had some kind of safe situation in which we could have told someone, imagine how many of them could have been saved. Nothing's changed; who protects kids from their priests? Who can break through that brotherhood that encompasses the world and hundreds of years of secrets and traditions? The church is not its people; it's the organization, the tradition, its leadership; all levels of it; its mysticism; its dogma. It's still governed by laws made hundreds of years ago without question. There are priests in schools and churches all over the world; hundreds of them, who are destroying the lives of children and their families, in essence, they are destroying what we know of the church and the children will go without resolution, a few of the priests will be punished, money will be paid, the majority of the guilty priests will remain guilty, and active in their Holy Orders and life will go on. No one saves the children; there's nothing but damage control." Gary said and opened another bottle of beer.

"I don't look forward to seeing him, but let's confront this bastard, but let's just tell him who we are and what he did and leave it at that. I heard he has cancer and is dying and that's why they're having this party." Trey said. Let the bastard die."

CHAPTER FORTY-EIGHT

John decided to take his grandmother to the anniversary banquet honoring the priest he knew nothing about, but Gary wanted him to attend, and had paid for their tickets. He hated banquets with their chicken, rice, frozen peas, and fake chocolate mousse for dessert, but his grandmother was excited.

The affair was being held at the Wortham Center. John was the Wortham's biggest fan. It had the most dramatic entrance as you walk through the double doors facing the escalator that rose through massive multicolored brass ribbons that seemed to float up to the lobby. The door pulls were replicas of the brass ribbons, and he always felt that the building that housed the Houston Grand Opera and the Ballet Company was the best Houston had to offer in its impressive theater district.

Gary greeted them at his table and introduced his date, and the dates of Trey and Jeff. Everyone was happy to see Jeff with someone after the divorce. She was an old girlfriend from school that had recently moved back to Houston; divorced with a daughter and seemed very cozy with Jeff.

Trey was with someone he said he met the week before and was banquet material, whatever that was, and Gary was with a co-worker he dated from time to time.

There were the usual speeches and introductions and the old priest seemed genuinely gratified with the accolades.

Gary's mother and a friend of hers shared their table and she couldn't stop talking about how privileged she was being the chairperson of the affair, and how wonderful Father Connor was. He couldn't help wondering why Trey, Gary and Jeff seemed so distant when Gary's mother talked about the priest and was even more surprised to learn that he taught them when they were boys. John just chalked their attitude up to their feelings being similar to his about banquets and nothing more.

The dinner was splendid, nothing at all as he expected which made the evening more pleasant that he assumed and his grandmother was enjoying herself which made it even better, John was thinking as he watched Gary Sanford cross the room to greet Father Connor.

Gary walked his mother who stood talking to his former teacher and felt the chill of rage rise from his feet making him wonder if his feelings were evident to the people surrounding him.

"Here he is Father. You remember my son, Gary, don't you?"

"My, how you have grown up to be such a fine man. Your mother was just telling me that you are a lawyer; that makes us all look good, son.

"I can't tell you what it means to me to be here tonight." Gary said staring at the priest, "You are responsible for the man I am today in every way. I'm sure you remember my friends Richard Peterson and Jeffrey Harrington." Gary said as his friends approached the group. "We all became lawyers, and we all hold you responsible for our lives as they are. You can't conceive of the influence you've had on all of us." Gary told him.

"I'm so happy you feel that way. All of you are a tribute to the school's commitment to a comprehensive well-rounded education; I couldn't be more pleased." As the priest held out his hand to shake Gary's, Gary grabbed the old man, hugged him, and whispered, "You killed me, you old bastard. You'll die in pain and burn in hell for what you did to us." Gary let go of him and said," take good care of yourself."

The three men walked away, leaving the priest shaken and paler and more afraid of his impending fate.

"Are you ok, Father?" Gary's mother asked him in concern.

"Oh, I'm just fine; just a little tired from all this celebration. I think I'll find my driver and start for home. This has been wonderful, Mrs. Sanford, you'll never know what it meant to me."

Gary's mother thought it strange how Father Connor's demeanor changed after talking to her son and his friends, but she dismissed it thinking the priest was overcome with the evening and seeing how well the boys grew up.

CHAPTER FORTY-NINE

Herman Walker was out of his league and he didn't like the feeling of being intimidated by a client he knew nothing about. He was confused about what information his client had that would be of any value to the police about the murder of his son's teacher. His client was belligerent, and hostile toward him in the same manner he was to the two detectives. The compensation for these appointed cases wasn't worth the work he put into finishing law school, he thought as the detectives entered the room.

"My client will answer your questions regarding his whereabouts last night and the night Mr. Danford was killed, and then we're leaving." Walker advised the men.

"Mr. Davis, where were you the night Mr. Danford was murdered?" John asked the suspect.

"Her name is Shirley Mathis; I go to her house most nights after work. I was there last night until you saw me going home. The night of the murder, I was with her, because my son told me his teacher wasn't in school the following day, and he had worked hard to finish a science project that was due that day; and his teacher never showed up."

"We'll need her address and phone number", Andy said and handed Davis paper and pen.

"My wife thinks she knows about this, and she just might, but I don't want you to tell her because, I don't need that shit from her. I'm going to do what I'm going to do, so you can leave her out of this." He said and wrote the requested information on the paper and handed it back to Andy.

Andy left the room to visit Shirley Mathis, knowing she would verify his alibi.

"Mr. Davis, I want you to go over each visit you had with Mr. Danford. How many times did you meet with him?"

"Twice"

"Tell me about the first time. Did you call him, or did he call you?"

"I called him and told him that I was going to call the police and tell them what he did to our son. He wanted to talk to me before I called the police. I thought he would get away with it because of who his father is."

"Did Mr. Danford come to your house?" John asked.

"He called first, said he wanted to talk to me about what happened. At first, I didn't want to see him at all, but then I wanted to hear what he had to say. When he got to my house, he said he wanted to talk to me alone without my wife or son. He told me that he thought that my son misunderstood what he was doing. He said that my son was upset about something and he held him and maybe his hands touch where they shouldn't have, but it was just a mistake. He said that if my son didn't change his story, he could lose his job and might even go to jail. He told me he could write us a check for fifty thousand dollars if we would consider asking our son to understand that he didn't mean him any harm. I asked him where he touched my son, and he said between his legs but wouldn't say why when I asked him. He just said it was all a mistake and he wanted to make it up to all of us. I told him it would cost him more if I like what my son has to say before I decided. I still didn't like what he did, but I didn't want anyone to find out about it and make things bad for my boy. He left and said he would be back the next day.

I talked to my son and he told me he wasn't upset about anything. He said the teacher told him to stay after school because he wanted to talk to him about something. He said when he went in the room; his teacher said that he just wanted to spend some time with him because he thought he was a good boy. Can you believe that shit? Danford locked the door and closed the blinds and said he just wanted to relax; he sat down and put my son on his lap and started to rub between his legs. My son said he felt his teacher's penis get real hard and he jumped off his lap and left. I told my boy that people would say ugly things about him if he told anyone else about what happened. I told him that his teacher was a son of a bitch, and was wrong for what he did, but I told him that I wanted him to keep it to himself to protect him, not Danford. I didn't care what happen to that freak and I was glad when I found out some-body killed him, because he needed killing."

"Did you kill him, Mr. Davis" John asked him.

"No, I didn't kill him. I'm no saint, but I ain't no killer."

"When did you see him again?" He called me the next evening and asked if he could come over. I told him he could, but my wife wouldn't be home because she went to Louisiana, because her sis-ter had a baby. He said he wanted to talk to me alone anyway. He came with his father."

"Reverend Danford was with him?"

"Yeah, all smiling and trying to kiss my ass, but I saw right through him. He didn't want anyone to know his son was a sissy. The Reverend started talking about how God could punish my fam-ily with stories about his son that could hurt God's church, and how he knew that I wouldn't want to do anything that would hurt God's house. His son just stood there saying nothing like the sissy he was, and let his father do all the talking. I was getting real pissed off with him telling me God was going to punish my family when he already punished his family with his sissy son. Then the preacher said he wanted to help my family so we could put some money away to send our kids to college because God told him that we were led to them through God's grace and we should answer the call to righ-teousness, whatever the hell that meant. He took a check out of his pocket already made out to me for the fifty-five thousand dollars, and said it was from God and, that God had plans for my children through the church, and that I would have to protect God's church and my children by accepting the check, or he couldn't be held responsible for the wrath God could bring down on my house. The bastard was threatening me in the name of the Lord."

"Did you take the check at that time?" John asked.

"You bet your ass I did. I wasn't afraid of God, because I knew all that God stuff, he was spittin' out of his mouth was bullshit; I was afraid of him. He made me feel like he would bring down something on my house, and it wouldn't be rain. The man is going to protect that church no matter what he has to do, and I didn't want him to do it to my family or me. Believe me, he's not what he appears to be; there's something in him that's not like any preacher I ever saw, if you know what I mean."

"What happened after you agreed to take the check?"

"Not much. The preacher told me to keep all this to myself because it wouldn't be a good thing to, how did he put it?" The man paused and looked up to the ceiling. "Oh, I know," he said, derange God."

"Did he say defame God?" John asked him.

"That's it, denigrate, whatever that means. They left after that speech and I never saw either one of them since."

"Mr. Davis, I appreciate your help; you're free to go now." John told the man and his attorney.

CHAPTER FIFTY

Andy returned to the station and reported that he found Will Davis' alibi, confirming that he was with her, and said she didn't care if his wife found out because she had nothing to lose since she didn't have a husband.

"Do you ever think we could host a trash talk show?" He said to no one in particular.

"On the way back here, I was thinking we might need to find out why the killer used that apartment where he killed Danford and how he got a key." Andy told John.

"I've been thinking about that too," John said, "he probably couldn't kill him at home because of the victim's family; he had all the privacy he needed with the others. Another thing I haven't figured out is where are the hands?"

Andy listened to the tape interview of Will Davis while John continued looking through the records of James and Barbara Evans.

"Reverend Darren Danford is someone we need to take a closer look at." Andy said.

"You're right about that, but what is his connection with the other three. We know that Darren knew the doctor, but I don't know about the Evans yet. One thing ties them all together, and to their killer." John said.

"Are we looking at Danford as the killer; the preacher himself?" Andy asked.

"The preacher himself is definitely at the top of the list; he's been playing banker with the church funds, harassing and intimidating people, compulsive, obsessive and motivated. I think he could be a cold-blooded killer, wash his hands, and give a sermon preaching thou shalt not kill. I look forward to watching him prove himself innocent of the killings; we already know he's a gangster in cleric's clothing. I have to agree with Will Davis; the preacher will do anything to protect him, *and* that church. He *is* the church; he sees nothing else. His family is a tool to his trade more like, accoutrement."

"Speak English, John."

"The preacher had obvious contempt for his son, and hasn't spent a minute mourning, but has spent hours praising his God for liberating him from the depths of what he calls lascivious wickedness, whatever the hell that is."

"You're probably right about the preacher and his son; he is dirty, but how dirty and what can we prove?" Andy asked.

"I want to talk to Paul Hutchinson about what he knows of the Danford men, father and son. They actually filed a report then had the kid recant, and that smells bad. I called him earlier and told him to get his ass down here this afternoon. I want him to explain why he took the money, selling out his own son. He let the man rape his son and gave him a walk for money. There's got to be more to it, and the Hutchinson's may be as dirty as their benefactor."

"Then lets find Danford senior's wife and find out what her story is about the whole sick clan." John said.

Andy called the home of Paul Hutchinson and was told by his wife that he was on his way to see him and John. Just as he hung up, he spied their suspect walking toward him.

"Mr. Hutchinson, we want to ask you a few questions about your relationship with Darren Danford, and you will tell us what we want to know, and I see no reason why you can't be home in time for dinner." Andy told the man.

He walked Mr. Hutchinson to an interrogation room where John was waiting for them.

"Mr. Hutchinson, can I get you a cup of coffee or something cold? John asked and sat down across the table from him.

"No, I'm alright."

"Then we'll get started," John said. "When did you first meet Danford?"

"I saw him from time to time at the school. He was my son's teacher, so I saw him at open house and sometimes when I picked my son up after school."

"You filed a sexual abuse report against Mr. Danford. Tell us about that."

"My son came home one day saying his teacher kept him after school and put him on his lap, and started to mess with him, so I went to the police. I couldn't believe anyone would do that in a school; not a teacher."

"When did you see Mr. Danford after you filed the report?"

"The next day, he came to the house."

"Did he call you first?"

"No, he just showed up with his father. I was shocked to see his father because of how famous he is around here."

"What did they talk about?" John asked.

"Mr. Danford introduced his father, and then his father asked to speak with me alone and Mr. Danford left the room with my wife. Reverend Danford said he was really sorry for what my son thought happened, and that it must have been his mistake because his teacher wouldn't do anything to hurt him. I told him that was bullshit. My son knew what was happening to him because I told him to watch out for that kind of stuff, if you know what I mean. I couldn't believe a grown man had to bring his father to clean up his shit like that."

"What did Reverend Danford say to you?"

"Like I said, he was sorry for what my son thought happened. Then he said that his son could go to jail and lose his job, and that his family would be ruined. I told him he could kiss my ass if he didn't think what his son did hurt my family. Then he said he could talk to some of his friends and help me find a better job. I asked him why he cared about my job if he didn't think his son did anything wrong, and he said that he just wanted to spread some of God's grace over my family. I couldn't believe this guy; he was acting like *we* did something wrong. He kept that grin on his face the whole time like he was kissing my ass, but when I think back on it, he was making me kiss his."

"What do you mean by that, Mr. Hutchinson?" John asked.

"Well, you know, the way he kept saying that his son didn't do anything wrong and that my son made a big mistake, and we shouldn't have told the police anything about it. He kept saying this could ruin his son's life and he never had any concern about my son, and he was really pissing me off.

Then he said everyone would be better off if my son told the police he made a mistake and it didn't happen at all, but I said no.

"What made you decide to drop the charges? John asked.

"He gave me a check for sixty thousand dollars. I could tell you I felt sick about taking the money and selling out my own son; and I did feel sick, but at the same time, people like me never see that kind of money and I couldn't trust the preacher to leave us alone.

"Why do you say that Mr. Hutchinson?" John asked leaning closer to the man.

"He said people could find out about the charges and make things tough for my family; and the way he said that was like he would be the one making things tough for my family. He has this way of talking and looking that makes you feel like he's in charge of everything; kind of like the Godfather when he was so calm and kind, but you knew he meant business or your brains would end up on the floor. That man is not the usual preacher; he's a real scary guy.

"Did he say anything that directly threatened you and your family?"

"No. Mr. Garrison, I wanted the money, but I was scared of that man and I don't know how to tell you why, but I was scared.

"What did you tell your son?" Andy asked.

"I told him that Mr. Danford was wrong for what he did to him, but no one was going to believe him but us, and then I told him I wanted him to tell the police he made a mistake, and that's just what he did and that was the end of it. I never saw them again. When I heard Danford was killed, I was glad the bastard got what was coming to him and you have every reason to think I did it, but all I can say is I should've for my son.

"Did Mr. Danford say anything to you at all after you took his father's check? John asked him.

"Nothing. He was still in another room with my wife, and his father was still telling me how I was doing the right thing, and that God would bless my house. He started to pray but I told him to stop. He said God would not favor us if we didn't honor his agent. I told him we had nothing else to talk about, so he called for his son and they left.

I took my son to the police station and he said what I told him to say. Then I went to the school and made them transfer my son to another teacher and that was it. I know what you must think of me and I don't blame you, but I did what I knew was best for my family. People like us can't do anything to change people like them; that's just the way of the world, Mr. Garrison, and it ain't never going to change." He said and sat back finished with his story.

"Mr. Hutchinson, that's all for now; we may need to talk to you again, but you can go now." John told the man and held out his hand. Hutchinson was reluctant to take John's hand; he felt humiliated and emasculated after telling his story but was grateful for the genuine grasp of the man who had not judged him.

John watched the boy's father walk away broken and ashamed for protecting his son the only way he knew was available to him. Reverend Darren Danford is a scary man, he said. What made him so scary and what was he capable of doing to cause enough fear in the people he controlled, including his son who was obviously completely controlled by his father to the extent that he didn't seem to have the character to provoke enough sympathy to mourn his death by anyone.

John thought about all of the victims and how they were connected to Danford's father, if they were at all. They were all sexual deviants; intolerable to the minister and his ministry, but not to the point of exhibiting any trepidation for the children whose innocence was made vulnerable by acts of those four people who are now dead. John tried to find anything inside himself that could justify sympathy for the four victims, but he understood the feelings of the two fathers; they were hurting children; he would do his job and catch the bad guy, because it was his job.

CHAPTER FIFTY-ONE

Andy located the senior Mrs. Danford living in Akron Ohio and working as an emergency room nurse at a local hospital. John brought his Captain up to date on the investigation and it was decided he should go to Ohio and visit the preacher's wife.

"Andy, while I'm gone, go over the Evans' files and see what they were up to. We don't have a connection between them, Hargrave and Danford. There has to be something, and it could be in those files. Also, I think it's time to find out everything we can about the Reverend Darren Danford. I want to know everything about him since he was born; he doesn't scare me, but he just may be scared himself, and if he is, I want to be there when he cracks."

"I'll be here when you get back; just don't find some young thing and run off and get married at least until we break this thing open." Andy said.

"I'll keep that in mind." John said.

John was already annoyed when he turned onto I-71 from the Akron airport driving the brightest yellow Mustang convertible known to mankind. He felt like he should be in a cage with a cuttle-fish bone and a swing.

He wondered what brought Mrs. Danford to Ohio and what she would tell him about her life with her husband, and there was every indication that he was still her husband.

He turned on Nordica, the street where Mrs. Danford lived and was grateful the drive from the airport was direct and swift following the GPS on his phone and stopped in front of the house that displayed the address Andy gave to him.

There was no answer when he rang the bell several times and John decided to wait for the occupant to return, since it was just past five o'clock. He felt conspicuous in the yellow car, so he called the local police and told them who he was and why he was in a car waiting for Mrs. Danford, just in case a neighbor reported a stalker.

John watched her park her car in front of her house and walk to her front door. He approached her and introduced himself and waited to be invited inside, which he was after she carefully inspected his identification.

Mrs. Darren Danford was a beautiful woman who appeared comfortable in her skin and not intimidated with the man she let into her home. She excused herself after offering John a drink that he refused opting instead for a clear head feeling drawn to this woman he never met, but had hoped for some time in his past, of that he was sure. While waiting for her return to the room, he tried to imagine her living with Darren Danford and nothing came to mind that resembled the church pastor.

She returned wearing a blue cotton caftan and thong sandals that showed her Corvette red toenails. Her hair was pulled back in a ponytail clipped with a mother of pearl barrette. He surprised himself with the detail of her appearance and had to bring himself back to the now of his mission.

"Mrs. Danford we are investigating the death of your son and I have questions about him as well as his father, your husband. It is not our intention to invade your privacy and I hope you understand that we have to consider anything involving your son that may lead us to solving this crime and bring the person who committed the murder to justice.

Although I cannot relate to your loss, I am sorry for the loss of your son and I will make this as comfortable for you as possible." John told her.

"Mr. Garrison," she said, "Darren was not my son."

John didn't know how long he was silent, staring at the woman who was not Darren Danford's mother; the last thing he expected to hear on this information junket. He had to gather himself after being thrown completely off guard, which was unfamiliar to him.

"You seem surprised, Mr. Garrison; are you?" She asked.

"I've been told not to assume; I should take heed lest I fall." He said paraphrasing a scripture he thought he heard once. "Was he your husband's son by a previous relationship?"

"Actually, he wasn't Darren's son either, Mr. Garrison. I think you didn't do your homework very well." She said smiling warmly, tongue in cheek.

What could he say, feeling humiliated and needing Andy for backup and hoping he would have a sudden heart attack that would explain his inadequacy and ineptness? He searched for a response and nothing happened.

"Why don't I let you tell me about your relationship with Darren Danford; both of them?" He heard himself plead.

"I'd rather answer your questions." She said.

"When did you become acquainted with Darren Danford Jr.?"

"I had been married to Darren Sr. for a year and a half when it became clear to me that our relationship was troubled. My husband had no interest in me in an intimate way and he was no longer sleeping in our bedroom. He spent most of his time working to raise money to build his church, and I worked to support us.

One evening my husband brought a fourteen-year-old boy home with him and announced that he intended to adopt him and give him his name. The boy had been living with his fourth foster family since his parents lost their parental rights for reasons I was never told and my husband wanted to give him, as he described it, a good home. I was taken by surprise since we had anything but a good home, and had never discussed, and had no plans to raise children. As a matter of fact, I was planning divorce since I refused to have sex outside my marriage and had none within it.

I told my husband that I would not consider adoption under any circumstances. Before I had a chance to finish my thoughts, my husband slapped me causing me to fall on the floor. He then beat me until I was unable to move. My eyes were blackened, several of my teeth were knocked out, my jaw was broken, and I was unable to speak. One of my shoulders was dislocated and I remember the pain of my shoulder was so severe, I prayed to die. While I was lying on the floor, I heard my husband call the police and report that an intruder came into my house and attacked me. He then told the boy to follow along with whatever he tells the police." She told him.

"Mrs. Danford, had he beaten you before?"

"No, that was the first and last time."

"When the police arrived, did they ask to see your husband's hands?" He asked her.

"They didn't have to because he told them that he and the boy walked in on the intruder and he beat him before he ran away, so his hands became a nonissue. I was taken to a hospital by ambulance and my husband followed in his car and stayed with me through the night and portrayed the distraught husband.

Understand that by this time, my husband had a modicum of celebrity in the community and was in favor with some very important people in the community. Many of those people were sponsoring fund raising events for the church, and he was careful to always appear above reproach in all aspects of his life. He was not in a position to lose the momentum, or to allow him to be compromised in any way. He was prepared to protect his achievements regardless of the consequences, and he was convinced that there would be no consequences. He started to believe that he was invincible, and it appeared that he was.

His church was not a church to him; it was his personal empire. It was of him and about him and would not exist without him. He wasn't able to separate himself from the church. He was the church.

"Did you tell the police what happened?"

"No. No one would have believed me, and my mouth was wired. I left the hospital on a Friday morning after receiving a message from my husband saying he and the boy would not be there since he was going to Lake Travis for the weekend. I was relieved to know the house would be empty for the entire weekend and I would have time to decide what I should do about my marriage.

I assumed the boy was staying in our guest room, but when I looked inside; there was no sign of anyone having been there. I walked into my husband's bedroom and found the bed unmade and the boys clothing thrown across a chair and, on the floor, and thought that that was strange. I went into my husbands closet to get some hangers and found a box labeled tapes on the floor.

John stared at the women mesmerized by her narrative.

"Next to the box were two video cameras and a digital camera, none of which I had ever seen. I opened the box and saw that it was filled with thirty-seven videotapes. My curiosity overcame me, and I put one of the tapes in the VCR and was sickened by the scenes of boys in various stages of undress in various sex acts. There were also scenes of young girls with boys and older men. I was sick to the point of nausea. I watched parts of about three of the tapes and couldn't stand any more. I went back in the closet and found three photographs on the floor that had been under the box. They were pictures of my husband, a young girl and the boy he bought home the night he beat me. There is no way that I could possibly find the words to describe how I felt, but I knew immediately that I had found my way out of the marriage, and the life of this despicable man.

I watched more of the tapes, hoping to see my husbands face and it was the tenth tape that showed my husband and different boys. I packed the tapes and photographs and all of my belongings for the remainder of the day and drove to my brother's office." She stopped talking and took a deep breath.

John was hoping he didn't display his shock and disgust. He was trying to maintain his composure in this strange house listening to a tale straight out of the dark side about a man who not only is a rapist, pornographer, and pedophile, but also maybe even a cold-blooded killer.

"Why did you go to your brother's office?" He asked her.

"My brother is a lawyer, practicing family law and I wanted him to file for divorce right away, and go over with him the terms I planned to demand from Darren. I wasn't comfortable using any other attorney considering the information I had about my husband, and my brother would protect my interest." She explained to him.

"You didn't come all the way to Ohio expecting to hear this sadistic tale, did you Mr. Garrison?" She asked the detective.

"To be honest with you, I don't know what I expected, but you're right, this is unexpected at best."

"I have no reason to fear Darren for the reasons others should fear him. I've never discussed this with anyone, but I think things are out of control and someone needs to know." She said.

"I stayed with my brother for the weekend and returned to my house along with my brother that Sunday when I knew Darren would be at home. He was surprised to see us to say the least. I was having a terrible time trying to talk, but I was able to tell him to send the boy away while we talked, which he did."

"What was the boy's name?" He asked her.

"Gary Holmes"

"I told him that I was leaving him and was filing for divorce the next day. He told me that he couldn't let me go because he had to maintain a certain image in the community. and he was not going to be divorced.

I told him that his image as a divorced pastor would pale compared to a pedophile pastor, and I watched the color drain from his face. I then told him I had found his stash of movies and photographs and that I had no intention of giving them back to him. I also told him that I made two copies of each and made them available to certain people in the event of my death, or the death of my brother or anyone in my family. That was a complete bluff; I never thought about making copies until I was sitting in front of him, and I realized my brother could also be in danger.

I wanted him to give me one hundred thousand dollars and a

monthly allowance of five thousand dollars for the rest of my life. I wanted the house sold and the proceeds given to me. I would have a quiet divorce, and he wouldn't see or hear from me again." She said.

"Did he have that kind of money?"

"I find this so amusing and unbelievable, but true. My husband was so charismatic, so loving and kind to his congregation, that several of his elderly flock, left him their entire estates when they died. They didn't bequeath it to the church as one would surmise; they left it all to him personally; I have no doubt it was their intent that the proceeds would be used for the church, but that would have been too much like the right thing to do. Darren had several hundred thousand dollars and people were still dying and filling his coffers. These people thought of him as their son, and since none of them had heirs, Darren became their only heir and he played them all."

"Did he agree to your terms?"

"He had no choice, and he knew it. Needless to say, he was dumbfounded when I told him what I found, and my plans, but he was helpless to act, and I knew without those tapes, he would kill me, and no one would be the wiser.

"Do you have the tapes now?"

"I have the tapes. I would understand if you thought that I should have reported Darren's activities, but knowing him as I did, there was no question that he would kill me, and he was in a position to get away with it and continue living as he was at the time. It was the only way I could protect myself, and I have no regrets whatsoever. That boy grew up to be Darren Danford Jr.; Darren raised him, but I don't know if he was ever adopted and I don't know how he explains my absence. I wouldn't be surprised if he never talks about me. He probably tells anyone who is curious that I left him for some scurrilous reason and since most people believe he created sunshine, he would have their sympathy and they would vilify me, which is fine because it's not about me anymore. I entered into a marriage that I believed would be sound and I was woefully wrong. Under ordinary circumstances, he would have made it impossible for me to get a conventional divorce, and I truly feel that I was given an opportunity that was best for me. I took advantage of the situation, and I've never looked back. I am financially comfortable. If Darren stops sending my monthly stipend there would be no adverse affect. I really am fine, and my mind is clear. I'm sorry that Darren Jr. is dead, but he was doomed the day he walked in our house." She finished her tale and walked to a closet and retrieved the videotapes and handed the box to John.

"These are yours now and I don't want to be involved in what you choose to do with them, Mr. Garrison. I have a life here that has nothing to do with who I could have been had I stayed with him. I don't know who he is anymore, and I don't want the involvement. I was not surprised to see you because I knew someone would show up sooner or later, which is why I kept the tapes, but turning these tapes over to you, leaves me alone to go on with my life without a trace of my life as Darren Danford's wife."

"Mrs. Danford, I appreciate everything you told me, I'm sure it was difficult to relieve those times. I'll do my best to leave you out of this, but please understand, that I can't make promises. The DA might want to talk to you, and he may decide that he has enough to move forward without your testimony; I'll tell him of your concerns." He told her.

"You should know now that I am no longer Mrs. Danford. It's Mrs. Sims; I have remarried, and I have three children, so you see that I have moved on and it wasn't at all difficult to relive those times, it was a part of my past, and perhaps I had to be there to get here. I have a good life. My husband is aware of everything I told you, and you have no reason to be sympathetic because my life has worked out very well." She said and shook his hand while walking him to the door.

John drove the thirty-five miles to the airport hoping to get a flight to Houston feeling his head swimming with the story he just heard about the pastor of Grace Memorial Church.

CHAPTER FIFTY-TWO

John took a flight to Dallas knowing he could catch a Southwest flight to Houston shortly after he arrived. He just wanted to get back to Texas anyway he could. He was still reeling from his meeting with the former Mrs. Danford.

He tried but couldn't get his mind off the woman he spent the morning with. She was calm, and so prepared to talk about her life during her marriage to the church pastor. He really didn't have any regrets.

These cases are getting more and more bizarre and sadistic he was thinking as he laid his head back hoping to fall asleep. He wondered if Andy found a link between the Evans and the other two victims, and Reverend Darren Danford. Everything pointed to the preacher but what was the motive. Intent and opportunity would be easy to prove, but the motive to kill Brian and the Evans' might be difficult unless they knew about his secret life or even involved in it.

He didn't fall asleep, but he didn't expect it to be that easy for him considering what was occupying his mind, and the packed airplane that was now descending into Dallas Love Field. He ran through the terminal carrying the box of tapes and found a flight boarding for its trip to Houston and was grateful for the lateness of the hour that meant the business travelers were gone for the day, and his boarding ticked was numbered forty eight; he wouldn't have to sit in a middle seat.

He finished writing his notes from his visit with the former Mrs. Danford and was looking forward to dinner with Andy so he could share this story that had blown his mind.

John drove home to shower and change and deposit the box he had carried from Ohio. He called his kids, then his grandmother and used his three-way phone feature to let them all talk to each other and was amused to hear the girls talk about their day and their plans for summer vacation. Sammy grew another half inch and Jessica was pleased to report that she still had a period every month, which pleased her father in ways she didn't understand yet. He made a mental note to talk to the girl's mother about the need for the sex talk and what Jessica's period meant. He realized that this was the first time he was glad the girls didn't live in Houston.

John told Andy he would report on his Ohio trip after they ate their dinner. He assured Andy it was worth the wait and John just wanted to eat in peace.

Andy told him that he had some luck with the Evans financial records. They were members of Grace Memorial Church and gave generously and often. James Evans sat on the Board of Directors along with the pastor. They had been members of Danford's church since before the current church was built. Both of the Evans chaired the building committee that was responsible for fund raising.

"They managed to raise over eight million dollars in less than four years plus another three and a half million willed to the church by members who died. Can you imagine anyone leaving that kind of money to a church?"

"You ain't heard nothing yet, my friend, finish your dessert; I've got a story for you that will fry your hair." John said.

They sat drinking wine while John told Andy what he learned from the woman in Akron. He didn't realize that he had been talking for the better part of an hour and there was more. He talked about the tapes and the boy who was Gary Holmes, now their first victim. He described the woman and her present lifestyle and status as married and a mother of three.

"Holy shit," Andy said and whistled like he does, "did you watch the tapes?"

"I haven't had time. I just went home to shower and met you."

"Well, what are we waiting for? Let's go see the tapes." Andy paid the checks and they drove to John's house.

"They're all pedophile freaks." Andy shouted and turned off the tape. "It's starting to all fit together. The preacher's going to Huntsville forever."

"I think there's more to this than we know right now. Besides being pedophiles, what else do they have in common? John asked Andy.

"They're all going to burn in hell?" Andy replied.

"Besides that; they all live or lived very well. Think about those houses. They all lived in incredibility expensive houses. The doctor could probably afford his on his own, but did you see his gadget toys and that car? The Evans lived in a mini mansion and both Danford's live grand. Where did all that money come from? I think they were running a porno ring, selling videos, and the Reverend is the Chairman of the Board. Think about it, all of them had photos and tapes. Why? All pedophiles and rapist don't keep visual records of their crimes, but all of the victims were connected by a Danford." John reasoned.

"All that is true and good, and we now have enough on Danford Sr. to put him away forever, but we don't have enough to prove him a killer and I think he is." Andy said.

"If we tip our hand now, we'll never get him for the killings, so we'll turn the tapes over to the DA, and ask him to wait until we clear these murders. Either way the Reverend Darren Danford is going down, before he goes to hell to settle with his friends. He can't pray himself out of this.

John and Andy met with their Captain and the DA the following morning and gave them their report, and requested a delay moving forward with the preacher and the evidence they had against him, to which they both agreed. The tapes and photographs were left with the DA along with the tapes found at the Evans and Hargrave houses.

John was thinking about the apartment where the body of Darren Danford was found and wondered again how the killer gained access and why he used that apartment. Whoever gave up the key, or lost it had some kind of relationship with the killer in a way they may not have considered. They may have met casually, and the key holder didn't realize the key was missing. The key could have been copied without the knowledge of the holder; somehow the killer had access not only to the apartment, but he had a key, and someone knows his or her key was missing, or perhaps the key was sold to the killer. Regardless, John had to connect those dots because they aren't getting closer to solving these murders.

John thought about Matt Porter, the maintenance man and decided to pay another visit.

CHAPTER FIFTY-THREE

The two detectives found Porter working on a leaky toilet in a vacant apartment, listening to Garth Brooks. He recognized the two and turned his radio off telling them he would be finished shortly.

"This apartment has been rented and I have to finish this before the people move in tomorrow."

Porter finished his work in the apartment, gathered his tools and led the two men to the clubhouse for their meeting. John couldn't help thinking how the room in which they were sitting contrasted with the maintenance man's appearance and demeanor. He looked so much like he meets in the woods with friends, wearing fatigues, face paint and carrying AK47's, shouting God Bless America, down with the Feds and remember Ruby Ridge and Waco. John didn't like being judgmental and felt like the bigot he thought Matt Porter was. He was ashamed of realizing that he too was capable of judging a man by his appearance and disregarding his right to be whomever he chose.

"Mr. Porter, I've asked you before if you ever lost your keys to the apartments, but I want you to think hard and try to remember if perhaps you laid them down somewhere, and someone could have taken them long enough to make a copy." John said to the man.

"No, I don't think anyone could have gotten to my keys; I have them on my belt the whole time I'm working here." The man answered.

"Do you ever have them with you when you've been off the property?" Andy asked. "Well, the master key is always on my key chain with my car and apartment keys.

I have those keys with me all the time."

"Do you ever go anywhere and put them on a table or counter or anything else? Andy asked.

"Well, you know sometimes when I'm at my night job, I might be carrying supplies, and I could put them down on something for a while, but I work alone, and no one would have a chance to take them."

"What is your other job and where would you put the keys?" John asked.

"I just put them on the floor while I carry my stuff in."

"Where is your other job?"

"I only work there three nights a week."

"Where?"

"Grace Memorial Church." He told the detective.

Bingo, Andy thought. John looked at his partner feeling they were finally accomplishing their objective.

The maintenance man didn't seem to be aware that his revelation might be the catalyst that breaks their case.

"Who hired you at the church, Mr. Porter?" John asked.

"The pastor's son."

"How did you know him?"

"I know this woman who goes to the church and she told me they were looking for someone to clean and do odd jobs on weekends, so I went over and talked to him and he hired me right away."

"How long have you worked there?"

"About two years."

"How often did you see the man that hired you? Was he ever at the church when you were working?"

"He was there a lot. He spent a lot of time with his father, and when they were fighting, he'd sometimes talk to me."

"Did you ever see or hear them fight?" Andy asked.

"Oh, yeah. They fought most of the time, a lot of shouting and some hitting. It was pitiful; you wouldn't believe some of the words the preacher used and the names he called his son. His son just took it; he never fought back. He was really afraid of his father. Shit, I was afraid of the man when I heard him screaming; and he hit him too. I couldn't believe it; it was really bad. I wouldn't let my father, or anyone treat me like that; I don't care who it was. He was always calling him a weak fag. He said he was stupid and a failure and fucking up everything. He always was telling him he wouldn't spend another dime for his fuck ups with those kids. He even said he would kill him if he didn't leave shit alone."

"Tell me exactly what he said when he said he would kill his son." Well, he said something like, you don't mean shit to me, you never did, and if you don't stop fucking with what I have here, I'll kill you in a way it would take days to identify you—something like that. I can't remember exactly word for word, but the preacher was always saying stuff like that. I really felt sorry for junior; he was a nice man. He always treated me really good, and I liked him."

"Did Mr. Danford ever have access to your keys?" John asked.

"Why do you ask that?"

"Mr. Porter, do you know the identity of the man who was killed in this complex?" "I do now. I didn't know when we found him. Who would've known with his face smashed in like that?"

"When did you know it was Danford?"

"When I read it in the paper. They didn't say where the apartment was, but I put two and two together. I knew it was him, and his father did it. I know that for sure."

"Mr. Porter, I think you know more that you're willing to tell us. How did Mr. Danford get a key to the apartment? Did he take it, or did you give it to him, and why do you have two master keys?"

Matt Porter lit a cigarette and lowered his head and said nothing for several seconds until finally he sat back and said, "I didn't mean no harm; he said he needed a place to, well you know; to meet someone, so I gave him the key. He always left it for me in the bushes like we agreed, and no one was ever the wiser. He just needed a place to take his women. I know it was wrong, but I didn't mean no harm. His father must've found him and killed him. I hate that I gave him the key now that he's dead, but his father would've found him no matter where he went.

"Why didn't you tell us you knew the victim, and your involvement with him?" John asked.

"I didn't want no trouble; you know what I mean; I'm on parole and I need this job. I never gave the key to nobody else; I swear. I mean he was a good man, and I knew he wasn't gonna steal nothin' or stuff like that; you know what I mean?" The man pleaded with the detectives.

"How many times did you give him your key?"

"Two or three; that's all." He answered. "Are you going to report me to my manager? I know she'll fire me, and I really need this job; I'm on parole. Can you help me out here?"

The two detectives looked at the man sitting in front of them and said nothing. John didn't think Porter had anymore information than he had given, but he wondered if the victim's father knew of the arrangement his son had with his employee who opened the door to his death, or maybe the man was right; the father would have found him anywhere. Why would his father follow him? John wondered. There was still much more, and the key to all of the murders was between Darren Danford and his father.

"Mr. Porter," John said, "we're not going to talk to your manager about this for now, so you need to go on with whatever you're doing and keep your keys to yourself. We'll probably be talking to you again, but in the meantime just make sure we can find you."

"I'm not going anywhere, and I'm real grateful to you for not telling on me, cause you know, I need this job really bad; I'll help you anyway I can. I really liked Mr. Danford, and I'm sorry for what I did; I'm really sorry somebody killed him; he just didn't deserve that."

John and Andy left the maintenance man to his thoughts of gratitude and guilt and wondered about the church pastor and why he would kill four people.

"We don't really know much about James and Barbara Evans," John said thoughtfully, "we need to start looking into their lives in every detail. We know about their sex habits, and what they did for a living, but who were these people, and how were they related to the other victims, *and* the church. Let's start with employees if any; they had to at least have a secretary, then family members and friends. Also let's get a criminal and civil background."

The Evans both worked out of their home, so the detectives drove to the house hoping to find a secretary or at least a housekeeper.

When they arrived at the house, they saw a small car parked in the back of the driveway, close to the garage.

A young man answered the door and identified himself as Jason Marks, the Evans secretary and boy Friday. He let the detectives in the house and told them he was there to clean up the office and gather his personal belongings. He left the room to make coffee for the two.

John thought the man seemed to be waiting for someone to visit him with questions about his employers and was willing to cooperate in the investigation into their murders.

He returned with a tray containing coffee mugs, spoons, napkins, steaming coffee pot, cream, and sugar, and placed it on the desk in front of the detectives. He sat in a chair adjacent to the two.

John thanked the man for the coffee while he and Andy settled with their mugs to question their host about every bit of information, he had about the doctors James and Barbara Evans.

CHAPTER FIFTY-FOUR

Gary Sanford was in his office preparing for a meeting with his client accused of selling Oxycondone to high school children, and an undercover cop posing as one of the students. Gary never liked the man, but his father was willing to pay a large fee for his son's defense in spite of the observation that his father was fed up with his son's criminal activities and lifestyle.

Oxycondone was the new hot drug of choice, and was either addicting or killing its users, making the courts hostile towards dealers. His client had been arrested previously for dealing the same drug and beat the charge on the technicality of a bad search. Obviously, his client learned nothing as evidenced by his carelessness of how he picked his customers. He was the twenty-four-year-old son of a successful dentist; educated in private schools graduated from dental school and was in his final year of residency. He told Gary that he started selling drugs in the eighth grade when he realized how many of his schoolmates smoked marijuana and some even cocaine. Since his was a private Catholic school, there never seemed to be any interest on the part of the faculty to stop or control use among the students, because the faculty refused to believe their students were involved. He first bought some grass from the school dealer to find out who it was then found out who his dealer was. It was that easy. His first investment was the five hundred dollars he had in his savings. He ran out of product within two hours of a school day and made a nice profit; it grew from there. He was always careful never to use his product because he never had the desire and had no respect for anyone who did use. He considered them losers, while he considered himself a businessman. His father still doesn't know how involved his son is in his business, nor does he know that his son was a millionaire, which was one reason his father was paying the bill. He was a major player and had no intention of spending time in jail. He had not been arrested for selling the drugs; it was a boy who sold for him and gave his client's name as the dealer.

Gary knew his client was going to walk on this charge also, since no one could identify him, but he didn't know how the boy knew about the man he sells for.

Gary argued with the DA that his client had a right to face his accuser and wanted the boy to identify him in person. The DA agreed to a line up and Gary told his client that would be the most expedient way to clear him if he was sure the boy couldn't identify him.

Gary and his client drove to the police station after he told the man to change into more casual clothing. He had arrived at Gary's office wearing a suit that was obviously custom made and his tie was perfect, though the people with whom they were meeting may not know it was a Hermes, it just looked very expensive.

The man balked at the idea that he should change his clothes, and when he asked his lawyer why; he was told it was because he looked a drug dealer; no one his age without any means of support could dress so well.

Gary sat in the room with the boy who accused his client and was saddened by his youth. He looked like a twelve-year-old, but the report stated his correct age at nine. He loathed his client's use of children. It was a form of abuse. The kid would probably spend time as a youth offender, maybe not for this charge, but there was no doubt he would do it again until he was caught, because the kid measured his value on the money he earned, and the juice he had in his neighborhood without joining a gang. He was without a clue as to the consequence of his actions and had no conception of his future. The kid's mother was in a drug program for the fourth time, and his father worked nights and could not provide adequate childcare, so he was free to roam the streets at night exposing himself to nightlife in his neighborhood that was rife with drugs.

Gary was convinced the child's father was aware of his son's activities, or else how did he explain his son's money and spending.

His client filed in the room behind the glass among four other men and stood staring at the glass knowing he would be going home sooner than the police expected.

The boy immediately said, "he ain't up there; he ain't one of them, bring in the other ones."

One of the policemen in the room asked the kid if he was sure and caught Gary's disapproving eye and walked away.

"Is this all you have? Gary asked the woman from the DA's office.

"You know it is and I'd like to know how your client got to the boy."

"I can't help you with that, so should I advise my client you will be dropping the charges today?" Gary walked out of the room wondering the same thing; how *did* his client get to the kid.

He took his client back to his office and told him that when he received word that the charges were dropped, he would not represent him again, explaining he won't handle any drug cases again. The man told his lawyer that he was willing to give him a large retainer to continue to represent him and Gary declined and walked him to the door offering to refer him to an attorney who would be better suited for him.

After the man left his office, Gary noticed his former client left the bottle of Oxycondone on his desk. He considered calling the man back, then decided against putting more drugs in circulation.

He thought about how many children worldwide were used and abused to make tremendous profits in legitimate and illegitimate business.

CHAPTER FIFTY-FIVE

John looked at the Evans' secretary and wondered how much secretarial experience he had before he came to work for the couple.

"How long have you worked for the Evans? John was the first to speak.

"Three years," he said, I met them when I was in college, and Dr. Barbara Evans taught one of my classes."

"How long after that did you start working for them?"

"This was my first job after I graduated. They were looking for a secretary and I needed a job before I started grad school—they worked in my chosen field, so it seemed right for me, and they agreed to give me the job." The man explained stiffly.

"What were your usual duties?" Andy spoke for the first time.

"I made their appointments; keeping their calendar, organized the files, typed all of the reports, did the banking of receipts and kept the books for their accountant. Then I did all their gofer work."

"What did that consist of usually?"

"I made their travel arrangements, bought gifts for clients, planned and organized parties and weekends at their house on Lake Travis when they entertained clients; things like that."

"What can you tell us about their clients?"

"What do you mean?" he said crossing his arms.

"Did they treat children, adults, families, groups?"

"They didn't have any clients like those; they stopped treating shortly after I started. Their clients are law firms only—for about the last two years."

"Do you have files on their private patients?" John asked.

"Yes, but you would need a court order to get those files. We have a privilege protection."

"Not exactly Mr. Marks; you don't have anything. Is there a next of kin for either of the Evans"? John asked.

"I never heard them speak of family, and of course they didn't have children. I know their parents have both passed on."

John looked at Andy who stood up and said, "I'm on it."

Andy left the victims' house on his way to beg for a court order to review their files.

John stayed with the secretary knowing he had key information about his employers that could connect them with the church pastor directly.

"What did the Evans do for their law firm clients?" John asked.

"They did some jury consulting, and expert testimony. They also evaluated clients of the law firms and testified regarding their findings." He explained.

"Do you meet with clients?"

"If it's someone being represented by the law firms, I administer the requested psychological testing, and the Evans evaluate the test results."

"Are the people you test charged with a crime of any kind?"

"Yes; all of them."

"What kind of crimes?"

"Most of them were charged with various kinds of child abuse."

"What kind of abuses?" John asked leaning forward.

"Beatings, neglect and sexual; the usual kind."

"Which of those kinds of abuses were the greater in number. In other words, were there more beating or neglect or sexual abuse cases?"

"Definitely sexual abuse, we had very little of the other kind. Sometimes there were people charged with more than one kind, but most of them were charged with sexual abuse.

John saw Andy drive onto the driveway in front of an unfamiliar car. He looked at his watch and was surprised that two hours had passed since Andy left.

Jason Marks answered the doorbell and John recognized Peter Altman, expressionless, standing behind Andy. Both men entered the house and John introduced Altman to the secretary. Peter Altman handed the secretary the court order and explained the conditions of the order.

"I have some boxes in the laundry room; I'll get them." The secretary told the group.

"I'll go with you." Andy said not trusting the man.

"What do you think you'll find?" Altman asked John when they were alone.

"Still trying to connect the victims."

"I know this is a difficult case for you and painful for Becker, but I have to tell you that we're all impressed with the way you're handling it. I also know you think I can't stand you, and you're right, but I know good work when I see it." Altman said to John smiling at the confused look on John's face.

"I appreciate that, Pete; I'm concerned about Andy too, not because he can't handle it; he can, but I think he expects too much of himself and hasn't moved on." John didn't realize how worried he was about his partner until he explained it to Peter Altman, the last person he thought he would ever share a personal feeling.

They turned toward the office when they heard Andy and Marks and saw them both carrying boxes. All four of the men pulled client files from cabinet draws and packed them in the boxes provided by the Evans' secretary and loaded the boxes in John's car.

"Mr. Marks, when I need to contact you; where can you be reached?" John asked.

"I just got an apartment," he said and wrote his new address and phone number on a piece of paper he found on the desk.

"I want to take one more look around to make sure we have all of the files."

"You have everything," Marks said panicked.

"Is there something wrong, Mr. Marks?" John asked, sensing there was more to the secretary than they had previously noticed.

"Oh no. I just wanted you to know that you have everything."

"Let's just make sure." Altman said and handed the secretary a search warrant for the entire house that he and John decided to use to surprise the man if they thought he might be hiding something.

"I'll call for some help; this is a big house." Andy said picking up the phone.

"I'll start upstairs, and you can stay with Mr. Altman while we conduct the search." John said to Jason Marks.

"Do I have to stay?" The secretary asked John.

"I'd like you to in case we have some questions about what we find.

"Do you have a reason for wanting to leave? John asked the man.

"No. I can stay; I just don't know what more I can tell you."

"Well, let's just wait and see; we may need your help, and I would appreciate it if you would make yourself available."

The man sat down and did not respond.

John started his search in the large master bedroom and found nothing unusual in any of the drawers. He looked under the mattress as well as the bed. He found nothing in the master bathroom. He went into a guest bedroom and found nothing. He went into a second bedroom and searched in the same manner as the other rooms. As he was getting up from the floor, he bumped his head on a framed painting on the wall. As he attempted to straighten the painting, he noticed he could pull it away from the wall and there he saw a wall safe.

John went downstairs and asked the secretary if he was aware of the wall safe. The man told him that he knew about it but didn't know anything about the contents. He said the Evans never opened it in front of him.

"Do you have the combination?" John asked. "No."

"Do you know if it was written on something?"

"I don't know."

"I'll look in the office." Andy said.

"Mr. Marks, you'll have to stay here until we can open the safe." Pete Altman told him.

John walked past the front door on his way to the second floor when he saw four uniformed policemen approach the house. He let them in and explained what he wanted them to do.

"One of you can take the attic, and one can help Detective Becker in the office."

He left the other two police officers searching the first-floor rooms.

John returned to the master bedroom looking for the safe combination and found nothing. He did the same in the other bedrooms and bathrooms. He looked under all of the furniture and throw rugs.

He heard Andy yelling to him from the first floor. "This might be it."

"I found it taped under the desk chair. Let's give it a try."

Andy started turning left and right to the numbers on the paper, but it didn't open. He started again and turned in the opposite direction.

"Maybe you need to make a complete turn then start right and left." Andy followed John's instructions and he was surprised when he opened the door.

"How did you know that?"

"Well, you see, in my earlier life..."

"Let's not go there." Andy interrupted.

"Whoa, what do we have here? Andy said as he pulled out four large accounting ledgers.

John and his partner looked thru the books and read the names and amounts that totaled millions of dollars.

"We'll have to match these names with the names in the files, but I can't imagine how they could have made this much money in their practice." John said.

"This is a hell of a lot bigger than we imagined."

I'll bet anything, that these books don't have anything to do with their practice, and the preacher figures in it somehow." Andy said.

"I think you're right; there's a bunch of money in here." John said patting the ledgers. He put them down on the bed and he, and Andy looked through all of the second-floor rooms again.

They walked downstairs; with John carrying the ledgers when they saw two of the officers at the bottom.

"There are no records or files in any of the rooms." One of them said.

"We cleaned out the office with the files we packed." Andy said.

They all heard the officer in the attic calling for attention. John went to the steps and saw the policeman standing at the top.

"Did you find something?" John asked.

"I think so," he said, I found some boxes up here; about twenty of them."

The officer handed the boxes down as each of the other men moved them hand over hand.

Pete Altman was the first to open a box.

"Tapes. Video tapes; hundreds of them." He said raising his eyebrows.

The videotapes were packed in moving boxes from a local moving company. They totaled thirty-six.

"Have you ever seen these boxes of tapes?" John asked Jason Marks.

"Never."

"Mr. Marks you can leave now if you want, but you need to keep in mind that this is a crime scene and, you are not permitted to cross that tape you see outside. Again, thanks for helping us out; we really appreciate it." John said walking Marks to the front door.

They watched the secretary walk out of the house and wait for the other men to move their cars that were parked behind his.

Andy came back in the house and asked, "why didn't you ask him about the ledgers?"

"I thought that was strange too." Peter Altman said.

"I think he has not only seen the ledgers but made many of the entries. Look at this," he said pulling a piece of paper out of his pocket, "this is his address and phone number he wrote down for me. Now look at these entries, the same writing. I didn't want to show our hand until we can get an expert to confirm; then well talk to him again." John explained.

"Aren't you afraid he may bolt on us?" Altman asked with the sound of concern.

"Not at all; he saw me with the books, and I know he thinks we can't accuse him or we would have. He's not smart enough to run. He'll be there when we need him and I'm sure we'll need him." John said.

"We have transportation on the way to move these boxes out of here." John told the four policemen, "we have a van on the way to pick up the boxes. We'll need two of you to ride with the boxes; we'll meet you to sign them in. We'll see you downtown, and thanks for your help."

They watched the van pull in the driveway, and everyone started moving the boxes into the van. When they were finished, the van and the police cars drove out of sight.

"Pete, thanks for coming and staying to help out; we really needed you today." John said and shook the prosecutor's hand with sincerity.

"It was my pleasure. I enjoyed watching the two of you work. I'll see you later." Peter Altman got into his car and drove down the street like a bat out of hell.

"You know, he might not be so bad after all." Andy said.

"He's ok; he's just a control freak, but when you think back on it, he has always helped us out; reluctantly, but he helped us."

"I'll see you on the other side." John said walking to his car, Andy following to his.

John drove away thinking about the tapes in all of those boxes knowing what they revealed, and not looking forward to seeing any of them. He had seen all the porno he ever wanted to see again.

CHAPTER FIFTY-SIX

Jeff Harrington knew he had been drinking too much and decided it was time to do something to deal with what he was hoping was not a one-way street. Nothing about alcoholism suited the image Jeff had created for himself. His life had been carefully scripted; he fitted comfortably into his creation—shallow and vacuous—lifeless. He didn't allow substantive relationship in his life other than Trey and Gary who he considered as shallow as he. He would never consider introspection; it wasn't a necessary tool. It would be useless since he was always aware that he wasn't willing to trust anyone or anything he couldn't control. Now that he had been faced with the abuse of Father Connor, his lifestyle gushed through the wall he built as shelter from anyone's attempt of dominance over him.

He admitted to himself that he married a woman who had no interest in anything except her comfort and gratification, which worked well for him until her complete betrayal that he couldn't bring himself to blame her, because he offered her nothing of himself.

He couldn't remember ever doing anything he wanted to do independent of what was expected of him by his parents, friends, and colleagues. He lost himself years ago to his parish priest and was burying himself with the vodka that he used to smooth the rough edges, or so he convinced himself.

If he was going to rid himself of his thoughts of the demon priest and live as chose, he had to get some counseling *and* stop drinking.

Jeff sold his house and gave part of the proceeds to his ex-wife because it was the right thing to do. He finally moved out of his friend's home into an apartment that he furnished in a style he was surprised to find complimented to him. He never considered anything like the style of furniture; he didn't care, but now he looked forward to shopping and buying accessories that he would come to consider his only.

He furnished and decorated his new home and started living alone for the first time in his life. The ownership of his space appealed to him in a way that was pleasing and comfortable.

He started to live as he pleased without ever looking over his shoulder listening for an objection or instructions; but he drank too much.

He didn't know if he was an alcoholic because he functioned well and never drank during his working hours. No one ever seriously told him he drank too much; it was understood.

He decided to find an AA meeting near his home, but true to his fashion, he did extensive research on the Internet and was fascinated by Bill Wilson and Dr. Bob Smith who founded the organization on the premise that only a drunk could help a drunk. It made sense to him to talk to someone who could relate to his alcohol use. If he continued to drink, he knew he would use Father Connor and his ex-wife Cheryl as his excuse, and neither deserved the credit.

Alcoholics Anonymous opened another world to Jeff—different from the one he created. No one had last names, and every walk of lifestyle was represented. He didn't want to make friends with anyone in his meetings, but he respected his sponsor who was older, in his sixties and had been sober for over thirty years. His sponsor had been homeless when he was Jeff's age, and had accidentally killed his only son by dropping him from the baby's changing table. He was drunk at the time, but no one tested him for alcohol, and he wasn't prosecuted. He punished himself by crawling in bottle after bottle until he woke up one cold morning and couldn't figure out what was smelling so putrid around him until he realized he had climbed into a garbage dumpster to get warm the night before. In typical movie fashion, his sponsor climbed out of the dumpster and moved into a Salvation Army shelter and was introduced to AA.

After a month of meetings with fellow alcoholics, Jeff admitted he was an alcoholic and resolved he could never drink again because he was enjoying life sober and in control. Counseling taught him he never had control. He surrendered himself to his parents, the priest, his work, and the life he existed within, that had nothing to do with the essence of the man he was meant to become.

He never dated in the conventional way since high school. He would meet women in bars, clubs or social functions, pass out his business cards and wait for a call from one of them. Occasionally he would go home with someone he met in a bar, but that was only instant gratification. He wanted a relationship with substance. He wanted to love a woman.

Jeff heard that Bridgett Lucas had returned to Houston after living in New York for ten years. He and Bridgett dated in high school. They both went off to college with the promise of maintaining the relationship, but letters from Bridgett became fewer and fewer and finally nothing. He saw her once during their first summer vacation from school, but he knew she had lost interest and he was heartbroken, but no one would know.

He decided to give her a call and reacquaint. His excitement at the sound of her voice surprised him, though relived when she seemed genuinely happy to hear from him. She had divorced and had a four-year-old daughter.

They met that night for dinner and went to Jeff's apartment later and talked through breakfast.

"Jeff has a girlfriend." Trey Peterson teased while they waited for Gary to putt. "You may be right," Jeff said feeling warm and content, "this could be the one."

Gary looked at his friend and wished this were the one; Jeff deserved a break as well as a healthy relationship with a woman. He held out no promise for himself; he wasn't willing to invest the time. He didn't need anyone; there was no room for anyone significant in his world.

CHAPTER FIFTY-SEVEN

Three months had faded into Houston's wet, but mild winter since the first murder, and John's frustration was growing since he couldn't identify the murderer.

Reverend Darren Danford was still the primary suspect, but he was illusive and seemed insulated from the crimes.

John read through the Evans' files and records, which were extensive. He took the entire caseload home with him so he could scrutinize the lives of strangers in a warm setting. He was working on the last box of files when he took a break to have dinner.

He decided to call Katherine Whitney and invite her to eat with him. Katherine loved Italian food, so he took her to Michelangelo's in Montrose for that small and cozy ambiance, and a great Merlot.

They were enjoying each other more than John thought he would, and he liked the feeling. Katherine was confident and generous with her laughter that ingratiated her in the lives she shared, without being offensive or cumbersome. John liked her sense of self and independence, and she was beautiful. He was drawn to her in a way that he had not felt in the past. They had been friends who slept together on occasion, but this night he saw more of the woman he only thought of as fun and sexy.

"How is that case you were working on with the preacher?" She asked.

"Not well," he said, "it's slow with more twists and turns than we can understand. We picked up some accounting ledgers you might want to look at if the DA gives the ok. You can offer your services on contract."

"I might just do that Detective; give me a name to call" she said and poured him a glass of wine.

He took Katherine home after dinner without a hint from both of them about staying the night. John felt different, but he pushed the thoughts of this woman to the back of his mind and chalked it up to the wine.

He arrived home to see Andy Becker sitting at his doorway grinning like the boy with a secret.

"Did she finally lock you out?" He asked his partner as he unlocked the door.

"She wouldn't think of it. It doesn't get better than me." Andy said walking to the kitchen for a bottle of beer.

"You didn't want me to read the sex stuff, so you missed out on what I found." Andy said.

"Andy, I'm sorry but I didn't think you needed to see any more than was necessary."

"You can't take responsibility of my emotions, John. I really am ok. This case has nothing to do with my family, or me. What happened to us, happened to us, and we can't change that. I know you meant well, but I can do my job, and be objective without going postal." Andy told him.

"Now let me show you what I found in those files you left for me." Andy said handing John a file marked Brian Hargrave.

"He was a patient?" John asked looking at the file.

"He was a patient and one sick ticket. He treated with James Evans for five years until about a year ago. He liked adolescents and cruised the streets for his prey. According to his file, he was never a threat to his patients, which seems odd." Andy said.

"Not really," John said, "he had to maintain appearance, and the status quo. His patients were protected from his depravity because they were the tools of his trade. I think he liked the lewdness of cruising; it was so removed from the persona he exhibited publicly."

"How did that file get in your box?" John asked.

"It was among the battered and neglect files, and I couldn't help wondering why."

"Well since you're here, let's go through this last box."

The two men read the files taking notes on each. John glanced at Andy from time to time and saw nothing but a detective doing his job.

"Jesus, look at this," John said, handing a file folder to Andy, "it's a record of boys and girls used for the movies. Look at the names beside the names of the boys."

They were staring in shock as they saw the names of Darren Danford and Brian Hargrave.

"They provided the kids; what if the Evans made the movies?" Andy said.

"The Evans didn't make the movies; we didn't find any equipment in that house.

The last box didn't contain patient files, instead, they read file after file of names of boys, and girls with filming dates meticulously catalogued by names of participants, and dates of shooting, distribution, and destination.

"Here's something," Andy said, "rent receipts for a warehouse downtown paid by Videos Etcetera. Wonder who owns Videos Etcetera, as if we don't know."

"Maybe we don't." John said.

"Maybe we do," came the response.

"This has become the most disgusting case I've had." John said.

"We still don't know who killed them." Andy responded.

"Tomorrow, we visit the warehouse, but first I'm calling Altman to get another search warrant" John said.

Andy took another bottle of beer out of the refrigerator while John called the Altman, who wasn't pleased by the intrusion.

"You can always go back to sleep," John said, "we need to search the warehouse as soon as possible, and if you're real nice to me, you can go with us."

"I'll meet you there at ten o'clock; good night." Peter Altman said and hung up his phone.

They were parked in front of the warehouse waiting for the prosecutor to arrive with the warrant they needed to search the premises. The location was in disrepair, in a seedy part at the edge of downtown near the new baseball stadium. The area was slated for renovation to include lofts, restaurants, and clubs, much like the renaissance taking place in the theater district. It was morning and the two detectives were obviously out of their element to the passersby.

Pete Altman arrived followed by two city vans, and two marked police cars.

"I thought we could use transportation; you never know what we might find in there, so let's go find some more secrets, and dash someone's dreams."

They knocked on the door that was opened by a small well-dressed woman clearly in her sixties. She was polite when they identified themselves and showed her the warrant. She told the men that she owned the property and rented it to a company that used it for storage. She was there to pick up the rent check that was always left for her. She seemed annoyed at having to pick up the check, but said the renter refused to use the mail. She went on to explain that she only had a key to the front door since the renter changed the locks to their storage area. She didn't mind as long as they paid on time and didn't damage her property. She required a two-thousand-dollar deposit.

"Can you tell us the name of the woman who rented the property?" John asked her.

"She said her name was Helen and didn't give me a last name.

"Who signed the lease?" John asked her.

"A nice man whose name is James Evans. I've only seen him once."

"Did he tell you anything about his business when you met with him?"

"He told me he just needed the space for storage, and the only time anyone would be on the property is when they are putting something in or taking it out, so I don't have any idea what kind of business he is in."

"Ma'am, we're going to execute the warrant now, but we will need a copy of the lease. I'm going to have one of these officers go with you to your office to pick it up. Is that ok with you?" John asked the woman.

"Oh, that would be just fine. Can I ride in the police car; that would be so exciting?" "Sure, you can, and the officer will bring you back to get your car." John told her. "No, no, that won't be necessary I walked over here. Its not far—good exercise."

"Ma'am, aren't you concerned with your safety walking in this neighborhood?" Andy asked.

"Young man, I grew up not far from here and I've done business in this neighborhood for more than forty years. On the contrary, I feel safe here; it's my home. These people you see out here are either poor or sick; I don't judge them or fear them. They're no different than you or me; they made the wrong choices. They respect me because I trust them enough to walk around the area knowing I'm a rich old woman. I don't believe any of them are threatening. Now come along officer, I can't wait to tell my daughter about this. My children don't think I have enough excitement in my life; they'll never believe this." She said and followed the policeman to the waiting car.

"The storage area is locked, so we're going to have to break it down." Andy said.

"No, we don't Andy, we'll just break the lock with cutters. You're watching too much television." John said.

The men walked into the enormous room and saw hundreds of packing boxes similar to the boxes they removed from the Evans mansion. There was not even a chair. All of the boxes were sealed and addressed.

"Look at these addresses," Altman shouted at the others, "they're addressed to Shanghai, Singapore, Bali, Nigeria, Granada, Brunei; can you believe Brunei? Here's one addressed to someone at the Sorbonne. This is amazing."

"There's a whole lot of people who aren't going to be happy when the mailman doesn't show up with their goodies—sick bastards." Andy said.

"Wait a minute, we don't know what's on these tapes yet." Altman said.

"Yes, we do," said John, we know very well what's on those tapes. This is a huge business encompassing the entire world. We know so far that James Evans is involved and perhaps his wife. What we don't know among other things is the filming is not done here. If we watch some of the tapes, we might get a clue to the location and who else is involved. John walked around the huge space and found a clipboard that held shipping dates. The boxes weren't scheduled for shipment for another week on scattered dates after that.

"We've got a lot of work to do here. We have to replace the tapes with something else for shipment. We don't want anyone to know we know what's going on here and that we have their tapes. We'll have to find something of equal weight and repack the boxes and let them go." John said.

"Don't you think whoever else is involved will know we were here?" Altman asked.

"No one around here would talk to anyone. It's not what people would do in this neighborhood. No one will want to be involved." John explained to the naïve prosecutor.

The entire back wall of the warehouse opened to the street and they decided to truck in new boxes filled with dirt and re-label each for shipping. It took three days and nights to complete the job and they were sure no one was the wiser. Few people walked behind the building and two uniformed officers stood outside to protect the activities inside. The dirt was trucked inside, and they were able to close the door behind the truck. A plan was put in place to have the building staked out on the shipping dates to make sure the boxes were moved out without suspicion.

John, Andy, Altman watched several of the tapes in an effort to identify the filming location. All of the tapes they watched were filmed in a bedroom that was well appointed and tastefully furnished. They watch bits and pieces of five tapes from each box, chosen randomly. The filmmakers used children; boys and girls of all ages between what looked like the age of seven to sixteen. Some had sex with adult men and some women and some of the children had sex with each other. All of the adults were filmed with their backs to the camera, in an obvious attempt to protect their identity. Each child was filmed in plain view. The location in each tape was the same bedroom.

When they viewed the last tape, John, Andy, and Pete Altman went to a local bar with the sole purpose of getting drunk.

"I've prosecuted dozens of sex abuse cases, but I never imagined this crime was so vast and heinous. If our killer is trying to stop these people, he has my vote." Altman said.

"People don't realize that entire communities are being destroyed when our children are destroyed, and we just watched children being destroyed. What kind of adults will they be, as if we don't know, and who seems to care? We are outraged when we hear or read about child abuse, but less than a few days later, we don't even remember the child's name, because we don't want to face the reality that it can happen to our own children." Andy said. "Parents and those without children have to unite to protect all children. This will not end with a conviction in this case, it will continue because no one is addressing the real problem which is the security of our children." He went on. "If Danford is the killer, it obviously isn't for the sake of the children; that's for damn sure."

"I don't think he's our man," John said," he needed all of them. I have no doubt that he is involved in the porno business, but I just don't think he's a killer. He wouldn't let himself to be that exposed. He would consider it dirty work, and from what we've seen in the stream of commerce of the porno enterprise, if he wanted them dead, he wouldn't do it himself. I don't think it's him; it wouldn't serve his purpose. The victims may have profited, but the pastor was their employer."

"Who could the killer be?" Altman asked.

"I hate saying so, but I have no idea. Whoever it is so good at what he does, he's left no clues, but I think he was aware of the porno operation and everyone involved." John told them.

"Do you think Danford is the next victim?" Altman asked.

"I don't know. What I think is, whoever it is, killed his victims in a way that would punish them to the extent of their involvement. They needed to be destroyed. The best way to destroy the victims was to kill them in the most humiliating way. He didn't want to just kill them; he wanted to disgrace them at the same time. What is the best way to destroy Reverend Darren Danford? Expose him as the leader of a vast worldwide pornography ring. Why kill him? It's too easy for the pastor. He needs to be destroyed. What's worse than a pedophile going to prison? A pedophile that is a prominent church leader going to prison." John speculated.

"You could have something there, partner. I hate to admit that I can't find anything that leads to the preacher either. After we iden-tify the filming location, we need to focus on our killer, and the location may be a clue." Andy said.

"You know what I hate about all of this?" Andy asked, "some lawyer could find some twist in the law to either get Danford off or lighten his sentence."

"It won't happen, Andy," Altman said, "I promise you that. That's why I've been so careful to do everything possible to help you two gather the evidence and protect it. Why do you think I've been hanging around? So, no one would have an opportunity to taint any of the evidence. If this preacher is involved like we think he is, who knows what influence he has in your department and mine?"

John was impressed with Pete's honesty and trust in Andy and him. He smiled to himself thinking how he and Andy thought of Altman as a complete dick.

"You know what we should do with murderers and rapists?

Andy asked them, feeling lightheaded but good, "instead of spending a fortune housing the bastards for killing people, we should sentence them in the same way they killed. If someone is beaten to death, then the killer should be beaten in the same way, to death. If he stabs someone twenty times, someone stabs the bastard twenty times. Think about it; we wouldn't have to build more prisons. Killers are going to think long and hard before they commit their crime knowing what's in store for them up the river. We can always find some sick son of a bitch to carry out the executions. Why let these bastards either stay in prison where they have three squares a day, television, phones, school, church, all the drugs and sex they want, while their victims are dead, and their families are destroyed. Why let them lie on a comfortable gurney and go peacefully to sleep forever when they shot some kid in the head three times. The system sucks at best."

"I should never say this, but everything you said has merit even though we're all drunk, your system sure would save a lot of lives and money." Peter Altman said raising his glass.

Andy smiled at the prosecutor and raised his glass thinking to himself, you just don't know how serious I am, Mr. Altman.

CHAPTER FIFTY-EIGHT

J eff had been seeing Bridgett several times a week since their reunion. They spoke daily, and for the first time he felt relaxed, and in control.

He loved her and wasn't afraid to tell her he wanted to marry her. He didn't have to talk it over with his friends or parents, it wasn't about them; it's what he wanted.

Bridgett's four-year-old daughter warmed to Jeff's attention, creating another outlet to channel his acceptance of himself. Jeff was happy, and he walked in new shoes.

Bridgett Lucas moved to New York City after her college graduation and married within a year. Her husband had the right job, look *and* she thought, direction, before his cocaine habit influenced his ability to work or function in any productive capacity. Bridgett was on the fast track as lobbyist for an environmental protection group while raising their daughter. She divorced shortly after she realized her husband had no inclination for change or adulthood. Her decision to return to her hometown gave her and her daughter the warm circle of family and familiarity to redirect their lives and give her daughter the security she would need to fill the void left by the absence of her father.

The feelings growing within her toward Jeff were no surprise because he was always easy to love, but eliciting his courage to open himself to love anyone provided her with a motive to move away so many years ago. She watched him peel away the insulation that was his shield against exposure of his inability to share himself.

She fell in love with him easily knowing she could live without him but living with him would compliment her in ways of fulfillment only he could provide.

They drove to San Antonio to surprise Bethany with visit to Seaworld, Jeff's first trip to the park. He never took the time or had interest in organized activity, but he was drawn to the antics of the whales and dolphins and found himself fascinated by a world he had only heard about. He wondered what else he was missing besides large fish.

Sunday morning, Jeff slept late after returning Bethany and her mother home from San Antonio and was awaken by banging on the door that startled him. His mother stood in front of him frenzied out of breath.

"What's wrong?" He asked his mother, closing the door behind her.

"What's wrong with me? What's wrong with you? I've been calling you since Friday evening and you haven't returned any of my calls. We were frantic."

"Mom come in and tell me why you were frantic, because we haven't talked for a day and a half. I was out of town yesterday, and I turned my ringer off last night so I could sleep. We had a long day. What's the problem?" He asked his mother annoyed with her intrusion.

"Couldn't you have told me you were going out of town? Is it too much of a problem to let us know where you are?"

"As a matter of fact, it is a problem letting you know where I am. Have you forgotten I am a grown man, and I don't think I have to advise you of my comings and goings on *your* regular basis? You're being ridiculous."

"Jeffrey, I respect your independence, but I was just worried that something may have happened to you."

"If something happens to me, you'll get a call from someone eventually, so you're wasting your time waiting to hear from me. I'll call you when I want to talk to you; in the meantime, I have a life of my own and I'm going to live it on my own terms."

"Jeffrey, you seem distant and I'm not sure I'm comfortable with that."

"I think you're not comfortable with me making decisions without your input and acceptance. I don't need your input. I appreciate your concern, but rest assured, there is no need."

"Can you at least tell me who you were with?" His mother asked.

"I could, but is it necessary?"

"Is it a secret?"

"No, I wouldn't think so, but what difference does it make who I was with? I'm here with you now."

"Jeffrey, I can't believe the change in you. I think it has something to do with those AA meetings. I can't understand why you would expose yourself to that element; you're nothing like those people. None of this makes any sense to me."

"I understand how you feel, Mom, by I expose myself to that element because I am of that element, I'm an alcoholic."

"You're not an alcoholic."

"Mom, I am, and I'll always be whether or not you approve or accept. You didn't make me an alcoholic, you didn't encourage me to be an alcoholic, and you can do nothing about me being an alcoholic. You don't even have to address it. This is my stuff; it's not going to fall on you; it's not about you."

"You stopped drinking, if that's true, how can you be an alcoholic and why keep going to those trashy meetings?"

"I've only stopped drinking; I'm still an alcoholic; only dry. These people relate to my disease and are the only people who can help me deal with it productively. So, you see Mom, these people as you call them are a lifeline for me and will share my path to sobriety. You can't walk that path with me because it's not about you, or who you want me to be. It's about who I am, and I am my own man who happens to be an alcoholic, so why don't you run along now and let me go back to sleep, and I'll take you and Dad to dinner tomorrow."

"I don't know what your father is going to think about all of this, but I'll go and leave you alone."

"I know what my father thinks, and he's ok with my choices. Drive careful Mom, love you much."

Jeff crawled back in his bed smiling at the thought of his mother learning that her little boy is no longer a suckling. He turned the ringer on just in case Bridgett called. He felt the freedom to rest and fell asleep.

He grabbed the phone when it rang and heard Trey's voice teasing.

"Your mother is a crazy woman looking for her little boy."

"She didn't find him," he told his friend, "she found a man."

"She gone and I'm going back to sleep without you. Thanks for the heads up, but you're late."

"That's cool; want to hit some balls later, and you can tell me about your love life, and I can tell you about my lack of one." Trey said.

"Meet me here at five, good night."

He was still in bed when he heard the doorbell, then heard his friends open the door with the key he gave them in case of emergencies, of which this was not one.

"What if I was in here with someone?" He asked Trey and Gary.

"We would sit quietly and watch. What would you want us to do?"

"I'll take a shower and you can buy my dinner."

His friends watched Jeff leave the room.

"He's changed," Gary said, "and it looks good on him; you too," he said to Trey, "are we growing up?"

"We're growing right." Trey responded. "Seeing our old teacher opened a big door thanks to you for forcing us to face him, I'm actually seeing a shrink, and have already broached you know what secret, and it wasn't hard at all. I needed to get that shit away from me, and what's left is that I'm pissed off that the old bastard got away with it, and more than likely hurt a lot of kids like us."

"He won't get away with it, he has to die with it."

CHAPTER FIFTY-NINE

John and Andy were at work early meeting with their supervisor and the prosecutor. The DA wanted the porno case wrapped up before the end of the month, so they were more pressured to find the killer first.

"The prints lifted from the boxes didn't tell us anything, which means our principle suspects either handled the tapes with gloves or wiped everything down." John said.

"The woman who met with the warehouse owner was named Helen. Do you think the widow is involved?" Andy asked John.

"She's been on my mind since I heard her name mentioned, let's visit the widow.

John called Mrs. Helen Danford and asked her if she had time to meet with him this morning. She was very agreeable telling him she would be home the entire day.

"I'll get a description from the owner and meet you at the Danford's." Andy said.

John finished with the report he was writing and drove to the Danford home and saw Andy's car in front.

"She described Helen Danford."

John was disappointed and didn't like the feeling. He liked Mrs. Danford, or he didn't like feeling like a fool.

They walked to the front door and rang the bell. Mrs. Danford answered and showed them into her living room.

"I have fresh coffee ready for you and hot muffins." She said.

Andy had poured himself a cup of coffee and was finishing a muffin before John sat down.

"Thank you, Mrs. Danford, neither of us have eaten; this is very thoughtful." John said.

"Tell me what you two have been up to since we last spoke. Do you know any more about my husband's murder?"

"We've been working hard on it, Mrs. Danford and we're expecting a resolution soon. Can you tell me about the warehouse you inquired about downtown?"

"Of course, I can. My husband wanted to rent it to store some of the property owned by the church. As a matter of fact, I was just packing my husband's clothes, so my father-in-law could store them until the church clothing drive. I don't know how I'll get them all downstairs."

"Did your husband sign the lease?"

"Either he, or his father. I not sure which."

"Perhaps we can help you bring the boxes downstairs." John said.

"That would be wonderful. I started packing them in boxes after you called this morning. I have more boxes in the garage, but you can go upstairs and start bringing the other boxes downstairs, I'll meet you up there.

The two men climbed the stairs and looked in the bedrooms for the boxes. They found them in a sitting room at the end of the hall. They took the boxes two at a time to the garage.

Mrs. Danford was packing the rest of the clothing when they went back upstairs.

"This is the last of them." She said to both of them.

"This house is beautiful ma'am; do you mind if I see the other bedrooms up here? Andy asked.

"I don't mind at all. I'll show both of you," She said.

Helen gave the detectives a tour of her second floor that consisted of five bedrooms and four bathrooms. There was a loft used as a television room.

"This is really nice" Andy said entering a room. "My wife would love this furniture. Mrs. Danford, I have a camera in my car, do you mind if I take some pictures of your bedrooms for my wife? She wants to re-do our house and I'm not much help, but if she sees this, it might give her some direction."

"Be my guest Mr. Becker, and I'd be glad to talk to your wife anytime about the best places to shop for the best bargains. You can take these last boxes down, while I freshen your coffee."

"Thanks ma'am, I'll get my camera."

Andy carried the last two boxes to garage and retrieved his camera to photograph the bedrooms for Beth.

They finished their coffee after Andy had taken all the photographs he wanted. They thanked their gracious host and left her standing in her driveway waving.

John drove away and couldn't stop grinning.

"I thought I was going to jump out of my skin," John said, "you were brilliant, and played her so well with those photographs. I'm buying your lunch for the rest of the week."

"I was going to let you buy my lunch anyway; you have money, and I have a wife who shops; you're right though, I am brilliant." Andy said laughing.

"When did you first notice it?" John asked.

"The minute we walked in. I took pictures of every nook and cranny.

They both beamed with the satisfaction of stumbling into the location where the videos were filmed.

"She's a part of the operation. That nice old lady said the secretary's name was Helen, but who thought Helen Danford. They filmed those kids in her house; how sick is that?" She's a mother and she let children be raped in the same house where her own children sleep." Andy said. "All these bastards are going down; way down for this. This bitch jeopardized her own kids; their father is dead and she's going to prison with their so-called grand father. What kind of shit is that?"

"I can't comment on the woman; my mind is blown. She has the arrogance of her father-in-law. She gave you permission to photograph a crime scene in her house because she thinks we can't touch her. These people are amoral at least and immoral at best. We have everything we need to put these people away, but we have nothing on our killer. I'm convinced that whoever he is, knew about what they were doing and killed them to stop it. We're looking for a vigilante, and he succeeded; now we have to stop him. John said, pulling into the parking lot of Mama's Café.

CHAPTER SIXTY

*H*e played his music and was transported to New York in the fifties, wishing he could have experienced the transformation of the music genre.

He thought about his victims and the children they damaged or completely destroyed and felt tears of rage as well as sorrow. He wondered how many children grew up only to commit suicide, spend time in prison, ravaged by drugs or alcohol or worse, victimized children the way they were victimized.

It was never ending in its scope and carnage. He felt helpless to do more to stop the madness that had become the fear of every parent.

He did what had to be done without reservation. He was fortunate to overhear that conversation between the preacher and the two men, one of which was the preacher's son only the year before. Who could be so obtuse as to have a conversation about abusing children in a bathroom without checking stalls?

He wondered if the police were able to connect the dots and find the warehouse. He didn't want to kill the preacher; he would rather he live out his life behind bars, but if he had to, he would kill the bastard in a heartbeat in the warehouse.

He thought he left enough clues to keep the detectives on the right track to expose the pastor's business interest, but they will never solve the murders without his help, which he will give in time.

There was more to do to bring everything to a close and put minds to rest. He planned to destroy the pastor and his vile business along with his partners. He was putting everything in place to leave those behind who were deserving, a clear conscience and peace of mind, and those who were not deserving even enough to die, an overpowering sense of guilt and remorse for the rest of their lives.

In its time, there will be no more, no more that he can prevent.

He was determined to comfort those people who loved him so that they accepted what he had to do and understand he had no other choice. In his entire life, those same people never judged him; he depended on them never changing.

The music played on.

CHAPTER SIXTY-ONE

John and Andy dressed to blend in the area of the warehouse and sat across the street drinking water from a bottle in paper bags. They sat on the ground and waited for the truck to arrive to ship the boxes of dirt.

A dark gray Mercedes parked across the street from the two detectives; the driver sat in the car waiting for the UPS truck to pull in front of him. The driver got out and opened the large door and let the UPS driver in to pick up the boxes.

John and Andy watched as the driver of the Mercedes stood outside of the building waiting for the UPS driver to load the boxes. There were two detectives in the building across the street from the warehouse filming the shipping activity.

When the boxes were secure in the truck, the driver handed a receipt to the other man and drove away never realizing he was about to ship dirt to all parts of the globe.

The large door was closed, and locked and Reverend Darren Danford got into his Mercedes and drove away.

"I'd feel a lot better if we could get the preacher inside the warehouse, and Mrs. Danford's hand in the cookie jar too." Peter Altman said to John and Andy during an early morning meeting. We have all the physical evidence we need, but we need them holding a smoking gun."

"There's a silent alarm in the warehouse. Why anyone would be stupid enough to have a silent alarm system in a warehouse filled to the brim with contraband is anyone's guess, but they have a nice system that alerts their local constabulary. John told the gathering.

"We could send in one of our own as the UPS driver, have him get Danford inside on a ruse and have the landlord call Mrs. Danford to report the alarm and ask her to go to the property."

"What if she calls Danford on a cell phone to have him handle the alarm? Andy questioned him.

"That's the easy part. We'll determine who his carrier is and have them turn the phone off as soon as the landlord makes the call. When she arrives, our mailman who will be wired, will ask some questions to get them to admit ownership of the boxes and we'll be ready to read them their rights, and the drinks will be on me." Altman said smiling.

"I know you're both disappointed about the killer still out there, but you did an outstanding job on this case. This is probably going to the biggest of its kind and you did it alone." Altman told the two detectives.

"Thanks Pete, but we weren't the only one who broke this case, without your help and the help of the killer, there would be no case."

"We're getting still shots of all of the kids in the videos to turn over to Missing Persons, and the FBI; Postal Service is getting involved because some of those boxes were labeled with Postal Service air bills and we haven't even addressed the fraud perpetrated on the church." John said.

"It's amazing how an operation of this size could be operated with so few people." Andy said.

"The next shipment is tomorrow, so we have to work fast. You make the arrangements with UPS and the phone carrier, and we'll talk to the landlord." John said to Pete.

Betty Ann Webster was a newly promoted detective John had worked with in the past on a couple of open and shut murder cases. He liked her ethic and attitude, and he took her with him and Andy to talk to the landlady. They explained that Detective Webster would wait in the real estate office for their call, to signal the call to Mrs. Danford. Detective Webster agreed to meet the landlady in her office at eight o'clock the following morning.

John and Andy took the rest of the day off for no other reason than they were dog-tired. They planned to meet at seven o'clock in the morning.

John called Katherine Whitney's cell phone hoping she would answer. She stayed on his mind since their last dinner together. He was unfamiliar with his feelings and longed to see her again. This wasn't about sex; he really wanted to spend more time with her.

"Called ID tells me it's the detective calling." He heard her voice and felt his stomach do something he hadn't felt since he was fourteen.

"I stand accused," he said, "take the rest of the day off, buy me dinner, and I'll rent a movie."

"Who's getting the short end of the stick, Detective?"

"Let's wait and see after the movie or dessert, whichever comes first."

"How about, I'll buy *you* a drink at the Red Cat, you buy dinner, and I'll rent the movie."

"See you at the Red Cat at five thirty." She laughed and hung up.

He sat at the bar staring at the door saw her backlit by the sun; she was silhouetted in the doorway inviting him to walk over to her.

"We only have time for one drink," she said, "we have early dinner reservations and I'm hungry; about you?" He kissed her and walked with her back to the bar.

"What made you take off so early today? Is everything ok?"

"Everything is fine now. I wanted to see you." John answered, never taking his eyes off her.

"That's nice," she said.

John woke up at five o'clock and dashed to the gym working out with Gary Sanford. He had an early morning with Andy and a busy day ahead, and he wanted his head clear.

"Late night? Gary asked.

"Great night." He answered.

"You look different; better. What going on with you?

"I can't believe it, but I think I'm falling in love."

"You too?

"Who else?" John asked.

"I think Jeff is going to ask Bridgett Lucas to marry him. He hasn't said anything, but I know it's coming."

"That's good news. I hope you're right about Jeff."

"Who's the lady? Gary asked his friend.

"Katherine Whitney."

"You're kidding; she's perfect. Go for it man, you can't go wrong."

"I think you're right. She is perfect for me and I want to see where this takes us."

"Congratulations John, you deserve it, I mean that."

"I'm going to bring the kids down here for a weekend to meet her, and if all goes like I think it will, I'm going to ask her to move in with me. I'm ready; I didn't know this two weeks ago, but it's right for me now."

Gary watched his friend work out and felt happy for him and Jeff. They both deserved to be happy, and both have great partners. Life was falling in place for his friends and he felt content.

"I heard about your the addition to your collection." "When do I get a chance to hear it? It's a classic, I'd kill or die for a copy." "You may not have to do either, my friend." Gary said.

CHAPTER SIXTY-TWO

The boxes that remained in the warehouse contained the tapes the police replaced after it was decided to attempt the arrest of the Danford's on the property. The boxes had been repacked, sealed, and marked for shipping. They didn't want to take the chance of arresting the couple and be convicted of dealing in boxes of Texas dirt. The boxes were in their original location by five thirty the morning they expected to ship.

The detectives were waiting across the street with an arrest warrant for Darren Danford Sr. and Helen Danford.

The wait was long and stressful. They knew they didn't have room for any mistakes that might compromise their case. Reverend Danford was well known and respected; one mistake could give him a walk because of the outcry. They could lose credibility that would take years to regain.

John saw the UPS truck park across the street. A few minutes later, Danford arrived and unlocked the door, waiting outside, like before. The undercover police officer stayed inside and waited for the signal that the call had been made to the landlord. They would have to wait until it was confirmed that Mrs. Danford was on her way. The undercover policeman was given a signal to start loading boxes. They knew there was plenty of time since there were ninety-three boxes scheduled for shipping and it would take time to load all of them. The policeman was instructed to tear two of the boxes, which would give him the excuse to call the preacher inside.

John's cell phone rang, and he almost dropped it in his attempt to answer, he heard Betty Webster's voice on the other end; "she's on her way now."

They had an officer in an unmarked car parked across the street from Mrs. Danford's house waiting for her to leave; when she did, he reported to Webster, who reported to John. Everything was a go.

The officer followed Mrs. Danford downtown and called John and gave him her location when she was two blocks away from the warehouse. John gave the signal to the UPS undercover to call for the pastor, which he did. Danford followed the officer into the warehouse, just as Mrs. Danford arrived and parked her car in front of her father in law's car.

Darren Danford was startled to see Mrs. Danford. She explained that she received a call about the alarm, and she couldn't reach him on his cell phone. She said she called the police and explained it was a false alarm and they cancelled the call.

In reality, the police would have answered the call regardless, but apparently these people didn't have that information.

"After these are gone, we're finished. They're all sold and we're going out of business.

"It couldn't have been done without you Helen." Danford told the wife of his son.

"Darren was just too weak to know how good he had it. Why he wanted out, I'll never understand; the money was incredible and so easy. Whoever took care of them all did us a favor; it's all ours as it should be." He went on.

"It was worth every penny." They heard her say.

"Look at these two boxes over here, they're torn, and you need to tape them shut before I can finish loading." The UPS man was heard saying.

Danford took a role of tape he had hanging on the wall next to the clipboard and taped the boxes.

"Are all these boxes yours?" He asked the preacher.

"They were until this lady and I sold them to the people you're shipping them to today. They all belonged to us, but this is our last shipment; were closing shop and moving on." Danford told the policeman.

John, Andy, Peter Altman, and four-uniformed officer entered the warehouse.

"Darren Danford, I have a warrant for your arrest for child pornography and the sale of pornography, child endangerment and rape" John said and read him his legal rights.

"Helen Danford, I have a warrant for your arrest for pornography and the sale of pornography, child endangerment and rape." He read her rights to silence and legal counsel.

They handcuffed the couple and led toward the door. They both seemed to be in a stupor and said nothing while the police officers walked them to waiting cars.

"You have no idea how this will destroy you Mr. Garrison." Danford said.

"You don't know the power I have in this state. I will personally destroy you and your partner, and you will be begging for food when this is over. How you can expect anyone in this city to believe that we would be involved in something so heinous as your charge against us is more than ludicrous, its contemptible. I will spit on your grave before you see me in prison."

They walked away and rode in separate police vehicles. John and Andy said nothing. They left a team to load the boxes and return them to the other evidence they collected.

They wanted to complete their reports before the end of the day when they both planned to drink their dinner and try to sleep off the events of the morning.

John didn't expect to feel as he did about closing this part of their case. He was disgusted with the people he had just arrested. Two people who appeared beyond reproach; respected in the community, and treated as the civic leaders they were, who instead used their positions to devastate children and families throughout the community and beyond.

John worked on reports throughout the day finishing late in the evening. He saw Andy dozing in his desk chair.

John was exhausted and forgot he had to drive Andy home because he picked him up that morning.

Andy opened his eyes; "are you finished?"

"Yes," John said, "let's go."

"You go ahead, Beth is picking me up; I'm taking her to dinner. Go on home and I'll see you Monday."

"Have a good dinner and kiss Beth for me."

"Kiss her yourself, she right behind you."

"You look awful," she said to John and kissed him on the cheek. Come to dinner with us."

"Thanks, but I need to go home and chill." He looked at his partner and said, "Thanks for everything."

"My pleasure. You did good, boy."

"What have you two been through?" Beth asked her husband watching John leave their office.

"It's been a tough one, but not tonight. Let's get out of here and forget."

CHAPTER SIXTY-THREE

John felt used by this killer they found so illusive. He didn't feel accomplished by the arrest of the Danford's. This killer, this man who is killing to right a wrong led them to the Danford's and their enterprise as part of a mission. He didn't know anything more about this killer, who John found daunting in his ability to fade in and out of the shadows of these crimes of molestation and terror.

The death of Darren Danford created no loss for his family with perhaps the exception of his children who may loose their mother to a prison term. No family has come forward to claim the bodies of James and Barbara Evans only the executor of the estate, who is an officer of their bank. John wondered how a couple with a successful legitimate business, not have a warm circle or support group of friends.

Brian Hargrave was the only one with a grieving family and friends; he was also the only one who didn't seem to mesh with the others, perhaps because he did have a support group, or perhaps he wasn't involved in their business; it wasn't consistent with his character portrait and lifestyle. He was a physician who was gay and used boys on occasion. Nothing they knew indicated his involvement with the others, so why was he killed?

When the killer met Darren Danford and Brian Hargrave in the bar the doctor may have let slip that he had an interest in children beyond his medical practice, thus sealing his fate, and providing a motive as victim number two.

John was convinced this was only about child abuse and nothing more. The pornography business was a bonus; a gift from the killer, which meant the killer, may not have completed his mission. John knew that the victims were random to the extent of the killer's chance meetings in the bar; their shared relationship was coincidental. He was convinced the killer planned his mission long before Darren Danford lost his hands.

There was no evidence to trace to anyone and no witnesses.

He drove to P&D's to talk to the bartender who saw a man leave with Danford.

It was early for the happy hour crowd and John was hungry. He ordered the chicken salad sandwich the owner recommended previously and it was as good as he bragged.

He was weary but wouldn't allow himself to feel defeated in spite of his lack of clues to this mystery.

He was sitting at the bar along with three other men having a late lunch with a familiarity that told John they were regulars as well as friends. The booth directly across from the bar was occupied by two women having a drink and engaged in an animated dialogue.

His eyes followed the room up the stairs to the lounge and he thought he recognized a man walking by, then out of sight. He immediately dismissed the recognition as nothing more than a look alike of a friend who would have no reason to frequent the bar especially before four o'clock in the afternoon.

"You know it's a shame about that Danford guy and Dr. Hargrave." John heard the bartender lament. "They didn't seem like chicken hawks; I would never have guessed it."

"Describe the man you saw walk out with Danford that last night." John asked the man.

"He had sandy colored hair that was kind of thick and long to about here," he said pointing to his lower neck. He wore shaded glasses that was kind of brownish with gold rims. He had a thick mustache that was real neat; about six three and well built."

"I'll need you to give that description to one of our sketch artists in the morning." John gave him his card and agreed to meet the bartender in his office at eighty thirty in the morning.

"Have you seen this man since Dr. Hargrave was killed?

"Yeah, he's been in a few times since. As a matter of fact, he came in about a half hour before you came, but I haven't seen him since, so he must have left from the upstairs exit."

"You have an exit upstairs? Why didn't you tell me you saw him today when you were describing him to me?" John was obviously angry and frustrated. "Don't you know we're looking for a killer, and that man is wanted for questioning?

John hurried up the stairs leading to the second-floor lounge and saw only three men sitting together. He opened the door under the exit light that led to a small hallway with an elevator. The area was empty, and John wanted to kick the shit out of the bartender.

He checked both bathrooms upstairs and found both to be as empty as the exit area.

He went down the stairs and found the bartender and had to calm himself.

"I want you and the other bartender to meet me in the morning; if that man comes in here tonight, this is my cell number. If I find out you're hiding anything, or doing anything to interfere with this investigation, your ass is mine and I'll flush it down your own toilet.

John was breathing hard as sat in his car for several minutes inhaling his anger. He drove to a bar a few blocks away and drank his way into balance. He sat at a table alone enjoying the solitude, thinking about his meeting with P&D's bartender, still seething. The man described someone wearing a disguise; John had no doubt. The thick hair, neat mustache and glasses were all he saw, which was what the killer had in mind with the design. If he was still going to the bar, he wasn't finished killing. If he was still meeting men in that bar, those men are at risk. Just then, he felt his phone vibrate on his hip; answering it, he heard Jeff Harrington.

"I'm leaving the office in a few minutes, feel like a tall one? I called Gary but he isn't answering his phone. Have you heard from him?

"I can't make it tonight but give me a rain check. I can't help you with Gary, it's not my week." He heard laughter on the other end of the line.

"He may be in a meeting and not answering. I'll try to give you a call sometime next week, Jeff, but right now this case I'm working on is taking my time. Have one for me and we'll talk soon."

Before he had a chance to clip his phone on his waistband, it vibrated. The caller id read P&D's Club.

"He's here and getting ready to leave with someone; you'd better haul ass if you want to catch him. I'll do what I can to keep them here."

John was running to his car before the bartender could finish his report of the sighting. He approached the club within six minutes and parked in front of the door.

"They just drove away in Steve's car a second ago. I tried to keep them here, but your guy was in a hurry."

"Who is Steve?"

"Steve Brooks; a regular, been coming here since I opened the place."

"Let's go somewhere where we can talk." John said walking into the club.

"In my office." The owner said leading John upstairs to a small office in the back of the room. There were two straight back wood chairs with cracked vinyl seat covers in front of the desk cluttered with newspaper, hard-core porno magazines, two cigarette filled ashtrays whose color was now ashen and coffee-stained Styrofoam cups.

"Did you have a reason for not calling me when he walked in? John started the questioning.

"Why didn't you call when he walked in?"

"He was upstairs when I saw him talking to Steve, and I called you right away. I went upstairs to talk to them and offer them a drink on the house; that's when your guy said they had to leave, and they did."

"What do you know about this Steve Brooks?"

"He's a lawyer. Scum bag if you ask me. He represents chicken hawks and gets too many off on what he calls technicalities that we all know was scaring the shit out of the kids they fucked with. He's always bragging about his victories and doesn't give a flying fuck about those kids his clients groped and worse. He's the worse kind of fag; he's no better than those freaks he works for and they all should have their balls whacked off. Give me the job and I'll do it in a heartbeat. What's anybody else doing about it anyway? People like you go around thinking that all of us hit on every man and boy we see. You won't let us live our lives in our own way making our own choices. It's about sexual orientation, stupid. I'm not a fag when I pour your drink, pay my taxes, and worship the God of my choice. I like men, some men, no different than you like some women, so bite me and get off my fag ass with those thoughts that have nothing to do with the kids. You don't care about the kids; you care about why we do what we do and, that has nothing to do with keeping children safe from the scum balls that hurt them."

"Listen to me," John shouted grabbing the man by both shoulders, I don't have time to get into a political debate about choices, do you know where Steve Brooks lives?"

"He has a condo at Haven Hurst Manor, two blocks from here. I went to a party there once. Wait a minute I have his address and phone number."

He went to his cluttered desk and pulled out a Rolodex and jotted down the information and handed it to John. John called the number and was shocked to get an answer.

"Is this Steve Brooks? John asked before he heard the phone click dead. John called Andy and told him what was going on and told him to meet him at the Brooks address; "and you better bring some back up, even though we're probably too late."

John drove to the address and showed his badge to the guard at the entrance of the gated property.

"Has anyone driven out of here within the last thirty minuets?"

He asked the guard. "Not by car."

"Is there another way out of here?"

"Someone would have to jump the fence."

"There will be other police officers following me, just let them in, and direct them to the Brooks house."

John drove around the complex until he found the condo. Brooks' car was parked in front of the unit. There was no one in sight. John walked around the rear of the house and saw the fence that separated the property from adjacent complex. As he walked back to the front, Andy's car pulled up.

"I just arrived a few minutes ago. The security guard said no cars drove out within the last thirty minutes. Either he's still in there, left over the fence, or was never here in the first place. The bartender gave me the lowdown on Brooks; he's an attorney who represents pedophiles. He also gave me the address and phone number that I called and either whoever answered hung up when I asked for Brooks, or it somehow disconnected on its own."

"What do you really think is going on here?" Andy asked.

"I'm convinced the killer left the bar with Brooks car and planned to kill him tonight. I'm also convinced our killer answered the phone."

The lights rotating on the police cars that had arrived illuminated the area and were the subject of the onlookers peering through blinds and curtains. The door to the Brooks unit opened and a man stood in the doorway, backlit by interior lighting. John didn't expect to see anyone standing inside the house; he and Andy stopped walking toward the building not knowing who else was inside.

"Are you Steven Brooks?" John asked the shadow of a man in the doorway.

"Yes, I am, what's going on out here?"

"Are you alone Mr. Brooks?"

"Yes, I'm alone; what the hell business is it of yours."

"Mr. Brooks please walk toward me and take your hands out of your pockets before you start walking."

"I'm not doing anything until you tell me what the hell is going on and what you want with me."

"Mr. Brooks, we are looking for a man that is wanted for questioning in a matter we are investigating, and we have information that you may have met with him earlier this evening; now I am not going to ask you, I'm telling you to walk toward us after you take your hands out of your pocket and do it now Mr. Brooks."

The man stood facing John, looking around at the six policemen surrounding him, and slowly removed both hands from his trouser pockets, and walked to within a foot of John Garrison.

"Now will you tell me what this is all about?" He asked John.

"Is there anyone else in your house?"

"I'm alone; he's already gone."

"We'd like you to come with us to talk about your visitor."

"Why should I? Whatever you're investigating has nothing to do with me."

"Mr. Brooks, you may have entertained a man we are looking for, and that's why you should come with us."

"I need to get my keys."

"Where are they," John asked him, "we'll get them for you."

"On the table beside the door."

Andy went to the door and reached inside to retrieve the keys from the table and saw what looked like a round charm on the floor that was engraved with a P that was probably attached to a key ring. He left it on the floor, closed and locked the door.

"Get in touch with Pete for a search of this house and keep someone here to watch the place, send the others to search the fence for signs of anyone jumping then meet me downtown." John told Andy taking him aside. "We're going to need a forensics team in there; I'm hoping there was no time to clean up. If he jumped the fence, there is a complex on either side and he may live in one the three, because I don't think he drove a car to P&D's since it's only a couple of blocks away, and he wouldn't have to expose his car. This is the closest we've come to catching this guy, and I'm not going to let him manipulate himself back in his hole this time."

"I'll wait for Altman and see you later." Andy said, feeling elated getting closer to catching their killer.

Andy told John about the charm he saw on the floor.

"You did the right thing leaving it on the floor; it just could be the first or last initial of our man.

John left his partner and the others on the property while he drove what might have been a victim and the only eyewitness, for questioning about his recent guest.

No matter how well planned; there are no perfect murders. There's always a mistake somewhere in the course and scope of the plan, or execution; one only has to see it, John was thinking. A cold unsolved murder is just that, unsolved because no one saw the mistake. This killer's mistake has become clear; he made too many trips to P&D's for his victims.

CHAPTER SIXTY-THREE

*H*e put his earphones in because they made him feel more alone in his house than he was and stared at nothing while he listened to the perfect sounds that no one he knew could appreciate, angry with himself for making the most careless of mistakes. Overexposure. He had become complacent and arrogant with his mission.

He lay there for several hours awake and incensed at his behavior that appeared common—normal, traits he was careful to avoid in anything that mattered to him. He was loathing the person he had become, to right the wrong that had become pervasive, yet he wondered if he would have been capable of this violence had he not been robbed of his ability to trust and love. Was he no more than a cold-blooded killer taking revenge for those who were unable to protect themselves, as he once was, or was this his assignment to do what no one was willing to do?

He had his music and nothing else but rage. The music made him move and breathe and think, but the musician was dead because that same music no longer had enough meaning for him to play on.

When this ends, it will be written that he was psychotic and had a dysfunctional relationship with his mother. He heard himself laughing thinking about what shrinks would do without mothers to blame for everything. He had no relationship with his mother at all. There was no common ground, no love, no sharing, no bond, and no reason for a relationship. She was stupid and shallow, and nothing about her was attractive to him. He didn't understand the need for mothering other than maintenance for a time, then perhaps friendship if there was common ground; otherwise, maintenance was sufficient for him. He didn't care enough about either of his parents to blame them for being what they were; they just didn't matter. However, he had to acknowledge the fact that if they made other decisions about his welfare so long ago, so many lives would have benefited, but that was then, this is now and he does what he does because I want to, he told himself.

The music played on; he turned off the light and listened.

CHAPTER SIXTY-FOUR

Trey Peterson left his psychiatrist's office drained from his session in which he described his abuse by his teacher and priest. He had never discussed it at this length with anyone until now and was astonished at its effect after so long living in denial. The clarity of his disclosure was overpowering, and he was lost in the distance of time. His emotions were threadbare; he only wanted to be alone. He couldn't remember a time when he welcomed solitude; there was always someone in his bed, his house, his office and his playgrounds; everywhere there was someone who promoted his denial and provided a forum to be who he thought he wanted to be without substance or commitment.

He left a message for Jeff telling him he wouldn't be able to play golf the next morning, but he didn't say he would be staying home to think, because he realized he had to learn. He knew he had to make decisions about how he would plan his life from this day of reckoning. No matter how he lashed out, or who he destroyed in the process, nothing would change about his past; nothing could make it right without his putting it behind him without the denial that had served him well.

A man he trusted and even loved when he was a small boy had abused him. That is what happened thirty years ago, and he had been punishing himself and the others ever since without the satisfaction of resolution; he raged as his clenched fist drove a hole in his kitchen wall. His arm swept across a countertop scattering coffee mugs, bottles, and canisters.

He never allowed himself to love a woman because he was in

fear of not having the ability to sustain a relationship as well as exposing his past. The rejection he expected was crippling. He never made love to a woman. He masturbated in them without any interest in their pleasure.

Trey sat unaware of the darkening room from the setting sun or his eyes overflowing down the sides of his face. He was scared, and the feeling was familiar; he felt it for the last thirty years. Controlling his life now was the only option for survival he was willing to consider. Talking to his friends about their shared abuse was not his idea of rehabilitation since Gary and Jeff were fighting their own demons and were bumping into each other with every remembrance and attempt of dissolution.

Jeff was trying, he considered. He was seeing a shrink, stopped drinking and might have the beginnings of a relationship that could be sound if his newfound independence from the chains of parents and friends, and those all-consuming expectations was any indication. Jeff is looking good to recover and recuse himself from the conflict that dictated their lives far too long.

There was always a dark sense of destiny that enfolded Gary, he thought of his oldest friend. To the unsuspecting, the three friends shared everything, but their sharing was superficial and aloof. He wondered how their lives would have differed had they not been abused and locked down.

He felt a pulling in his stomach remembering his priest touching and threatening him into the silence that would control his life. He heard his own scream before he realized he was in the present. He screamed and cried and screamed until his throat was dry and his face was wet, and he was spent knowing the man he was meant to be without the pain and fear that had rendered him powerless.

He would make a difference as he exposed the abuse of children that were unable to protect themselves and stop the madness that has destroyed so much innocence regardless of the cost.

His doorbell shattered his thoughts and brought him into the room that was now dark. He heard Jeff's voice calling to him, and the incessant doorbell. He yelled through the door to wait while he splashed cold water on his face, not wanting anyone to witness his catharsis. He felt the throbbing in his hand and saw blood still rolling down his fingers and remembered the kitchen wall. Cold water rinsed away the blood; a square adhesive pad covered the broken skin; the throbbing was more painful.

"Your message sounded strange. Are you ok?" Jeff asked his friend.

"Everything's ok. I had a tough week and decided to take some time off and chill.

Nothing's wrong; you can go home now Mommy."

"You don't look ok; do you want to talk?"

"No, I'll be ok, really. I just need some down time; I'll call you in a couple of days."

"I don't believe you, but I'll go and let you do whatever it is you have to do, but don't think you can get rid of me that fast; I'll call you tomorrow."

"I did get rid of you that fast, I'll talk to you soon."

Jeff Harrington walked to his car worried about his friend who never in his memory was mysterious or distant.

He wanted to tell his friend that he was engaged to marry Bridgett, but this was not the time.

CHAPTER SIXTY-FIVE

Steven Brooks sat arrogantly in the wood chair slightly leaning, and unscathed as he listened to Detective John Garrison explain that they were investigating a homicide that may involve a man with whom he left the bar earlier in the evening.

"Who was the man you drove away with from P&D's, Mr. Brooks?" John questioned.

"I met him tonight at the bar; we had a couple of drinks and shot the breeze a bit and, I invited him to my house when he said he might need my services for a problem he had. The place was too busy and getting loud, and I didn't want to discuss business there when I lived so close."

"What is his name?" "Ray Dorfsang."

"Did you ever see him before tonight?"

"No, I met him for the first time tonight."

"How long were you in the club with him, Mr. Brooks?"

"Oh, about an hour or so."

"What did you talk about?" John continued questioning.

"The usual; you know, golf, Enron; small talk, bar talk. I told him I was a lawyer and we talked about my practice, and he seemed interested in the cases I handled and told me he thought I might be able to help him out. Considering the type of cases I usually handle, I thought we should talk in private and my house was closer than my office, so I suggested we go to my house."

"Who drove?"

"I did. He said since I lived so close, he could walk back to his car, so we took my car."

"Did you go straight to your house?"

"Yes. He answered.

Andy walked into the room and stood in the corner. John excused himself and walked out of the room followed by Andy.

"Pete is at the house with a forensic team and the search is on." Andy reported.

"There is a housing complex on both sides of the property separated by fences. He could have either jumped them or walked out the front entrance under the unseeing eye of the security guard. When I drove out, the guard was listening to music through headphones reading a comic book and never looked up. I don't think he knew I was there." Andy went on.

"We just got started here. He gave a name, that I doubt is real, and Brooks met him for the first time tonight. He took him home to discuss a possible case the man wanted Brooks to consider and that's it so far.

The two detectives returned to the interrogation room where Steven Brooks sat without concern.

"You know," Brooks said, "you could have saved the trouble of a search warrant; I would have given you permission to search my house."

"We appreciate that Mr. Brooks. "Now tell us what you did when you arrived at your house." John asked staring at the lawyer seated across the table.

"He sat in my study while I went to the kitchen to get ice. My phone rang and I was rather surprised when he answered. All I heard him say was "no" and then he hung up and said he forgot about an appointment he had that night and left without another word. I looked at my caller ID, and saw the call came from came from you, and knew why he left; I recognized your name from seeing you around the courthouse. He probably saw the name in the papers. He's killing child sex offenders, isn't he? He figured since I represent them, I'm just as bad. The man came to my house to kill me, didn't he?" The witness was now sitting straight with a look of terror.

"We don't know that yet, Mr. Brooks. That's what we're trying to determine. Can you describe him to a sketch artist?" John asked acknowledging the change in demeanor of his witness.

"I'll do what I can, but when I think back on him, he looked like he was trying to alter his appearance with a beard, thick mustache and baseball cap. He wore gold-rimmed glasses, shaded brown."

Steven Brooks sat with the police artist and gave vivid details of the man who may have brutally killed four people.

Andy was pouring stale coffee in his stained mug when Peter Altman walked in. Pete was enjoying himself with this investigation; Andy was thinking watching the prosecutor walking toward him grinning with satisfaction.

"We found a clear shoe print on a utility box next to the fence and lifted prints from the house and fence as well as Brooks' car. There were no prints on the charm; it looks like it was stepped on more than once. We should have word on the prints in a couple of days." He told John and Andy.

"Did you get anything useful from Brooks?"

John relayed the information Steven Brooks had given during the interview and returned to the interrogation room followed by his partner.

"Mr. Brooks, did the man tell you anything about the reason he may have needed your help?" John asked after sitting down.

"He didn't have the time. After the phone call he left right away, and that was the end of it. Well, there might be one more thing; he may be an attorney."

"What makes you think that? John said with a look of surprise.

"Nothing specific; just using the lingo naturally as lawyers do especially talking to other lawyers."

After their witness left, John and Andy compared the sketches described by the bartender and Brooks and they agreed both looked like disguises.

They had their first concrete lead to this mystery, and the killer might be a lawyer who killed for reasons known only to him. It was obvious that he met all of his victims at P&D's, and all of the victims had pornography and child sexual abuse in common, but what did they have in common with the killer, John wondered as he scrutinized the files again and again trying to find the key to the mind of the man who was ridding the world of monsters.

CHAPTER SIXTY-SIX

Jeff Harrington didn't regret losing Bridgett when they were too young to out picture their consciousness, and too naive to understand the need.

When he was with her in school, he loved her, when she married and moved out of his life, the memory of his love left him shallow without direction; when she returned, his memory restored, he would marry her.

Jamaica was their choice of playground, love nest and wedding location. Bridgett said yes to his clumsy proposal before he gave her the ring, he had since the day after their first night together.

Before he had a chance to give her the ring he brought the day after their first night together, Bridgett said yes while the deep golden sunset of Negril went unnoticed. They planned to get married the following week on the beach allowing another opportunity to view the sunset.

The villa overlooked the ocean and was spacious enough to host their guests that included parents, Gary, Trey, John, Jeff's secretary and two of his partners.

The wedding and reception plans were completed within a day and the couple flew home to make their announcement.

Jeff's parents were taken by surprise, and his mother balked at the suddenness and short notice, complaining that the cost of flights would be exorbitant. Her son relieved her fears of the expense by offering to bear the cost of the trip for his parents.

Jeff met Gary and Trey for lunch and made his announcement recruiting both as best men.

"Seven days; why so long?" Trey said sarcastically.

"Because I thought you'd be busy tomorrow." Jeff said laughing.

"You've been planning this for a while, haven't you?" Gary asked knowing the answer.

"I wasn't going to let her get away this time, and I've waited long enough."

Jeff called John Garrison who was surprised as well as pleased with the couple's decision. He was grateful for an opportunity to get out of town and away from the mire he had wallowed in for too many weeks.

He was happy for Jeff and could see the change in his college friend who never seemed relaxed; it was encouraging to see him meld into his own manhood.

John felt compelled to conclude his investigation; it was wearing on him as well as Andy. What started as a violent killing has evolved into the heinous destruction of children by some of the city's leading citizens.

He had a sighting and physical evidence that gave him his first glimmer of hope where there was none.

He needed Jeff and Bridgett's news to wash away the filth he was living.

CHAPTER SIXTY-SEVEN

John and Andy drove to Steven Brooks' town house and stopped behind a familiar car stopped at the guard gate. John followed the car onto the property and recognized the driver and parked behind his car.

"John, what are you doing here?" Trey Peterson asked getting out of his car.

"Following up on a case, John said surprised, "what brings you here?"

"This is where I live as of a couple of months ago."

John was baffled, having been to Trey's house a few months ago for dinner and this was not the house that greeted him.

"Does this have anything to do with the onslaught of the police force the other night?" Trey was curious.

"Were you here?" John asked him.

"Austin," he answered, "I had a meeting that lasted late, so I stayed the night and heard about it when I got back. What's going on?"

"Do you mind if we come in?"

"Not at all."

Trey's garage door opened by remote control as he drove in followed by the detectives who parked in the driveway and entered the garage.

John noticed lawn equipment beside Trey's car that included a bamboo rake that looked vaguely familiar. The men entered Trey's new home through the kitchen door as the garage door closed seemingly without provocation.

The hole left in the kitchen wall from Trey's fist was visible to the detectives as well as the ace wrapping on Trey's right hand. They were seated in the den of the luxury town house, and John was not comfortable questioning an old friend about his possible knowledge of murder.

"I see you have your own lawn mower; do you have to maintain your own grass here?" John asked him.

"Not hardly; all that stuff belongs to my friend Gary who left it here to make room in his vehicle. He was moving something and needed the space. I forget it's here; it's been months; if fact, I had to move it to this place."

"Do you know anything about Steven Brooks?" John asked him.

"I didn't know Steven Brooks until I heard about what happened at his place, and I still don't really know what happened; just that he was taken away, and his house was searched. I can't help you; I don't know anything."

They left through the garage, and John looked at the bamboo garden rake leaning against the wall and realized a rising sense of recognition.

"Aren't we going to see Brooks?" Andy asked as they drove off the property without stopping.

"I don't think he can tell us anything else. I need to buy a rake."

CHAPTER SIXTY-EIGHT

The bridal party was scheduled to fly to Jamaica mid morning without Jeff who had a deposition in the afternoon and planned to fly out first thing in the morning.

John, Gary, and Trey drove to the airport together, all anxious to spend time celebrating their friend's good fortune as well as down time.

They arrived on the island where cars were waiting to transport them to the villa where they would witness the nuptials and spend a weekend of celebration.

The scent of tropical flora permeated the estate, and the sound of the waves swept over the party away from the mundane of the lives they left behind.

Jeff called shortly after they arrived and said he was finished with his work and would be in the air early in the morning.

John, Gary, and Trey found a golf course in short order and spent the rest of the day engaged in Jeff stories, drinking and the game of their choice.

Jeff's partners and secretary arrived later in the evening and they had dinner on a veranda overlooking the ocean as the much-heralded sun set slowly behind the horizon. The curried goat and rice prepared by the live-in staff was eaten with flourish and the rum punch flowed until the last of the party, which happened to be Gary, went to bed looking forward to seeing Jeff and celebrating the wedding he longed for.

Jeff slept very little with fretful periods that finally ended when he gave up earlier than usual, looking around the room and laid back into thoughts of marriage to Bridgett.

He took a shower and finished his packing. He decided to leave for the airport early rather than waiting around with nothing else to do.

He entered the freeway and saw that traffic was already heavy with construction restricting lanes causing the congestion. He called Bridgett and told her where he was and would be early for his flight so that nothing could keep him from catching the plane. He saw the traffic moving to the right lane and stop ahead. As he waited to move right looking into his mirror, the bobtail truck struck him without warning, crushing him against his car. Jeff heard nothing; he felt no pain and died on his way to be married.

Gary was cleaning his golf shoes when he took the call from Jeff colleague giving him what details were available. Jeff was lying in the county morgue-awaiting autopsy instead flying to Jamaica as he promised.

He dropped the phone and stared at Trey who had just walked into the room buttoning his shirt.

"What's up?" He said. "He died." "Who died?" "Jeff."

"What are you talking about, who died?" "Jeff." Gary told his friend not feeling the tears rolling down the sides of his face. Trey grabbed Gary's shoulders shaking him, "tell me what you're talking about. What do you mean Jeff died?"

"He was on his way to the airport when he was hit head on by a truck and died at the scene. He's dead, Trey. Jeff is dead."

Trey sat down feeling his soul leave his body, as his head grew lighter. He tried to picture his friend dead, but there was nothing to see except Jeff driving to the airport. Jeff couldn't die; he was their friend all of their lives. He would always be.

John walked in seeing both men distraught and learned of the tragedy. He poured them both a drink and called Andy for details of the accident.

"It happened quickly; there was no suffering. He died on impact. I don't know what to say about your loss. I can't imagine what you're going through, but I'll do everything I can to help. Do you want me to tell Bridgett?"

Both men hadn't thought about anything but Jeff. Gary finished his drink; "we owe it to Jeff to tell her."

"Ok, I'll make arrangements to get everyone out of here and back to Houston today." John said after pouring each of them another drink.

The funeral was small and intimate the way his friends thought Jeff would have planned had he the chance. John watched Gary and Trey stand over their friend's grave in the same stupor he saw when they were told of the accident. Jeff's mother couldn't be consoled and blamed everyone and everything for the loss of her only child; the son she lived through and for, to the sacrifice of everything in her life. Her life was now empty of everything that had meaning and would never change. She would not allow anything to fill that void; the life she knew had ended on highway 45 and she never considered the driver of the truck because it was too easy to hold him responsible when she could blame the blameless giving her no resolution.

Bridgett looked weary with grief but was prepared to pick up the pieces and raise her daughter without Jeff who she loved. She held dear the time they had together and was sustained with the memories. She would be ok, John thought watching her.

Jeff changed his will shortly before he died Trey explained as Jeff's parents, Bridgett, and Gary met in his office. There was an insurance policy with his parents as beneficiaries. He left his cars to Trey and Gary and the bulk of his estate to Bridgett and her daughter. Jeff managed his money well and left Bridgett and her daughter a generous trust that would provide a substantial income.

Gary and Trey felt as if they had lost a limb and could feel the fathom pain of their loss. Trey discussed his grief with his psychiatrist that explained that he would never get over losing his closest friend; he would have to work at getting on with it only.

Gary resented the untimely death of his friend after he just started coming to terms with the rape and terror, he lived with for too long at the hands of the monster who they believed would care for them. His loathing consumed him; he thought of nothing but his friend lying cold in the ground and the priest who had killed the best part of him so long ago.

It was time for him to finish what he started so many months ago when he learned the priest had cancer and would die without acknowledging the evil that he was.

CHAPTER SIXTY-NINE

John walked into the police station carrying the bamboo rake he bought before he left for Jamaica to attend Jeff Harrington's wedding.

"Ok, will you now tell me what you are doing with the rake?" Andy said. John was going through the photos of the Evans'. When he found the ones he was looking for, he showed them to his partner.

"Look at those lines and remember the bamboo shards found in the carpet. It was a rake; a bamboo rake." "Just like the rake we found in your friend's garage, who happens to be a lawyer."

"Don't even go there, Andy. Trey Peterson is not a killer."

"And his last name starts with a P. Coincidence? I don't think so partner."

"I think so partner." John said annoyed but questioning his judgment.

John left the rake and photos with Andy after he received the forensic report that showed fingerprints of Steven Brooks, his son and his housekeeper who had cleaned earlier in the day. The hair in the carpet and upholstery was accounted for and nothing indicated that Brooks had a visitor. The charm was dirty from a shoe. The footprint on the utility box was that of a Doctor Marten's loafer size eleven.

John called Trey Peterson and arranged to meet with him at his house at five thirty. He would either rule Trey in or out as a serial killer.

While he waited for his evening meeting, he did a background check on Trey and found nothing significant other than the schools he attended and his law license and a myriad of traffic violations. Trey went to Catholic elementary and high schools with Gary and Jeff. He had a vague hunch and drove to Saint George's school and met with the principal, Father Robert Cummings. The priest examined the detective's badge and gave him a list of the three boy's teachers during their eight years at the school.

John spent the afternoon looking for complaints against any of the teachers and found seven against one man, Father Davis Connor, who taught all three of the friends until the middle of their third year. None of the complaints involved Gary, Jeff, or Trey.

John didn't like what he was thinking. He may have just established motive for his friend.

He decided to visit his grandmother before seeing Trey.

"Don't jump to any conclusions why I'm here, he said to his grandmother while hugging her, "I have some time, I haven't eaten today, and I was wondering how you were since I haven't seen you in over a week."

"And hello to you too, little boy. I'm glad you have the time; I'll fix you a very late lunch and I'm doing fine; still sleeping with the next-door neighbor's husband."

"You better be careful, Grand, his wife may be packing a gun the next time she's here playing bridge." "I'm not worried about her, she too busy packing her fat gut, now tell me what's really going on with you, and I'm sorry about Jeff. He was too young to die and he always looked so sad to me, as if something terrible hurt him a long time ago."

"Maybe something did hurt him a long time ago, but he seemed to be coming to terms with his demons too late to matter.

"You're not coming to terms with your own demons, son. It's time you accept the fact that someone who probably will never be caught, killed your parents and you have to stop looking for him in every case you handle. You joined the police force over my objections and concern to catch your parent's killer, you obsess over all of your cases and your life is limited to your job, children and your grandmother in that order and I think something is very wrong with that picture.

You are young, tall, dark, and handsome with money of your own. You're a great catch; why don't you let someone catch you and move on with your life?"

"You're right about some of that crap; I have money because my parents died, and I will never stop looking for their killer. I'm not hurting any longer, I mean that; loving grandparents raised me and I'm grateful, but I won't stop looking for him, Grand, please accept that I owe it to myself and them.

He finished his meal and said good-by to his grandmother and drove to meet Trey Peterson, hoping to rule him out of this killing.

He arrived before Trey drove up and opened his garage. He left his car outside behind the Porsche John recognized as once belonging to Jeff Harrington.

They greeted each other and went into the house.

"You don't look comfortable, John. I'll fix us a drink and you can tell me why you wanted to meet."

John emptied his glass before he sat trying to be balanced enough to question his friend without bias.

"Trey, you know I am investigating the murder of Darren Danford and three others and all of them are connected with a group of pornographers.

The man were looking for may have visited your neighbor, Steve Brooks, who said he thought he may be a lawyer. The man got away on foot, and we don't think he had to go far to his car or house. We have evidence that a bamboo rake was used at one of the crime scenes, and a gold charm with the letter P engraved was found in the Brooks home.

Trey you are a lawyer, Steve Brooks is your neighbor, you have a bamboo rake in your garage and your last name starts with P and your key fob looks like something is missing."

John stared at Trey Peterson who was not at all as incensed as thought.

"If you're waiting for me to react, I have no reaction. I am a lawyer, Brooks and I are neighbors, I did lose a signet charm and I had a bamboo rake in my garage. I can't explain the similarities John. I am not a killer.

"When you were in grade school did Father, Davis Connor molest you and your friends?"

"Could you be more direct?" Trey was sarcastic. "It looks like you've been working hard John."

"Trey, I am doing my job. I don't want this to work against you, but I have to follow through on everything that's pointing to you. I'm not liking this at all, now tell me about the priest."

"I won't talk about my friends; it's not my right to do so. I was in the second grade when Father Connor started on me. At first there was groping, a lot of it, then he moved on to masturbation in front of me and then he used my hand to masturbate. One day early the following school year he was gone."

"Trey, I'm sorry for bringing it up, but" Trey stopped him with his raised open hand. "Don't apologize John, I can talk about it now that I'm finally seeing a shrink. It's been buried too deep for too long and it's time to end it. There are still too many kids out there being raped and I want to be in a position to counsel with them and their families. You see John, I am aware that I just gave you a motive, but if let myself give in to my desire for revenge, that priest would have taken everything. I won't let him have that control any longer. I can do better helping those kids one on one than killing the bastards who are fucking with their lives. Don't worry John, I don't blame you for your suspicions, I would have them too with the same information, but I'm not your man. I'll be around if the DA wants to talk to me."

"One more thing, what size shoe do you wear?" "Nine. I wasn't endowed like Gary and Jeff who were a full size eleven and I envied them for years." He concluded laughing.

"I'm off the clock and ready to drink." John said. "So am I my friend."

John and Trey had three more drinks before he was ready to leave. He wasn't convinced that Trey was unscathed by the inquisition, but he felt justified as he drove home thinking about his parents and the man who killed them.

CHAPTER SEVENTY

Gary was in a meeting when Trey called. He was meeting with a former client who wanted to thank him again for saving him from a long prison term and assure his attorney that he was getting too old to stay in the business of selling drugs.

Gary told him that he wasn't willing to represent him again under any circumstances. The man went on and on about how this was the second time he escaped a long stay in prison.

He told Gary about a time over thirty years ago when he and his brother were stoned and wanted to break into his teacher's house and steal the money, she was holding for a school band fund raiser. Gary told him he didn't want to hear about it because he would be required to report him since he was not representing him, and that crime had nothing to do with any crime in which Gary was involved as his attorney.

"Just let me finish, I've never talked about this to anyone since my brother sixteen years ago."

He went on about how they entered the house through the patio door that was easy to open. They thought the house was empty and the two separated to look for the money.

"I was looking in the kitchen when the teacher's husband came at me with a gun yelling at his wife to call the police. My brother came up behind the man, grabbed the gun and shot him then turned around and shot his wife who was my teacher. I remember how she looked at me when she fell. We got the hell out of there and never did find the money. I really felt bad about the whole thing especially when I found out they had a son who wasn't in the house. We never even thought about killing anyone; it just happened. I'll tell you one thing; I've never held a gun since. I often wondered if anyone's doing time for what we did. I know you can't tell anyone what I did, but I just had to get it off my chest. Thanks Mr. Harrington you won't be seeing me anymore.

Gary turned off the tape and put it in an envelope. He sat thinking about the man who killed John Garrison's parents, just walked out of his office.

Trey was waiting for Gary to conclude his meeting. He sat down and asked Gary for a drink.

He told him about the visit with John Garrison.

"John was right to consider me; look at the evidence he has. You're going to have to represent me if it comes to that. I'm not worried; I just don't feel like going through it."

Gary felt tired and didn't feel like going through it either.

"I'll handle it," he told Trey, "let's just wait and see what they do next."

"I told him about Father Connor; I didn't mention you and Jeff." "What did he say?" "He felt bad, but he already suspected. Apparently, there were some complaints filed against the padre."

"You realize you gave him motive." "I know and I told him I knew, but it's not about me. Killing those people isn't going to stop the madness. Children have to be protected by not being as assessable to these predators. If windows aren't broken and they gain entry through those windows, someone didn't lock the window. If a kid can be enticed from the front of their house, they're not being taught how to avoid these people. I'm not saying that all of it will stop, but a lot of can be prevented."

"That's all well and good, Trey, but the bastards need killing." "I agree, they do need killing, but it's about the kids; somebody has to make the kids safe. If I thought I could do it, I would have killed that priest a long time ago. I've never fucked a woman without thinking about what he did to us and I'm tired of thinking about it. I don't want to be there any longer. It's not where I belong. He took us there, but it's up to us if we choose to stay and I'm not staying. He can't hurt me anymore; he can't hurt us anymore Gary. Didn't we learn anything with Jeff's death? Life is shorter than we ever dreamed it could have been. Jeff tried, I believe he really tried toward the end, but he never accepted the fact that it happened, it was not about his failure or shame and he wouldn't let it go.

It's over, Gary; it's over for me anyway."

He listened to his friend and knew Trey had conquered the demon. The shame and rage they shared since childhood was left only for him and he couldn't dispel what he held dear and was still useful.

"I'll talk to John tomorrow morning when I see him at the gym and find out where they are with the case. I don't think they have enough against you to matter. Meet me at my house tomorrow for lunch, I'm not going in so we can have time to prepare for whatever they think they have." John said and walked his friend out of his office.

CHAPTER SEVENTY-ONE

John Garrison sat in his living room thinking about his friend who killed four people. He never saw it coming but as he looked back on the victims, crime scene and evidence they now had, it was clear that he played golf with the killer every Saturday morning.

His friendship was unchanged, but redemption was not within his power to grant.

Trey was right, interdiction was not the issue; this is about the children who are used by all of us to justify our own excesses and exhibit them to validate our self worth, we leave them without the security of our commitment to cherish them at least as much as we do our automobiles that we lock away from intrusion.

John barely remembered living with his parents and longed for their protection for the pain he was now feeling.

His job was clear; he had to stop his friend he held close for so long, from killing and lock him away.

He opened another bottle of beer and picked up the newspaper that was full of news of the Danfords and their former enterprise. These were the real killers who would use their money and power to escape the consequences of their atrocious and evil deeds. They killed the spirit and innocence of whose names they wouldn't remember or may have never known. Their debt would never be fully paid because they could only assume the damage was greater than the damage to themselves. They'll spend a short time in prison and return to a society who will forget their sins and welcome them back to a life they forfeited and will never deserve.

The church is crumbling as auditors have invaded with their

calculators and tsk tsk tsk's that won't last long enough to invade our memory.

He went to bed early looking forward to meeting Gary at their gym in the morning; he had a lot of his own rage to work off.

It ended as it began with no resolution or release, he told himself while he prepared for the final murder.

His plans worked well for him; there were only the clues he planted in plain site. John Garrison deserved to solve this, and he believed his friend has done just that. He knows, as well he should. Had anyone else led the investigation, there would never have been a solution because the victims themselves elicited no sympathy from society. They needed killing.

He was nearly finished and prepared to move on having made his statement. There was no remorse, only satisfaction and joy. There could be no peace and he was prepared to live without the hope that escaped him each time his teacher touched him and made him feel shame and fear and loss.

It was time for the teacher to die for what he did to so many of us; more than he knew or wanted to know.

He wrote the letters to be sent the following day and then it would be over. They all deserved it. They deserved it well. It won't happen again.

CHAPTER SEVEN-TWO

John was on a treadmill when he saw Gary walk through the front door carrying a bag. It was early and only a handful of the early morning faithful were on hand to see the sun rise after they finished their workout.

Gary stepped up on the treadmill next to his friend and started out running without a warmup. He ran a full thirty minutes and finished his routine after working several weight machines.

John followed him to the steam room where they were alone and spent. They were silent for several minutes lowering their heart rate and gathering their thoughts.

"I met with Trey yesterday. He told me about your visit and suspicions. You don't really think he could be capable of murder do you John?"

"No, I don't think he's capable of murder. Tell him there's no reason for concern."

"Good, Gary said standing up to leave, "I'm going to shower and get back to my house. I have some things to take care of and Trey is meeting me for lunch, so I'll tell him we talked. Take care, John and thank you for more than you know."

Gary shook his friend's hand longer than usual and left the room to shower feeling refreshed and renewed.

John lingered in the steam a while longer sweating out the disappointment and anguish, he felt since he solved the murders that consumed him for the past four months.

John met Andy Becker for breakfast and told him that he knew who the killer was.

"I need you to trust me with this, Andy. I'll let you know when its time to make a move and I'll want you there, but right now I'm asking you to say nothing and just trust me." Andy never saw his partner in such a state and obliged him because he did trust him to do the right thing regardless of the outcome.

CHAPTER SEVENTY-THREE

Trey rang Gary's doorbell several times before his friend answered.

"I thought you might have a partner for a little afternoon delight." Trey said with a wide grin walking to the kitchen. "What's for lunch and don't tell me to make a sandwich. Can we just once not listen to Bird? It's not that I don't like Mr. Charlie Parker, but have you considered a limit to this torment."

"Young man, don't you know by now that there is nothing more substantive than the mellow sound of the Bird himself. I've spent almost twenty years teaching you and Jeff and you still don't get it. He lives in his music; he is his music and I've become his music as well. Listen to it and what do you hear? You hear a place that is safe and at peace with the world. You hear the yellow in daisies and the taste of sweet corn, the warmth of the morning sun and the tingling of fresh snow on your face. You hear all there is and ever needs to be. This is his gift. This is his music. This man; this Bird, this Charlie Parker."

"What's for lunch?" Trey pronounced as rhetoric, having heard this homily repeated incessantly throughout the ages.

"Caesar salad, Mushroom stuffed ravioli, the wine of your choice and Focaccia with pesto olive oil, followed by espresso, rum soaked pound cake with raspberry sauce; all of which I prepared myself with only you in mind."

"All of which you picked up prepared at Magiano's, my best friend the liar. Who loves you more? Only you would think of my favorite meal, now are you kissing my ass or do you just love me like you should. I think I'll kiss you." Trey said salivating over the fare being removed from containers.

"Let's don't and say we did." Gary said sitting down to lunch.

Gary enjoyed watching his friend celebrate their lunch, which was the first time they spent together celebrating anything since they buried Jeff.

"Since you're the only one left, I want you to keep a copy of my will that I changed after Jeff left us for parts unknown. I've left you everything except my music collection that I want you to give to John Garrison, since he's the only person who feels the music, as it should. Wait about six months before you let him have the collection. I have every song, album and cd catalogued and insured. I'm counting on you do take care of it just like I instructed. I bought the plot next to Jeff, so bury me there."

"Hold up a minute, are you planning to check out soon, if so, I'm busy this week and next."

"No, I just want to make sure you take care of my affairs when I die. You never know what's going to happen or when. Just handle it."

Gary told Trey about John's decision not to pursue him and they talked about missing Jeff and the plans Trey had to open a facility to counsel abused children and their parents. He wanted to work with other organizations to create a paradigm that will teach parents, teachers and children how to protect themselves from predators and the importance of reporting family abuse.

Trey was finally where he should be and doing what he wanted on his own terms and Gary was gratified that his friend was healing and using his experiences positively.

He cleared the leftovers and prepared for his date that evening.

John spoke with his ex-wife for over an hour finally convincing her to move back to Houston with the children. He needed to be with his girls' full time and wanted them to know that he was always available. She told him that she had considered the move very seriously for several months for the same reasons. She wouldn't have problems with a transfer within her company and just needed time to sell her house.

His relationship with the girl's mother was never strained regarding the welfare of their children and for that he was always grateful. His children needed both of their parents and he needed his family.

He called his grandmother who was elated with the news knowing her great- grandchildren would give John the balance he needs.

He then called his partner and arranged to meet him in the morning to arrest the man who killed Darren Danford, Brian Hargrave and James and Barbara Evans.

He was feeling free of the grief he allowed himself earlier as he drove to meet Peter Altman for dinner to tell him about the pending arrest and why he wanted to do it his way. John didn't expect Pete's understanding and was prepared to argue for as long as it took to convince the prosecutor, but not only did he understand, but was sympathetic and supportive.

He went home and didn't think about it anymore that night; he had to do the right thing because it was the right thing to do.

CHAPTER SEVENTY-FOUR

*H*e wrote letters to explain his motive and included tapes for his friends. He finished cleaning his house and sent the letters and tapes to his friends and family via over night delivery.

While he was out posting his letters, he went to a liquor store to restock his bar. He returned home satisfied that all was in order and he had only one more murder to commit before it all ended and his mission complete.

He showered and dressed in lightweight wool slacks and cotton shirt and sat in his living room after pouring a double shot of Glennfidch. He took four of the pills he confiscated from a client and enjoyed his scotch for as long as it lasted which was the rest of his life.

CHAPTER SEVENTY-FIVE

J ohn and Andy approached the Memorial home of the killer and rang the bell several times to no answer. John knocked and called out to no avail. They tried the door that was unlocked and walked into the house that was lit seemingly from the night before. John had been in the house many times and the pain he felt was crippling as he walked into the living room and found his friend sitting in a club chair; his head against the back; a glass on the floor beside the chair under an extended hand that previously held the glass.

John found the envelope with his name on the table in front of the dead man. He opened the envelope and read the letter inside.

Dear John,

I have no doubt that you figured it out before you found me. I hope you know how sincerely sorry I was to see you involved in this investigation since I expected you to be in Seattle with you children when this began for you.

It began for me so many years ago and I decided to kill pedophiles when I was still in high school. I'm not going to belabor my reasons; I think you already know about Father Davis Connor's raping, my friends and me and who knows how many others.

I won't try to justify my actions; I have no reason to do so. It's what I wanted to do; I was compelled with satisfaction.

You are better served knowing how I selected them and why I killed them in that manner. I met with a client last year at P&D's Club for lunch and sat at a table next to Darren Danford and both

Evans who were talking about their film enterprise and how they selected the children. They were sincere in their conversation that involved casting (their words), filming, marketing, packaging, and shipping. I can't describe my shock and disgust. From the start I couldn't believe Darren Jr. could run the kind of business the scope of which they spoke until his father walked in like Darth Vader in total control. He was angry with them for insisting on the meeting place since he thought he would be recognized. He took over the meeting and that was also the first time I heard the name of Dr. Brian Hargrave the pediatrician. Dr. Hargrave provided boys and girls for their "casting" after he used them for his own gratification and rated their performance.

They were so involved with their meeting; they never once noticed me staring at them. I stayed after my client left to hear as much as I could. I followed the Evans to their home since I knew it would be easy to find Danford and Hargrave.

I chose Danford first because he disgusted me to the point of hatred, and I couldn't kill him enough.

I returned to the club many times over several months watching Danford and Hargrave who were regulars. I wore several disguises that would confuse anyone who thought they could identify me to your sketch artist.

I met Danford at the club his last night and followed him to an apartment where he had a key for reasons I didn't ask and didn't care. I know the cleanliness blew you mind and that was part of my plan to throw you off only you knew all along that I killed him in the apartment. It wasn't hard to do. He wanted to take the pills after I told him the sex would be better. He took an overdose with several glasses of wine and died shortly thereafter. I waited all night before I beat him and removed his hands, obviously I used plastic tarps and cleaned the already spotless apartment. I took the dishes because I didn't know if he ever used any of them and I wanted his family to suffer a little about his whereabouts, which is why he lost his hands as well as he didn't need the hands that destroyed so many children.

The apartment was isolated enough to allow me to clean, vacuum the carpet and leave without interruption. I took everything I used as well as his hands to my deer lease where I put the hands in a woodchipper and burned everything except the kitchenware that I left at the door of a church off of 290.

Brian Hargrave was chosen because he was a pediatrician who worked with children every day and raped children at night; the conflict overwhelmed me. His seeming innocence and well meaning disgusted me. I decided on asphyxiation because it was humiliating, and he needed the exposure. The lemon wedge was a great prop.

The Evans did what they did as a couple. I broke into their house while they were out, and saw the records they kept of their films and watched a couple in which they participated. Watching her having sex with little boys sealed her fate. She was a slut of the first order. I killed them the way I found them on the tapes; you can fill in the blanks.

I made my final decision for obvious reasons. I don't belong in prison any more than I belong on earth any longer.

Again, I hope you can accept my apology for your involvement, but if I chose to be caught, I'm convinced you are the only one who could succeed.
As always, I remain,
Gary Sanford

John replaced the letter and gave it to his partner, then sat down and sobbed uncontrollably and Andy gave him time with his friend before he called for the medical examiner and Peter Altman.

Gary Sanford's mother answered the door wondering who would be visiting so early and found the FedEx man with a letter package; she signed and was surprised to see that it was from her son.

She returned to the kitchen and her coffee and opened the letter.

Dear Mother and Father,

I expect you to be more shocked than saddened by the end of this morning. I'm not able to expect more from either of you.

You will learn throughout the day that I have killed four people over the last several months and I do not apologize to anyone for their deaths. They did to other children what Father Connor did to me so long ago.

You either never believed me when I told you about the priest or you didn't care; I have no doubt that it was both. You wouldn't allow for embarrassment.

Father, you, and I haven't had a conversation since I was a child, not because you didn't know how, but because you had nothing to say to me, because I was nothing to you.

I stopped hating both of you a long time ago until I felt nothing and that is why I didn't kill you as I originally planned. You need to live with what you did, not die because of it. I want you to always know that you should have protected me from our priest instead of allowing him to rape me until I was in the third grade. Did it ever occur to either of you that I couldn't possibly have created that story, what did I know about rape when I was only seven?

I have left instructions with Trey, who is probably reading his letter at this same time. He will take care of my burial and I don't want you anywhere near my funeral.

I have nothing more to say to either of you, not even good-by.

The letter was unsigned.

She was convinced that her son was playing a sick joke and she would give him a piece of her mind. She called his house breathing heavily and was surprised to hear an unfamiliar voice answer.

"This is Gary Sanford's mother, to whom am I speaking?" "This is Detective Andrew Becker ma'am." "Let me speak to my son." "Mrs. Sanford, I'm afraid that won't be possible." "Just tell him I'm on the phone and I need to speak with him right away. Tell him I just received his letter, and I am not amused." "Mrs. Sanford is there anyone with you?" "No. Why?" "Mrs. Sanford, your son is not able to speak with you because he died sometime last night. I'm so sorry."

Andy heard the woman on the other end screaming and was helpless when the phone went dead.

John was still in the living room when Trey Peterson burst through the door and ran into the living room finding his friend cold and lifeless.

"Jesus Christ. Jesus Christ Gary, what have you done?"

He didn't realize John had grabbed him to stop his shaking.

"I was here yesterday for lunch. He told me about his will and gave me instructions and I thought it was because of Jeff dying so soon and he just wanted to make sure he had everything in place. "My God, he's my brother; my world. How could this have happened?

He sent me a letter and told me he killed those people. Is it true, John?" "It's true. He left me a letter explaining everything. There is too much going on this morning, Trey. We're going to have to take him and try to sort things out tomorrow. Are you going to be ok?" "I don't know John; my brothers are gone, and I don't know what to do. I don't have anymore friends."

"Yes, you do." John said and held Trey until he stopped sobbing.

The medical examiner had unbuttoned Gary's shirt that flung open at his chest while he examined the body. John took one last look at his friend and smiled when he saw the tattoo over his heart. BIRD LIVES.

John noticed that for the first time since he met Gary, there was no music and that was sad, very sad.

John finished his lengthy report and went home early to re-member his friends as they once were. He saw his neighbor run-ning toward him carrying a FedEx letter she said was delivered after he left this morning.

He poured himself a drink and sat down and read the note from Gary Sanford.

This is not a part of your evidence and I did not represent the man when he told me his story that is on the tape, so use it as you see fit. It was the least I could do for you. Please keep an eye on Trey; he'll need you. Make sure he continues to see his shrink and understands that no one loved him more than I. In time, I'm confident you will understand. You never have to accept it and you never have to defend me, just understand.
Be well and have a great life.
Gary

He listened to the man on the tape confess to the murder of his parents.

CHAPTER SEVENTY-SIX

Trey moved into Gary's house and felt at home surrounded by the memories of his life with his friends.

The caterers were arriving for the party he was giving for John Garrison's birthday. He owed John for keeping him together after they buried Gary and helping him open Sanford House. The facility was now fully staffed and opened for business and Trey was free to live the life he wanted for too long.

He had enough money to leave his practice and would receive his PhD in Psychology at the end of the term. He was where he belonged.

He missed his friends every day, but he knew they were pleased with his choices.

Father Connor died shortly after Gary and before he could be arrested for rape, but not before the formal accusation.

The Danford's were sent to prison long enough to lead them into old age.

The house was filled with John's well wishers including his children and their mother who Trey was hoping would re-marry his guest of honor, but in the meantime, they seemed to be enjoying the courtship.

"Your gift was too large to wrap so it will be delivered to your house tomorrow, so be there." Trey told John. "What could be so large?"

Trey handed John a card and opened it to find Gary Sanford's signature. A note fell to the floor.

You are the only one who would appreciate and care for my music. Enjoy every song, every note. You deserve them all.

Just do me one favor, every time Trey is in your house, play Bird and think of me.
Love,
Gary.

ACKNOWLEDGEMENTS

This book was written on a dare; could it be done? Could a murder be committed and not solved until the murderer allows the solution?

I am deeply grateful for the encouragement and assistance of people in my life that believed in my ability to meet the challenge.

Thank you, Sandra Newmark Stephens, my oldest and dearest friend, for the advice, support, and encouragement.

Erie Calloway Smith helped me with editing and encouragement.

Will Burrows, my brilliant cover artist, who nailed it. Thank you, Will.

The following offered their support and advice in many ways, without which would have made this project more difficult.

Thank you, Jennifer Green, Wennette Pegues, and always, Gabby.

This book is dedicated with love, to
My Jennifer
David W. Green
Wayman Anderson
Gordon Cooper
and
Children, everywhere.

CPSIA information can be obtained
at www.ICGtesting.com
Printed in the USA
BVHW071125250621
610447BV00002B/210